The Path to Freedom
Task Force 125, Book #1

I0613301

Lisa Pietsch

Table of Contents

Copyright

The Path to Freedom
Copyright © 2025 Lisa Pietsch
(Defiance Press & Publishing, LLC)

All rights reserved. No part of this publication may be reproduced, distributed, or transmitted in any form or by any means, including photocopying, recording, or other electronic or mechanical methods, without the prior written permission of the publisher, except in the case of brief quotations embodied in critical reviews and certain other noncommercial uses permitted by copyright law.

This book is a work of fiction. Names, characters, places, and incidents are either products of the author's imagination or are used fictitiously. Any resemblance to actual persons, living or dead, or locales is entirely coincidental.

Published by Defiance Press & Publishing, LLC

Bulk orders of this book may be obtained by contacting Defiance Press & Publishing, LLC. www.defiancepress.com.

Defiance Press & Publishing, LLC

281-581-9300

info@defiancepress.com

Task Force 125 Series

One

Some time ago...

It was one hundred and four degrees in the shade, and the Algerian sun was taking no prisoners. Vince was soaked in his own sweat and anxious to get out of this place and into a nice dark bar somewhere. Something about this extraction made him itch.

His gut told him something was off.

Vince couldn't understand why he hadn't heard from Chris yet. Chris was a communications expert. The only time he was ever quiet was when there was bad news. Vince adjusted his radio earpiece and checked his ammunition one more time. Crouching behind a gardener's shed wasn't the most comfortable position he'd ever been in, but he'd set up ambushes in worse places.

"Chris, I know you're four miles away, sitting in front of a radio console, in an air conditioned room but we could use some communications out here. Do you have radio contact with Dana? She knows we're here, right?"

"Jesus, boss. You're not gonna believe this. She's telling him."

Despite the heat, Vince's blood turned to ice. If Dana blew her cover, the whole mission would be scrapped and they'd never get her out without a firefight. "Say again?"

"Her radio works fine." Chris let out a deep sigh that came through loud and clear on the radio. "She's ignoring my communications. She told him. She fucking told Carlos!"

Vince heard the confusion in Chris' voice. Years in Force Recon taught him to keep a cool head when everything went sideways. "Okay, boys, change in plans. Drug dealers aren't known for their compassion. We gotta get her the hell out of there before they kill her…or worse."

"They're moving," Jason's voice came over the radio as a whisper.

Vince knew Jason would have a clear shot at the chopper on the helipad from his position on the beach, just out of the sightline from the glass front of Carlos' mansion. He took a mental inventory of Jason's gear. The M-60 machine gun would do some serious damage and the Stinger missile launcher was a last resort.

Vince watched as Dana and Carlos left the mansion, arm in arm, and walked toward the helipad. "Damnit, she's right next to Carlos. I can't get the shot. Can anybody take out Carlos? Jason?"

Jason's cool, confident voice came through on Vince's earpiece. "I can take Carlos out easy, but a 7.62 is gonna go through Dana, too. That's the smallest round I'm packin' today, Major."

Vince knew Brian was positioned behind a well, ten yards to his right, between the gardener's shed and the house. "We need to try to get her out of there alive. You got a clear shot, Brian?"

Brian's voice came back over the radio. "Negative, Vince. I've got bodyguards in the way."

Shit! What the hell was Dana thinking? Did she honestly believe a drug dealer would fall in love with a CIA agent? Did Dana really think Carlos would let her live after being told she had shared his secrets with the CIA for the past three months?

Vince checked the magazine in his machine gun and then the handgun on his left hip. "Okay, Chris. If she's still listening, tell her to stay out of the way. Carlos needs to be taken out with or without her help. If we don't get the shot now, they're going to take her up in that chopper and we all know she'll be dumped before they land."

Vince watched Dana carefully for the slightest opening to shoot Carlos.

Vince's team had been tracking Carlos for months before they managed to plant Dana undercover as his lover. Dana had been in deep cover with Carlos for three months now. The team finally had the information they needed about how Al Qaeda had raised their most recent infusion of cash. Vince and the rest of the team were here to pull Dana out and clean up the bad guys.

Now the stupid bitch had gone too far and fallen in love with the guy.

What does she think, they'll fly off into the sunset together?

His gut had told him she'd never complete the mission, but she had all the training with high scores so the Agency green-lighted her.

Chris had briefed Dana on where the team would be set up so she could get away from Carlos safely.

Vince expected her to duck and cover but she stopped on her way to the chopper with Carlos and turned directly toward Vince's position. She yelled to be heard over the noisy coastline. "Don't do it, Vince! I m going with him. I don't want to go back."

Too many years as a U.S. Marine gave a man certain instincts. The hairs on the back of Vince's neck stood up. He knew this operation was going to end ugly.

Carlos smirked and held Dana as close to him as possible.

It ain't love, honey. You're a hostage now and everybody knows it but you.

Jesus! How could the agency hire such a fool?

I should have followed my gut when I met her. She was wrong for the mission.

No time for regrets now.

Carlos' bodyguards opened fire on the gardener's shack that Vince was crouched behind. The dry wooden walls offered no cover. Splinters flew at Vince but he felt nothing but the adrenaline powering through his body. His senses heightened. He could smell the gunpowder in the air and heard the *buzz* of each bullet that flew past him. His eyes focused only on the enemy. His body responded the way it had been trained to in combat. Steady hands returned fire with his Mac-10 as he instinctively rolled away from the shack and just below the ridgeline where he had more cover but could still see Dana and Carlos. The air was thick with dust and bullets as Vince's team, set up in a semi-circle around Carlos' complex, rained hell on Carlos' bodyguards, who returned as much fire as they could.

Vince slapped his left hand over his combination earpiece and microphone to block out the noise from bullets overhead and ricocheting rocks. "She's getting on the chopper! Somebody kill that son of a bitch now!"

An audible *pop* rang out and one of Carlos' bodyguards dropped like a wet rag. A second crumpled to the ground as Carlos dashed into the chopper, pulling Dana with him.

Another bodyguard dropped. Brian was taking out whoever he could.

"Take the rotor, Jason! Take it out before it climbs." They couldn't let Carlos escape.

The familiar *dug-dug-dug* of Jason's M-60 was all the response Vince needed. He'd seen Jason hit running rabbits with that gun, but somehow the chopper lifted off the ground in spite of the hundreds of bullets assaulting its most vulnerable parts.

The decision had been made. Vince couldn't change the course of history now. "Carlos will torture her for whatever he can get and then finish her. We can't get her back, boys." Vince passed his hand over his clean-shaven head. "Jason, finish it."

The sand in the center of the compound swirled as the chopper rose into the clear azure sky.

What's going on in there?

Vince's gut dropped into his boots as Dana's familiar form fell from the chopper. While she flailed in mid-air, a Stinger missile hissed toward the helicopter.

Dana landed fifty feet from the beach and hit the water like a stone. Hitting the sea from that height would be the same as hitting concrete, and every bone in her body would be crushed.

Oh, Jesus Christ.

The Stinger missile sliced the chopper in two. Both pieces fell in flames on top of Dana's broken body.

Vince closed his eyes and let out a disappointed sigh. The sweet smell of burnt fuel from the chopper, gunpowder and salt mixed to seal yet another combat memory in Vince's mind. Yes, they found the information they needed on Al Qaeda and Carlos was out of the picture, but they'd lost an agent. Vince would need months to find a woman with enough training to replace her, and after this one's serious lack of good judgment, Vince wasn't too keen on going through the process again.

The next female they chose had to be tough as nails and cold as ice. They'd never find the right "swallow" for another Honey Pot mission.

Brian broke the radio's silence. "Hey, boss?"

"Yeah?" Vince dusted his cargo pants off. He noticed with surprise several wooden splinters had flown like tiny darts into his shoulder. He plucked the bloody bits of wood out of his right shoulder as one might remove lint from a sweater. He pulled his canteen from his belt to wash the tiny wounds, thought better of it and drank the water instead.

"Wasn't that chopper our extraction plan?"

"Yeah." Vince shook his head and stretched his legs for the walk into town.

Two

Friday couldn't come soon enough. Sarah reported to the Security Forces building where she would begin her out-processing for her deployment to Kuwait on Monday. Her first stop was the orderly room for the standard out-briefing.

The Sergeant working there pulled out his checklist. "Okay, take your boots off and step on the scale."

Sarah froze. She hadn't been expecting a weigh-in. If she had, she would have spent the past week drinking grapefruit juice and taking mass quantities of laxatives instead of drinking beer and eating pizza. The First Sergeant had planned to deploy her so she'd lose weight.

The Sergeant who weighed her didn't seem to be in on the plan. "Did you know you're over the weight limit?"

"Uh, yeah."

It's difficult to not notice an extra sixty-five pounds when you live with it 24/7, dipshit!

"I can't deploy you if you're overweight."

Sarah suddenly sensed every tiny hair on the back of her neck standing up. She shook off the sudden chill as she stepped off the scale and stared at the sergeant. "What do you mean? The First Sergeant had it all worked out for me to deploy so I could lose the weight in the first place. It's his plan."

The Sergeant cracked a half smile and shook his head. "You don't understand. If I send you like this and they weigh you on arrival, they'll ship you back and I'll have a lot of explaining to do." He walked back to his desk and sat, laying her personnel folder open in front of him. "Deploying to the Middle East isn't a spa vacation, Airman Stevens, it's your job and you're supposed to be fit for it."

"Look, I'm sure if you talk to the First Sergeant about this he'll explain the whole thing."

"The First Sergeant is out of the office today. I'll have to discuss this with the Commander. Have a seat."

Sarah sat in the waiting area, and the reality of what just happened hit her in the face like a bag of pennies.

That son of a bitch set me up. He knew I'd have to weigh-in today and he left the office.

Forty-five minutes later, the Sergeant returned from the Commander's office and motioned her over to his desk.

"Stevens." He pushed his glasses up on his nose and never made eye contact with Sarah. "Are you aware this is your third unsatisfactory weigh-in?"

Sarah leaned back in the chair and nodded slowly. "Yes." She had no respect for this little weasel.

I remember working with you. You couldn't even put your M-16 together after cleaning it.

"You know where you are in the weight management program, Sarah. You'll have to see the Commander."

Five minutes later, Sarah was called into the Commander's office. He sat at his desk while Sarah stood at attention in front of it. He frowned and shook his head. The shuffling of papers from the personal information file in front of him was the only sound in the room.

"You're a good troop, Stevens. Twice named Airman of the Quarter and even named Squadron Airman of the Year. You have excellent test and annual rating scores. You're one of my best Fire Team Leaders and a bang-up Desk Sergeant." He came around to the front of his desk and sat on the corner of it. He motioned to the chair beside her. "Sit down."

Sarah hadn't expected the Commander to be so informal. She sat stiffly in the leather chair.

"I don't want to discharge you, Sarah."

Sarah looked into his eyes and understood what was coming next. She adjusted in the leather chair, straightened her shoulders and took a deep breath.

The Commander rubbed his forehead. "Do you understand? Overweight, you're still the best troop I have." He stood from his seat on the corner of the desk and walked back to his high-backed leather chair. He motioned toward the phone on his desk. "I just spoke to your Lieutenant and he told me that at your current weight, you can carry the heaviest weapons and packs and still outrun anyone on an armed response. Your Operations Officer also gave you a glowing recommendation. You could have an amazing military career if it weren't for your weight."

Sarah looked at the Commander. He didn't look a day over thirty but she knew he'd been enlisted prior to becoming an officer. Once he became an officer, he was what the military called a fast burner. He made rank as quickly as anyone could and now he was the Commander of a police squadron. He was working on his own amazing career and she respected him for that. "Thank you, sir." She knew that "could" meant "won't" and her Air Force career was ending. Shame and disappointment churned inside her stomach. She never wanted to leave the Air Force this way. The many months of frustration at not being able to lose the weight had wracked her nerves. She'd soon be leaving the life she'd loved for years, but it was almost a relief to know she wouldn't be so stressed out over not measuring up all the time.

This is it. The big send off.

"Don't thank me. I can't help you now. You've tied my hands. I have to do something that no Commander should ever have to do. Stevens, I have to discharge one of my best troops and I'm not the least bit happy about doing it." He stared down at the papers on his desk and shook his head.

Sarah waited silently for the inevitable. She could feel her world crumbling down around her.

I still have Scott. We could always get married like we'd talked about doing.

"Nobody wants you discharged, but this is the United States Air Force. We can't afford to be kind and gentle. Rules are rules and we all have to follow them or else there would be chaos. I hope you understand that, Sarah. You've failed too many weigh-ins for us to continue this way. I have to recommend you for immediate discharge."

Deep down, Sarah had known this would happen.

"When this is all done, what will you do? Do you have a plan for your future?"

Not many career prospects for an overweight ex-cop. This is it. My career is over.

"No, sir." Sarah focused on the wall above the Commander's head and blinked back the tears.

I can't lose my military bearing now. The world is shaking beneath my feet. I didn't really plan for this. All I have now is Scott .

"Well, I suggest you get one together quickly because you'll be a civilian by this time next week."

"So quickly, sir?" Sarah had no idea it would happen so fast.

"Even Commanders have to answer to a chain of command. I can't protect you any longer." The Major shuffled through his desk drawers and pulled something out. Sarah stood as he came around the front of his desk toward her.

The Major offered her a white business card. "Here's a start."

Sarah took the card and read it:

Boot Camp

Specializing in Weight Loss

(702) 482-0623

Sarah glanced up at the Commander and blinked hard as tears welled. The Commander had prolonged this process for about six months now in hopes she would find a way to lose the weight. She had tried and failed so many times that it had finally broken her spirit. She took a deep breath and very sincerely said, "Thank you, sir."

His features softened and he seemed earnest when he said, "Look, this service is free, provided you make satisfactory progress. Given the nature of their program, I'm sure you'll do fine. You can begin a new future for yourself there. Please call that number when you leave my office." He reached out, shook her hand and then stood at attention. "Dismissed."

Sarah drove directly to Scott's apartment. After the morning she'd had, she really needed some reassurance that everything was going to be okay. Scott was all she had left now, and she really needed to be with him.

She pulled into the parking lot, and walked up the steps to his apartment. The door was unlocked, so she walked in and headed straight for Scott's bedroom.

Scott's voice carried down the hall. "Who's there?"

Sarah heard mumbling and shuffling in the bedroom as though Scott were talking to someone.

"Hey, it's me, Scott. I need to talk to you." Sarah rounded the corner and her breath clogged inside her lungs.

A completely naked man shot past her and into the master bathroom and slammed the door behind him. Scott hopped out of bed and pulled on a pair of jeans.

A knot formed in Sarah's stomach that made her want to retch. "Oh, my God, Scott! You've got to be kidding me." A massive vise closed around Sarah's chest. She gasped for a breath.

Gay? My Scott is gay? Scott is cheating on me with a guy? But how? Why?

"What the hell are you doing here?" Scott pulled on a T-shirt, and then pushed her out into the living room.

The room became a good forty degrees warmer as the adrenaline surged through her bloodstream. Her heart beat so hard it thumped inside her throat. She barely rasped out a question of her own. "What am I doing here? What am *I* doing here?" She pushed hard against his shoulder and he stepped back as she stomped forward into his personal space. "A more appropriate question would be what the hell were *you* doing in *there*? What is *he* doing here?"

Scott raised his hands in front of him. He wouldn't want to fight, but Sarah was too pissed off to care.

"Sarah, don't play dumb. You had to know."

Sarah's stomach churned with self-doubt. She refused to accept the blame, steeled herself and mustered enough strength to appear very cold and calm. "Did I? We've slept together¾often. All that talk about wanting a future with me was just a bullshit cover wasn't it?" She didn't let him answer as she paced back and forth between him and the hallway to the bedroom. Rage burned inside her. "I can't believe I fell for it. How long were you going to let me believe that everything was fine between us? How long were you going to pretend and keep having sex with me?"

I don't know who I hate more¾you for deceiving me or myself for being deceived.

There was silence except for the *click* of the master bathroom door opening.

The thunderous voice that Sarah always reserved for the words "Police! Open up!" suddenly burst from deep within her gut. "Stay in that bathroom, bitch!"

Scott shook his head and practically whimpered. "We were such good friends I thought you'd grow to accept it. I thought we could work out an arrangement."

The reality of his plan hit her like a bucket of ice water in the face. She gasped for a breath. "Work out an arrangement? Are you fucking kidding me? Do you actually believe I am so unworthy of a relationship with a real man that I would settle for being a fag's cover?"

Scott reached for a cigarette on the coffee table behind him and lit it as he spoke. "Hey, Sarah, you let yourself go. You used to be pretty hot but you're not exactly on anyone's most wanted list any more, if you know what I mean."

"You bastard." The vise continued to close around her chest and something finally broke inside. Someone completely unknown to her stood before her. He was hateful, selfish, self-serving and had the blackest of black hearts. Looking at him now made her want to vomit. There was a stink in the air she could no longer stomach. "You know, Scott, I would have moved mountains for you, but whatever you thought I was going to do for you, forget it."

Scott closed the distance between them and reached out to take her hand.

She flinched away and stiffened, hands fisted at her sides.

Scott puffed nervously on his cigarette.

Yes, it was fear she saw in his eyes.

"Look, we don't need to tell anybody about this. Right?"

Sarah pushed past Scott, nearly knocking him over, and stormed to the front door. "Your secret and your Air Force career are safe—for now. I'm certainly not ready to admit to anyone that my boyfriend cheated on me with a man. Oh, and I'll be a civilian by this time next week." The first smile of the day curved her lips. "Who knows, perhaps you will be, too."

You may have used me, but I own you now.

Sarah got into her Jeep and squealed the tires as she pulled out of the parking lot. The cars and traffic were a haze of colors as she drove across town to the house she shared with several other cops. At the first red light, she pulled a cigarette out of the box and lit it. The adrenaline was wearing off as the claws of reality began climbing up her spine.

I've managed to lose everything in less than a day. What the hell do I do now?

Reality hit. Her head throbbed. It would have to be made of Silly Putty to wrap it around everything she'd been through today. Sarah pulled over to the side of the highway as tears flooded her eyes and rolled down her face. She choked on her sobs and her body tried to vomit but there was nothing in her stomach but the twisted train wreck of love, hate, bile and loss.

The same thoughts and questions kept swirling around inside her head as she sobbed.

This isn't what I wanted when I joined the Air Force. How do I fix all of this? How do I create a life out of this huge pile of shit?

After what seemed like hours, the tears finally stopped. Sarah cleared her raw throat and rinsed it with the last swig of Diet Coke remaining in the can she'd left in the Jeep's cup holder last night. The warm, flat, sweet liquid did nothing to quench her thirst. Even her taste buds were too exhausted to care anymore. Exhaustion weighed on her body like a lead suit. Her muscles pulled at each other so hard that the simple act of driving became a chore. She was so drained and exhausted she could barely think.

Sarah pushed down on the clutch, slid the gearshift into first and continued the drive home. Fifteen minutes later, she parked the little, white Jeep on the street outside the brown stucco house that looked like every other house on the block.

It wouldn't be long before she couldn't afford even the rent on the one lousy bedroom in this cookie-cutter house.

Well, Sarah, you've officially hit rock bottom. You're so obese nobody will hire you for anything but a position as a lunch lady or a housekeeper. Your boyfriend prefers boys. You have no place to live and you have fifteen dollars in your checking account.

Then, a clear voice inside her mind that seemed far too calm to be her own spoke up.

You can either give up completely or you can look for the positive in this situation and make a fresh start.

Okay, it was inventory time.

No place to live, no significant other, no place to go, and as of next week, no job. It didn't look good.

At least there's nowhere to go but up!

She could always head back to South Dakota, but the last thing she wanted to do was to move back in with her parents. She had never been terribly close with her family, and when she joined the Air Force during a war, they hadn't understood the decision, nor did they approve.

The last thing she wanted to do was go crawling back to them and admit she'd failed at something else. She'd never hear the end of it.

Suddenly, the calm voice deep within her was back.

No, you will not give up now.

Life had great adventures in store for her, she knew it deep in her gut. Something good was going to come out of all this and she just had to ride out the shitstorm.

Her fingers nervously fidgeted with a small piece of paper in her non-smoking hand. When she looked down she understood that her options were limited¾to one.

Marilyn Manson's "The Beautiful People" played on the radio.

Yeah. I can be one of them.

That cinched it. She'd call the number on the card. Her first step in getting the life she wanted was to find a way, any way, to lose this weight and gain some control over herself and her life for good.

~~~

"Hey, boss lady! I thought you were processing for the sandbox today?"

Sarah wasn't expecting Jody to be awake when she arrived home.

"Change in plans." Sarah reached for the phone and dialed the camp to see if she could get in as soon as she was discharged.

The woman on the other end of the line asked only a few questions.

"Full name, please?"

"Sarah Marie Stevens"

"What base are you currently stationed at, Sarah?"

"Nellis Air Force Base"

"Okay. We'll call you back within twenty-four hours to let you know if we can take you." There was a click and then a dial tone.

It was peculiar that they'd want so little information, but she was in no position to question their methods. She just hoped they'd take her.

On Saturday morning, the phone rang at eight.

"Sarah Marie Stevens?"

"Speaking."

The woman on the other end of the line spoke quickly and didn't pause long enough for Sarah to ask questions.

"You've been accepted into our weight loss program. Pack one bag only. The required uniform is battle dress trousers, black T-shirt and combat boots. You'll have little need for civis, so don't bother packing any. Call this number to notify us once you've out-processed at Nellis. Then park your vehicle in the long-term parking lot at Las Vegas International Airport and standby there for your ride to the camp. Do you understand these instructions?"

"Uh, yes. Thank you. Thank you very much!" Sarah heard the now familiar click and dial tone.

The whole phone call lasted less than forty-five seconds. Sarah spent the rest of her weekend wondering where her future would lead. The only difference now was the fact that the light at the end of the tunnel wasn't a speeding locomotive. There was finally a glimmer of hope.

At nine-o-clock Monday morning, Sarah drove to base and reported to the orderly room. They gave her a checklist of things she had to do prior to her out-processing like returning any library books she may have from the base library, attending a three-day class in preparation for her civilian job search and speaking to a military mental health professional just so they could be sure she wouldn't off herself as soon as she got the boot.

Sarah just rolled with it and did what she was told.

When she reported to work for her last two days in the Air Force, things had changed. Her usually talkative coworkers only spoke to her when they absolutely had to. She had suddenly become invisible to all of them. The people she had thought were her friends now ignored her and spoke around her rather than to her. To them, she had done the equivalent of quitting the Air Force, and they took it personally as though she had quit them.

Sarah smoked a lot of cigarettes that week. She barely ate. There wasn't room in there for all the butterflies and food too. It was the roughest week of her life, but it would be over soon and her life would be back on track after a stay at the camp.

It was another hot day in Vegas when Sarah was led¾like the prisoners she'd escorted so many times herself¾to the military personnel office to sign her discharge paperwork.

The Sergeant who shepherded her to her final appointment had been her peer. They'd worked together for years and had a lot of laughs working as Desk Sergeants. Today he wouldn't smile or even make eye contact with her. This part of her life was over. She didn't want to waste her energy feeling loss and disappointment. She cut it loose. She cut them all loose. She felt liberated, light, free and ready to begin her new life.

At three-o-clock, it was finally done. She was a civilian.

She was free, but she had nothing.

Her severance pay would cover eight months of her Jeep and insurance payments. She hoped that boot camp would come through and help her lose weight quickly so she could get her life back on track.

She'd already packed her bag and dumped everything else she owned in storage. Her storage unit was paid up for the rest of the year. After that, she'd need to either pay month to month or pick up her things before the storage company sold them.

Sarah drove out of the Nellis main gate for the last time and pulled into a convenience store just a block away. She bought a can of Diet Coke, a pack of Marlboro Lights and made her phone call at the payphone outside.

Three

Sarah drove into the long-term parking lot at Las Vegas International airport about a half-hour later. She pulled her duffel bag and Diet Coke out of the Jeep. Then she lifted the soft, canvas top back up over the Jeep and snapped it into place. The soft top wasn't exactly a theft deterrent, but she locked the Jeep anyway.

As she pocketed her keys, she smiled to herself. Two keys were all she had to show for her thirty years of living. One key started her Jeep Wrangler, and the other opened a small storage unit, no bigger than an outhouse, which contained all her worldly possessions.

Sarah propped her duffel bag against the bumper of the Jeep, lit another cigarette and paced the width of her parking space. Halfway to the filter of her cigarette, a shiny, black Suburban with black tinted windows rolled up next to her.

The electric window lowered and the driver called over the rumble of the engine, "Sarah Stevens?"

Sarah nodded.

The driver tipped his head toward the passenger door, and motioned for her to get in.

Sarah stubbed out her cigarette on the sole of her combat boot and flicked the butt under the Jeep. She moved around to the passenger side of the Suburban, threw her duffel in the back seat and climbed into the front seat.

"I've seen these in convoys but never ridden in one. They're pretty nice."

He shrugged off her comment. "Yeah, they aren't bad, but when you've got something this shiny in the desert you're constantly waxing off the sand scratches."

The driver picked up a radio handset and keyed the mike. "Transporting Stevens to Thunder."

Sarah peered out the window into the bright Nevada desert as they drove out of town. The driver sat silently as though he'd driven this road a million times.

She kept her eyes on the road and focused on her future. It wasn't long before they lost sight of Las Vegas and any other signs of civilization.

They drove a series of dusty trails through the desert. Occasionally, a Joshua tree would rise over the horizon or a tumbleweed would roll into view. She was careful to remember the position of the sun, mountains, road and the time of day. If she was left out here, she'd know how to get back.

After about thirty minutes of driving, the Suburban came to a dry riverbed that crossed the trail. The vehicle slowed to a stop and the driver handed Sarah a blindfold. "Put it on. If you don't know where we're going, you can't give away the secret."

Nervous bubbles rose within her to a light chuckle. "You can't be serious. Are you afraid that hoards of fat people will rush the gates and demand you take them in?" Sarah grinned at how silly such a scenario would look.

The driver narrowed his eyes and glared at Sarah. "This isn't a joke. Put on the blindfold or get out and make your own way back to the airport. It makes no difference to me."

He seemed a little too serious for Sarah's liking, but she understood his tone. Since she had no intention of walking back to the airport, she tied the blindfold around her head.

I'm alone in the middle of the biggest cemetery in the country with this weirdo. This had better be worth it.

She reached into her right pants cargo pocket and curled her fingers around the handle of the bayonet she had stashed there. Somehow, in this very uncertain time in her life, it gave her a feeling of security to know she was armed.

Dressed to kill.

After more dips and turns through the desert, the driver said, "Okay, you can take off the blindfold now."

Sarah reached behind her head and untied the black cloth. She squinted and blinked back the harsh light of the desert as her eyes adjusted to the light. They were on a hill over a valley that could have been, and likely was, once used for nuclear testing.

A completely desolate desert location devoid of any plant life, the camp consisted of a multitude of metal, round-roofed huts and aircraft hangars.

Every hut and hangar was covered with desert camouflage netting. Several small white picnic tables, black trashcans and red butt cans were scattered around the buildings and shaded with camouflage nets on spreaders.

Well, at least it doesn't look like smoking is frowned upon here.

A handful of sand-colored, government-issue Hummers were parked near hangars under camouflage netting, but there were no civilian vehicles in sight.

The ride in was a bit bizarre but this suddenly feels right.

Four

The driver pulled the Suburban in front of one of the rounded huts and shut off the engine. "Get your bag, Stevens. This is where you sign in."

When she opened the door of the Suburban a blast of hot, dry desert air whipped through the vehicle. Sarah stepped out and retrieved her bag from the back seat before walking into the hut behind the driver.

The driver spoke to the tall, blond woman standing behind the only desk in the small room. "Hey, Mary. This is Stevens, checking in "

"Okay, Stevens, this is a pretty simple process so let's not muck it up with a bunch of questions. Have a seat." Mary motioned to a chair in front of her desk. "First of all, this is a co-ed camp. Any messing around with campers or cadre will get you both a one-way ticket out of here."

Sarah nodded agreement and then began reading and signing the paperwork Mary placed in front of her. It amounted to a non-disclosure contract and an agreement stating the four rules of the camp:

1. Sneaking meals would lead to immediate removal from the camp.

2. Leaving camp without permission would lead to immediate removal from the camp.

3. Failure to follow the prescribed schedule would lead to immediate removal from the camp.

4. Failure to lose weight at each weekly weigh in would lead to immediate removal from the camp.

Everyone at the camp wore combat boots, battle dress trousers and black T-shirts. Luckily for Sarah, she had quite a few of each since she used to wear them to work every day. She had expected to have little use for her uniforms after she left the Air Force, but then again, many of her expectations had been incorrect lately.

Thank God there's a uniform here. After eight years of wearing uniforms every day, I certainly wouldn't want to have to run out and spend my severance pay on a new civilian wardrobe in size extra massive.

The only thing that bothered Sarah about the uniform was the fact that the largest trousers she had were so tight she had to leave the top button undone. She managed to hide the open button with her elastic BDU belt, but having a button undone anywhere was an awkward feeling.

She just wasn't comfortable in her skin and hadn't been for some time now. Squeezing into tight, ill-fitting clothes just seemed par for the course.

"Okay, Stevens." Mary stood. "Let's get you to your quarters so you can get started."

Sarah stood, picked up her bag and followed Mary past the Suburban, a covered picnic area and a wide open space that could have been a parade ground.

Mary explained as they walked briskly toward a group of small huts. "Campers do not have access to washing machines or dryers, so rinse your clothes in the shower after each training day. The desert air will have your clothes bone dry by morning." The woman gestured to several rows of small huts. "The lodging situation here is pretty simple. Four rows of five small huts house four campers each." She opened the front door to one of the windowless huts and walked in. Sunlight blasted into the room from the open door. "You've got two bunk beds on the left wall and two on the right. You may recognize the green, government-issue blankets."

Sarah nodded. "This looks like a mini basic training bay. Of course, in basic, we had fifty girls to a room."

"Yeah, it's the same concept. There are four metal lockers there against the back wall. Pick one and unpack your gear. The latrine and shower are in the large building at the end of this row of huts, out the door and to your right. Your trainer will be in shortly to answer your questions and give you further instructions."

"Thank you, Mary."

Mary shook her head and smiled as she turned to go. "Don't thank me. You're about to work harder than you ever have in your life."

After all the draining, emotional crap in her life over the past two weeks, Sarah welcomed the challenge in Mary's voice and took a deep breath of the hot desert air.

I'm counting on it.

Sarah looked around. The hut had no frills, no windows, and no bathroom. A single light bulb hung from the center of the ceiling. The walls were made up of bare, whitewashed boards on each end and the underside of the arched corrugated metal made up the ceiling and side walls.

I drank too much Coke. I guess I'd better find that latrine.

Sarah dropped her bag in the first locker on the left and then ran quickly to the large building at the end of the row. The community bathrooms were built in the same manner as the huts only about twice as large. Each one had a row of four toilet stalls on each side, facing two opposing rows of four sinks in the center. At the far end of the building was a gang shower that could accommodate eight.

It certainly isn't a four-star resort but, then again, it is free.

When Sarah's trainer arrived, he apologized for being late and led her to the chow hall for dinner, where she officially began camp.

Breakfasts consisted of egg white omelets and grapefruit halves.

Lunches and dinners were made up of grilled, skinless chicken breasts and steamed, mixed vegetables. Occasionally they'd throw in a fresh salad of spinach, celery and tomato. No gravies or sauces and not a condiment in sight.

The only white foods served were chicken, pork and cauliflower.

Starchy carbohydrates like rice, potatoes or bread were never served.

In addition to breakfast, lunch and dinner, there were three liquid meals served every day. Several stainless steel dispenser tanks set up at each end of the chow line near the water dispenser tanks were simply marked *Vanilla* and *Chocolate*.

Soft drinks and milk were never served.

Although Sarah overheard many people complaining about the lack of more tasty and creative foods, she ate whatever they served and didn't complain. She was simply relieved to not have to plan her own meals, much less pay for them while figuring out how to make rent. The fact that the camp's program was free, including room and board, and Sarah could stay as long as she showed weight and or fat loss progress every week was good enough reason for her to keep her mouth shut and follow the rules.

The real beauty of this camp was she stayed so busy she didn't have to think about anything. She found it easy to lose herself in the constant activity.

As she lay in her bunk at the end of the day, Sarah and the other women made up for the lack of diversions by chatting and getting to know each other.

Melanie mumbled into her pillow, "I'm so wiped. If this is Phase I then what do they do to you in Phase II?"

"Oh, be quiet, you big baby," Dani chided. "I think I speak for all of us when I say your time might be better spent visualizing a faster running pace instead of whining." Dani took no prisoners. Melanie had a good six inches more leg than Dani but Mel was just a turtle when it came to running.

Mel rolled in her bunk and leaned over the edge to look down at Dani in the lower bed. "What do you mean by that?"

Tracey chimed in. "She means you drag ass, slowpoke. I don't mind that we all have to keep the same pace all the time, but you're killing us with that slow jog of yours."

"Sarah, do you think I'm slow?"

"Well, Mel, Dani is only five-foot-one and Tracey is five-five. If they were the ones setting the pace, I'd expect it to be a little on the slow side. But you're five-seven. Couldn't you stretch your stride a little?"

"Yeah, whatever." Melanie punched her pillow and rolled over in her bunk to face the wall.

"Hey, loser." Tracey kicked Sarah's bunk from her bed below.

Sarah smiled. "You kick me again and I'll make you sleep up here."

"Yeah, yeah," Tracey teased. "So, what do you think of our trainer, Steve?"

"I think he's a monster. He's six feet tall, six feet wide and nothing but muscle. How does a human being have dimensions like that?"

Dani answered before Tracey could comment. "Probably built 'em in an Oregon logging camp, cutting down trees with six foot trunks!"

Tracey ran her fingers through her blond hair. "And what's with that shaved head?"

"Receding hairline," Dani answered.

"Shaving the whole thing seems a little overboard in response to a receding hairline. But some chicks like that, eh, Sarah?" Tracey bumped Sarah's mattress from below again.

Sarah defended her preference for men who preferred not to hassle with a lot of hair. "Hey, I'm not saying every guy should be bald. But if a dude has nice eyes, a strong jaw line and a great body, who needs hair on top?"

Melanie added one comment before finally falling silent for the night. "I'll take any man, hair or no hair, at this point!"

~~~

Sarah stretched and looked down from her bunk to the door of the hut. The sun was just coming up and creeping through the crack under the door.

Bam, bam, bam!

Sarah jumped down off her bunk in a flash. Her heart racing. Steve's pounding on the door at the crack of dawn always surprised her, whether she was asleep or awake.

He followed the banging with the same phrase every day. "Wake up, girls! You have thirty minutes to dress, drag your butts to the chow hall for some protein and then assemble for your morning run."

"Jesus, Sarah." Tracey rolled over to face her. "Do you always wake up ready to fight?"

Sarah reached for her pants and slipped them on. "Pretty much."

"Steve sounds a little too energetic today," Tracey mumbled into her pillow.

Dani rolled out of bed and started dressing. "That's how they make us eat a breakfast of grapefruit and egg whites. I'm so hungry after these runs I'd eat fried grasshoppers if I had to."

"You are disgusting," Melanie deadpanned just before walking out the door.

Sarah pulled her hair back into a tight pony tail. "That would be pretty nasty, especially when he takes us to the gym after breakfast and makes us lift until we puke. At least grapefruit and egg whites don't look that bad when they come back up."

Tracey stood up from her bunk and slapped Sarah on the shoulder. "That's our Sarah, always sunny side up."

"Oh!" Sarah rolled her head back. "That was too lame even for a loser like you."

This is all very Spartan but the company sure is fun.

~~~

Sarah climbed into her bunk and collapsed face down on her pillow. "Oh, what a day."

"A hundred and ten degrees in the shade and he makes us do calisthenics right before lunch," Mel griped.

Dani rubbed her shoulders. "How about that hike? Rucksacks filled with rocks."

Tracey flopped down onto her bunk. "You gotta hand it to the guy. He is creative. I definitely prefer the hikes when we fill the rucks with canteens. At least we can drink the weight and sweat it out."

"I definitely prefer obstacle course afternoons over those desert hikes." Sarah rolled off her bunk and landed with both feet square on the floor. "No sense bitching about this anyway. We all seem to be losing weight and that's what we're here for. Let's go dig in to some of that grilled chicken and steamed broccoli, huh?"

~~~

Bam, bam, bam!

Sarah rolled over in her bunk. "Oh my God, are you kidding me? Today is Sunday, isn't it?"

Steve's voice answered from outside the door. "Wakey-wakey, campers. Time to see which of you are losers."

Sarah dressed quickly. Within a few minutes, all four women assembled in front of Steve, just outside the hut. They followed Steve as he walked toward the chow hall.

"Oh, no," Tracey protested. "I'm not eating before a weigh-in. Forget it, man."

"Take it easy, Ballantine." Steve laughed. "The weigh-in room is on the East side of the chow hall."

When they walked into the large room, Sarah couldn't help but be impressed with the efficiency. Other campers were already there, quietly lined up in straight rows in front of eight medical scales.

Steve directed them to a scale without a line and called Mel to the scale first. After weighing her, he reached into his cargo pocket for a small notebook and pen and noted her weight. "You lost eight pounds, good work."

Mel dismounted the scale with a smile.

26

Rising voices and a commotion two scales down drew Sarah's attention. "Hey, Steve, what's going on over there?"

"Hold on, I'll be right back." Steve walked over to the cadre member talking to a belligerent male camper. When he returned a few minutes later, he told the girls what had happened. "That camper was filmed by a security camera when he broke into the cadre kitchen last week. We would have let it slide if he'd still lost weight but he was up from last week. When his trainer told him to do the duffel bag drag and report to the command hut for transport out of here, he thought he could fight it."

"Damn. I'm too tired to work for food at the end of the day." Sarah was being totally honest. "Now, if you had a bathtub hidden somewhere, well, that's a different story. The first thing I want to do when I leave here is to take a long, hot, luxurious bubble bath. Aside from that, some sleep would be nice."

Steve shook his head. "Sorry, Stevens. No bath."

Dani and Tracey had both lost six pounds each. With dread in her heart Sarah closed her eyes and stepped on the scale next.

"Looks like you're down ten pounds, Stevens. Not bad for your first week." Steve scribbled something in his notebook. "Okay, ladies. You've earned your breakfast. Meet me back at the hut in thirty minutes for a hike."

Days turned into weeks and all four women in Sarah's squad continued to lose weight. One night, Sarah dragged her tired body up to her bunk and flopped onto her back after another exhausting training day in the sun. She stretched her sore arms over her head. When she dropped her arms, one hit something hard. "Okay, who threw a boot in my bunk?"

Tracey punched her pillow. "What the hell are you talking about?"

Sarah sat up and patted the mattress as she searched for the boot. Nothing was there. When she lay down again, she realized it was her hip bone that her arm had fallen on. Glee bubbled up inside her. "Oh, my God! I just found my hip bones." She touched them as though pinching herself in a dream.

Hello, old friends. I haven't seen you in years.

"'Bout time." Dani smiled as she hung up her wet pants to dry at the foot of her bed. "By the way, your ass isn't taking up nearly as much real estate as it did when we first got here."

"Speaking of asses." Mel sat up in her bunk. "Did you guys see those men watching us today?"

The bunk bed frame moved as Tracey sat on the bunk below Sarah. "Yeah, the ones all dressed in black?"

Dani lay down on her bunk. "Very mysterious."

Mel was true to form. "Did you see the muscles on those guys? Oh my God! They were gorgeous. I'll take an hour with one of them any day."

"Yeah, they were a good bit of eye candy." Sarah punched her pillow and lay on her side so she could see Mel and Dani in their bunks. "What do you suppose they're here for?"

"I think they're the food police. Checking up on who might not be losing as quickly as they should," Dani speculated.

"You would say that, Dani." Mel peered over the edge of her bunk to see Dani. "You're always thinking about your next meal. I don't care who they are, they're frigging hot."

Tracey's voice came from the bunk below. "And you'd say that, Mel, since you're always wondering when you're going to eat your next man. I agree though, they are pretty hot. I think they're just QC, you know, quality controllers to make sure the staff and campers are doing what they're supposed to do. What do you think, Sarah?"

Sarah leaned over the edge of her bunk to see Tracey. "I think Dani's stomach is growling a little too loudly, Melanie is a slut with an oral fixation and you're probably right, even though you are a loser."

Dani rolled over with a moan. "Sorry, guys. I can't help it."

"Guilty as charged," Melanie admitted with an ear to ear grin.

Tracey smiled up at Sarah and made an "L" with her right thumb and forefinger pressed to her forehead. "You're still a loser."

Sarah lay back on her pillow and stared at the ceiling. "Seriously, guys. They show up at any time of day and follow particular squads, like they're watching certain people. By their glances and hand gestures, they seem to be discussing us, too. I don't know who they are or what they're up to, but I suspect it has something to do with why this 'Boot Camp' is free." Sarah laced her fingers together behind her head and stretched her shoulders as she spoke. "People make millions running places like this. You can't tell me that somebody, just out of the goodness of their heart, decided to start a fat camp for ex-military personnel. That doesn't happen. There's a lot about this place we don't know, but we're so desperate for the service they provide, we don't care."

"We are all such losers." Tracey flopped over with a chuckle. "Now, shut up and go to sleep. You ugly bitches need some beauty rest. I'm tired of looking at the dark circles under your eyes."

Sarah smiled.

One thing is for certain. Those men in black are all so damned buff I'm just happy to see them whenever and wherever they might turn up.

Her body was starting to take shape, but her self-esteem and confidence weren't exactly overblown at this point in her life. Some things required more time.

Her thoughts turned to her friend, Laura, in England, who Sarah had always thought was so shallow and missing out on the joys of love. Laura would tell men she had no use for a long-term relationship and honestly meant it. Laura always had plenty of men to choose from, but she'd never commit to any of them. Men would follow her like dogs. Sarah now understood that Laura wasn't being shallow at all and just enjoying the upside without the hassle of the downside of relationships.

Yeah, Laura had it right all along! Laura was the one in control. Now I need to be the one in control. Control over my body and eating. Control over my mind and heart so I stop falling for, or settling for, all the wrong men. Yeah, control could be a better drug than carbohydrates.

This became the last thought, her personal mantra of sorts, before she dropped off to sleep every night.

~~~

Sarah adapted quickly to the schedule at camp and welcomed the simplicity of it. In just a couple months, her body fat dropped from over thirty-five percent to seventeen percent and her long limbs soon became lean and hard. She lost fifty pounds and found herself at a svelte one-seventy-five.

Instead of braiding it after her shower one night, she left her hair down and let it dry naturally. The many weeks of healthy living had done wonderful things for her hair. The long, shiny, voluminous waves framing the newly thin features of her face and accentuating her deep green eyes surprised her. She had never seen this woman in the mirror before but she liked what she saw.

Honey, I don't know who you are, but you're a welcome change from that fat chick I used to see all the time. Stick around. We could have some fun.

She was even stronger than she'd been when she graduated from the Security Police Academy. The activities at the camp were becoming less challenging. Her self-confidence grew and she often imagined what her life could be like if she never gave up control again.

Starting over. Where do I want to live? What do I want to do? I don't know how or where, but I want to finally do something exciting. I finally feel like I can do just that.

Five

Bam, bam, bam!

Sarah woke to see Tracey spring from her bunk.

"I swear, Steve, one of these days you're gonna knock that bitch clean off the hinges!"

"Damn, Trace." Sarah looked down from her bunk. "What the hell got into you?"

Dani stood and started to dress. "I'll tell you what it is. We've been here eight weeks now. Look at us. We're gorgeous. How much longer are they really going to let us stay?"

Sarah and Melanie each climbed from their bunks. All four women dressed in silence. Sarah realized she hadn't even begun to think about what she would do when she left the camp. Excitement about her new physique, uncertainty about her future and doubts as to whether she could maintain this new body out in the real world mixed and tumbled in her stomach.

Dani makes a good point. I think this may be a good time to start putting a plan together.

Sarah walked outside first to see Steve's smiling face.

As the others stepped outside, Steve smiled with a larger than usual grin. "Good morning, ladies. Shall we?"

The hairs on the back of Sarah's neck stood at attention.

As they walked to the chow hall for their Sunday weigh-in, Tracey leaned close to Sarah. "Did he call us ladies?"

"Something's up."

I weighed myself at the gym yesterday. I've lost fifty pounds so far. I can lose more. They won't kick me out.

Sarah was the first to step on the scale.

Steve checked her weight and smiled. "Great job, Stevens."

A thrill ran through Sarah like an electrical current. She'd bought herself more time to put her plan together. "Thanks, Steve. Just check me out next week. I'll do even better."

"No can do, Stevens. You won't be here. Pack your bag and report to the command hut."

"What?" Fear smacked Sarah in the head and her face dropped. "But I'm making great progress. Why am I being kicked out?"

Dani came to Sarah's defense. "That's messed up, Steve. Sarah is doing great and hasn't broken any rules. Why is she getting kicked out?"

Sarah felt as though her feet had been glued to the floor.

"Don't ask questions, ladies. You're asking for need-to-know information, and you don't. Good job on your weight, Dani. Get on the scale, Melanie." Steve turned and stared directly into Sarah's eyes. "Duffel bag drag, Stevens. Good luck."

Sarah took a deep breath and walked quickly out of the room. She clenched her hands at her sides and started to shake with anger. After the door closed behind her, Sarah vented all the way to her hut.

"What the hell? I need more time. That bastard. No explanation? No 'nice knowing you?' Duffel bag drag, huh? I'll drag my duffel bag back there and shove it up his ass."

Sarah took her anger and frustration out on the contents of her locker. She jammed everything in her bag, took one last look around the room and slung the duffel over her left shoulder. The door closed behind her with a final click and she walked the dusty quarter mile from her quarters to the command hut near the camp entrance. Sarah lifted her chin and stormed past a black Suburban into the command hut ready for a fight.

The same guy who had picked her up at the airport stood inside the command hut, near Mary's desk.

Sarah looked for Mary but she wasn't anywhere around. Sarah aimed her anger at the driver. "Look, this is bullshit. I followed every rule and lost a ton of weight. What's going on? Why am I being kicked out?"

"You aren't." The driver chuckled. "You're moving on up to Phase II, kiddo. Get in the truck."

Sarah tipped her head to the side. This didn't register. When she'd processed what he'd said, every cell in her body exploded with joy. "What? Are you kidding?"

"Would you rather go back to the airport?" The driver shrugged as he made his way toward the door. "It makes no difference to me."

"No, no, no!" Sarah turned to follow him. "Phase II. Where is that? What is that?"

"Short drive. More training and weight loss. What's it going to be?"

Sarah threw her duffel bag in the back of the Suburban and hopped into the passenger seat before the guy finished his question. "Phase II, man. Let's go."

The driver smiled, shook his head and sat behind the wheel of the truck. He picked up a radio handset and keyed the mike. "Transporting Stevens to Lightning." He nodded toward the blindfold on the seat. "Short drive."

Sarah tied the blindfold around her head without argument as her thoughts whirled about what was to come.

This is turning out to be more of an adventure than I expected! What's next?

Six

Sarah's body swayed forward in the seat as the Suburban pulled to a stop.

"Okay, you can take the blindfold off now."

Sarah untied the blindfold and squinted against the light. Once her eyes adjusted, she looked around and found a camp similar to the one she had just left, only this one had ten campers' huts and several more hangar-style buildings. There were more people moving around outside at this camp. They all seemed to be the guys dressed in black BDU pants and black shirts.

Damn. Those are some fine looking men!

Sarah made a mental note that getting laid by someone who looks like one of those men should be on her to do list when she finally left the camp. She hopped out of the truck and grabbed her bag from the back before following the driver inside the command hut. The man sitting behind the front desk was nothing less than impressive. His biceps were as thick as Sarah's thighs and his chest looked as if it was ready to burst through the black T-shirt he wore. He had a dark tan, sky blue eyes and a blond buzz cut. The tattoo across the top of his right arm read "Semper Fi."

A Marine. Of course. Nobody else builds them up quite like that.

"Morning, Stevens. Welcome to Phase II." His voice rolled like thunder.

Sarah was so distracted by his physicality that she never thought to ask this man's name. "Thanks. Good morning."

"Heard good things about ya. Hear you got potential. I s'pose we'll see about that."

"Thank you."

Potential for what?

"You'll be in hut number three, just across the way." He pointed straight out the door. "Your squad is short. Only gonna be two of ya but we can't afford to wait for two more. Need to get you both in training ASAP. That okay with you?"

The light blue eyes set in the smiling, tanned face distracted Sarah for a moment. "Yeah, absolutely. I'm ready to go."

"Good deal. Same rules here as before. Your training buddy ought to be here shortly so just chill in your hut for the rest of the day. Training starts tomorrow morning. The latrine is by hut number one and the chow hall is right next door here." The massive man stood and towered over her. He was at least six-foot-four. His blue eyes narrowed as he stared at her. "Don't go poking around in any of the other buildings or I'll send your ass home. Got it?"

Sarah nodded. "Got it."

"Dismissed."

Sarah slung her bag over her shoulder and walked out of the building. She pretended not to notice the stares from four guys, all dressed in black, who were sitting at a picnic table just outside the command hut. After taking a few steps she glanced back to see if they were still watching her and it surprised and excited her to see they were. The attention made her feel giddy and she suppressed a nervous chuckle. When Sarah arrived at her hut, it looked exactly like the one she'd left this morning. Sarah unpacked her bag and hung her clothes neatly in the first wall locker on the left.

I can't believe my luck. I'm staying at the camp, get to keep training and losing weight and I'll only have one roommate instead of three. Throw in a bath and I might think I'd won the lottery!

When she finished unpacking, Sarah picked a lower bunk because it meant less climbing at the end of the day and stretched out. A whole day to catch up on some rest and she fully intended to use it. She let out a deep sigh of contentment and fell asleep almost immediately with a smile on her face.

The recurring dream she'd been having for the past year, ever since she had arrived in Las Vegas started again. She was lying in the sun on a warm beach with the whisper of palm trees and the sweet smell of salt water in the tropical breeze. Crystal blue waters lapped at the shoreline. Only this time someone was with her. She turned to her left to see him...

Bam!

Sarah bolted out of bed, both feet on the floor and her fists in a defensive position. "What the hell?" She found herself staring straight at

Tracey who was grinning wide as she picked up the duffel bag she'd thrown on the floor near the head of Sarah's bed.

"Nice reflexes, loser."

Tracey is my training buddy? This is too good.

Sarah played it cool. "I was sleeping, bitch."

"Forget it, loser. Beauty sleep won't help you," Tracey teased. "Is this a sweet deal or what?"

"Yeah, I was just thinking the same thing."

Tracey sauntered over to the first locker on the right and began to unpack her clothes. "Did you see those guys out there? I thought I'd died and gone to heaven."

~~~

Sarah woke to the sound of firm knocking on the door of the hut. She sat up in the dark and looked for a sliver of light under the door. There was no light to be seen. Sarah rubbed her eyes and then flailed around until she found the string to turn their single light bulb on. She closed her eyes tight against the glare of the bulb. "Trace, get up."

Tracey pulled her pillow over her eyes. "I didn't hear the pounding on the door yet."

Sarah slipped on her pants and buttoned them. "I guess they don't pound here. It was just a knock."

When Tracey finished dressing, they both stepped outside to see their trainer waiting for them.

"Okay, campers. My name is Shawn. Your wake-up calls will be the same as in Phase I, but there will be a slight change in the training schedule. Hit the chow hall for your liquid breakfast and then muster back here for your morning run in thirty minutes."

Sarah and Tracey jogged over to the chow hall, drank a light protein fruit punch for their first meal and then made quick time back to their hut.

The routine was very much the same¾they ran and lifted weights in the morning, but their afternoons were focused solely on martial arts training. They trained for four hours every afternoon learning Krav Maga. The first few days exhausted Sarah, but she soon learned to enjoy the physical challenges of Phase II.

Within their first week, Sarah and Tracey became so accomplished at Krav Maga they had to start sparring with cadre instead of each other.

Sarah and Tracey knew each others' moves so well they could anticipate each others' attacks. Sparring with cadre challenged both women to excel. The cadre kicked their butts more often than not, but Sarah and Tracey were up for it. Sarah's self-confidence grew as she began to realize how physically strong and skilled she had become.

~~~

One night, Sarah and Tracey lay in their respective bunks chatting about life in general to avoid thinking about the aches and pains from the day's training.

"You know, Trace, I always thought if I was a good girlfriend, I'd get what I wanted and needed from guys."

"That's a sucker's bet, Sarah. If you want something in this world, you gotta take it."

"I think you're right."

"Sarah, stop being such a doormat. I don't know about you but I'll be ready to start breaking some hearts when I leave this place."

"You're absolutely right, Trace. It is about time I got a piece of the pie instead of being the one to bake it, serve it and clean up after some bastard has finished eating it."

"Frig the pie, Sarah. Eat the apple straight from the tree and send Adam packin', baby!"

Tracey was right. Sarah was ready to be a one woman wrecking crew and the determination carried over into her training.

The biggest difference with Phase II was the men in black were around every day. Sarah recognized one in particular who followed her and Tracey throughout their training. He had a massive build. She recognized his shoulders every time he showed up, but could never see his face since he wore dark sunglasses and a black BDU cap low over his forehead. Not being able to see his face created a delicious mystery in Sarah's mind¾a mystery she'd spent a great deal of time thinking about lately. Whatever this mystery man was up to, he provided great fantasy fodder for this now very physical woman who hadn't had sex with a straight man in a very long time.

One morning during their run curiosity got the better of her, and she decided to get some information from their trainer. "Shawn, who are those guys in black and what do they do here?"

Shawn kept running. "They're scouts."

Sarah stepped up her pace to run beside Shawn. "Scouts for what?"

Shawn glared at Sarah as he picked up the pace. "Any further information will be given on a strictly need-to-know basis. When you need to know, they'll be the ones to tell you. Now do you want to train or do you want to go back home and eat Twinkies?"

Sarah nearly fell over when Tracey pushed her left shoulder from behind. "Run, loser."

Tracey sped by as Sarah recovered from her stumble.

Sarah sprinted to catch up but her mind wandered.

What are they scouting for? Who do they work for? What do they have to do with our training?

Unanswered questions didn't stop Sarah from taking full advantage of what the camp's program offered. Her body had changed for the better and so had her mindset. This was a chance at a whole new and completely improved life.

I won't be here forever. I'm an excellent physical specimen now, but where will that and eight years in the Air Force get me? I'm thirty, homeless, jobless and have no possessions of note. I don't really exist, do I?

A smile curled her lips.

I can be anyone I want.

Seven

"Okay, guys. Time to pick a replacement." Vince sat at the kitchen table and opened his briefcase.

Will leaned against the kitchen counter. "What are you talking about?"

"I told Young we get to pick the replacements from now on. We can't assume the Agency knows what we need for our team. We know better than anyone, so sit down and start checking out these files."

Chris thumbed through the files Vince had placed on the table. "This is all well and good, boss, but how do we know if any of these are good looking enough to pull off a Honey Pot?"

"It'll be better to start blind." Vince pulled a cigarette from the box on the table and lit it. "Right now, we just have to find the ones who are qualified. We need language skills, good test scores, some sort of background that prepares them for the job. We'll narrow down the list and then get a look at each of them."

"Hey, how about this one, guys?" Jason pulled a page from a file folder. "Air Force cop with FBI training, maxed out her language battery scores and¼" Jason smiled wide. "Lots of heavy weapons certifications."

"You and your gun fetish." Brian closed the folder in front of Jason. "We need a babe that can work close up, not long distance, dipshit."

"Wait a minute. Wait a minute." Jason held up his hand. "Heavy weapons operators have a very short life expectancy. I think we can all agree on that no matter what branch we served in."

Everyone nodded.

Will sat down at the table. "What's your point, Jason?"

"Here it is¾a chick in the Air Force doesn't automatically get heavy weapons training. She has to request it and even then she won't get it if she's just looking for bragging rights. She's got to have the nerve to do it and the strength to haul the weapon and ammo. We need a woman with guts who can kick ass if she has to. This one¼" He held up the folder. "Is the one we need if she cleans up nice."

Vince set his cigarette in the ash tray. "Good points, Jason. I like his thinking. I say we check her out. Who is she?"

Jason read from the folder. "Sarah Stevens. She's right here at the camp in Phase II."

"I've seen that one." Vince pointed at the file. "She's pretty tough, but I don't know if she'll clean up to what we need. Jason, you and Brian check her out."

Eight

Five weeks into Phase II training, Sarah continued to drop weight. Not to mention, six hours a day of Krav Maga training did amazing things for her reflexes, and her self-confidence.

On the Sunday marking her fifth week in Phase II, Sarah weighed in as usual.

"One hundred and fifty on the mark, Stevens. Nice work."

Sarah raised her arms, fists clenched, in triumph. "This is huge. The least I've ever weighed as an adult is one hundred and fifty-seven pounds."

Shawn smiled. "Congratulations. Now tighten that belt and get off my scale."

Sarah looked at the baggy BDU pants that were once tight on her, rolled her eyes at her own foolishness and stepped down. As she stepped away from the scale, she wondered what size jeans she could fit into and grinned with her own silent excitement.

After Tracey weighed in, Shawn had some great news for them. "Okay, you've both got twenty-four hours of liberty. A bunch of us are going into Vegas for some R&R. We're not allowed to fraternize with campers, but we can give you a ride in, if you like."

"Sounds great to me. When do we leave?"

Tracey wasn't as enthusiastic as Sarah. "Thanks, but I think I'm gonna hang out here and catch up on some sleep."

"Are you nuts, Trace? As much as I could use some sleep, I'm ready to try this new bod in an old dress."

"Sarah, we'll be leaving from the command hut at sixteen-hundred hours. See you then." Shawn turned to leave the weigh-in room. "Enjoy your sleep, Tracey."

Sarah and Tracey followed Shawn out of the room and strolled to their hut.

Tracey elbowed Sarah. "What's this old dress you're talking about?"

"My little black dress." Sarah smiled. "I never thought I'd wear it again but I packed it for motivation."

Tracey held the hut door open for Sarah. "Okay, let's see this dress of yours."

Sarah darted to her locker and pulled out a pair of black, patent leather, stiletto pumps, a black mini skirt and a black, low-cut, thong leotard. Altogether, these items made up the little black dress she'd dreamed of being able to wear and feel good in once again. An outing in the city would be the perfect place to give the outfit a try. "After weighing two-twenty-five and feeling practically invisible in public, I'm ready to see if my seventy-five pound weight loss changes anything."

Tracey settled in to her bunk for a nap. "If it doesn't, you're doing somethin' really wrong."

Several hours later after Sarah dressed, she looked into the mirror and gasped.

Hello gorgeous!

She could barely believe her eyes. She looked spectacular from top to bottom. Her light brown hair fell over her shoulders long, lush and wavy. She ran her hands down her waist and hips, smiling with satisfaction at the hourglass shape. When she turned to the side, eyes still fixed on the mirror, she marveled at the perfectly flat stomach she'd never seen before. Her skirt hugged her hips and stopped mid-thigh.

Good God, look at those legs! This is beyond my wildest dreams.

Sarah tried to contain her giddiness while still hoping for a reaction as she walked to the command hut to meet Shawn for the ride to town. Two scouts were waiting with him, leaning against the black Suburban.

A long, low whistle sounded from one of the two scouts.

Oh my God, that's for me. Yes!

Sarah smiled at the whistler. He stood about the same height as Sarah and had short, light brown hair. He was cute in a devilish sort of way.

The second scout tipped his head toward Shawn but spoke loud enough so Sarah could hear. "Nice job, dude." He was a long, lean six-foot-five and had brown hair just long enough to run your fingers through.

Yeah, nice job yourself, stud. Thank your Mama for me.

The whistler looked wide-eyed at Shawn. "You've been training this one?"

Shawn smirked. "Yeah, but remember, she's been doing all the work." He smiled and nodded his approval to Sarah. "The boys seem to agree. You're lookin' good, kid." He opened the rear passenger door for Sarah and then walked around to hop in on the driver's side and start the Suburban.

Sarah smiled and her cheeks warmed. "Thank you very much. Compliments are always welcome." Sarah took a deep breath and sat back in the seat.

So, this is what fabulous smells like.

The man with the devilish smile climbed into the back seat. "Well, if that's the case, I've got a few more for you."

The tall hottie sat in the front seat. "Heel, Jason!"

Sarah looked out the window and couldn't stop smiling. Having her accomplishments acknowledged by a truck full of hotties drove home the idea that she really could be anyone she wanted to be. Her blood bubbled like champagne.

Yeah, this is good.

Shawn drove the shiny, black Suburban while Sarah and the two scouts rode in silence. Shawn was very careful to ensure Sarah wore a blindfold from the camp to the highway.

"Okay, I'll wear the silly blindfold, but I don't get all this secrecy. Come to think of it, I've never seen a mailman at this camp and even the business card I received from my Commander didn't have an address. You know, even the phone calls I had with a rep didn't last long enough to be traced." Sarah laughed. "You'd think it was a training camp for spooks or something."

Sarah's joke was met with tense silence.

Can it be?

Nine

Sarah noticed a different glow about the lights of Las Vegas. Instead of the place she never fit in, she now marveled at a city offering bright opportunities.

Shawn pulled the Suburban up to Caesar's Palace and stopped in front of the main door.

"Do whatever you like here in town but rendezvous right here at noon tomorrow. If you miss the ride, you won't be allowed back at the camp. Got it?"

"Pretty harsh, isn't it, Shawn? What if I'm a few minutes late?"

Shawn glared at Sarah in the rear view mirror. "Don't be."

Sarah nodded and took one last look at the guy in the back seat. The devilish grin shone back at her.

Who the hell are these guys?

Sarah stepped carefully out of the black Suburban, and strolled across the portico toward the main entrance of the casino. A small group of guys leaving the casino stopped and stared admiringly at her while the doorman grinned and held the door open.

Sarah glowed with pride, gave a saucy smile to the men and thanked the doorman.

I feel like Cinderella. I could get used to this.

Sarah strode through the lobby of Caesar's Palace and took a seat at the first bar she found. The bar was quiet which suited her just fine. She was looking forward to a nice cold Margarita and a cigarette.

The bartender smiled at her expectantly. "What'll it be, beautiful?"

"Cuervo Margarita on the rocks, no salt." Sarah opened a fresh pack of cigarettes, tapped out a Marlboro Light and took a deep drag as she lit it.

She reveled in the ego boost she received with each appreciative glance from men walking by. Each admiring stare made her feel more sure of herself.

"It's on me." The bartender flashed her a smile as he returned with the drink.

He must assume I'm playing one of these slots on the bar.

"Thanks, but I'm not gambling."

"That's not for gambling, lady. It's for sitting at my bar." He winked.

What the heck?

"Thank you, but what's the deal? Is it happy hour for chicks or something?"

The bartender leaned toward Sarah and whispered, "I don't buy them for every woman, only the gorgeous ones."

Oh, this is too good to be true. Cinderella finally arrived at the ball after all these years.

Sarah tingled with excitement. "Thanks for the compliment and the Cuervo." She lifted her glass and took a drink of the tangy goodness she so loved.

Vegas is good to beautiful people and it looks like I'm finally one of them. Excellent.

"No. Thank you. Guys like to frequent bars where there are beautiful women. Those same guys also like to appear important, so they tip big to impress the ladies." The bartender leaned across the bar and whispered, "I figure if I can get you to sit at my bar for a half-hour or so during the slow part of the evening, it ought to be good for at least an extra fifty in tips."

"Oh, I see." Sarah smiled and raised an eyebrow conspiratorially. "You're baiting the trap."

"You got it, babe." He reached across the bar to shake her hand. "I'm Mike."

"Sarah." She returned his firm handshake.

Mike turned and began restocking and polishing his bar while Sarah continued to sip her Margarita and puff thoughtfully on her cigarette.

I'm not invisible anymore. People see me now and I'm liking it! The free drinks are a nice bonus, too.

Only minutes after she and Mike finished their introductions, two men walked into the bar and sat on the stools to her right.

"Jameson on the rocks and whatever the lady is drinking," the man next to her said.

She turned to thank him and noticed he laid a hundred dollar bill on the bar.

Mike knew what he was talking about because the man made a point of loudly saying, "Keep the change, buddy."

Mike gave Sarah a knowing wink as he brought her another Margarita.

Sarah had no sooner pulled out another cigarette when the big spender had a lighter lit and waiting for her convenience.

Now this is more like it!

He was a middle-aged man with short, well-groomed, gray hair, wearing a dark suit, white shirt and a stunning royal blue tie. He had either left his wife at home or sent her off to a show so he could play man-about-town for an evening.

I've got nothing better to do. I can play along.

The big spender introduced himself and his friend. "I'm Dean. This is Matt."

Sarah turned to face Dean. "Sarah. Nice to meet you Dean, Matt. So, are you here on vacation?"

"We're in for a convention this week. Financial planners from Boston." Dean tapped his knuckles against the hardwood bar. "So, who manages your portfolio, Sarah?"

Sarah laughed. "I'm a long way from having a portfolio, but I'll look you up when its time."

Halfway through their drinks, Dean asked, "You play cards, Sarah?"

"No, that's a rich man's sport." Sarah took another sip of her Margarita.

"Well, how's about you be my lucky charm at the tables for a while?"

Sarah chuckled. "I'm not so sure I'd bring you much luck."

"I'm sorry. I'm sure you must have plans." Dean motioned to the bartender for more drinks.

"Actually, I don't have plans and it could be interesting to watch a game or two." Sarah slid her pack of cigarettes into the small purse slung over her shoulder.

Dean's face brightened with a smile. "That's great. See I just lost a bundle, but I've got a feeling you might change my luck."

"This is Vegas. Anything can and does happen." Sarah took a healthy pull of the new Margarita Mike set in front of her. The tequila began to warm her from the inside out and she was beginning to believe Vegas really could be a magical place.

"Shall we?" Dean's blue eyes sparkled as he stepped off his stool and motioned toward the card tables with his left hand.

Okay, but if you don't offer me a seat and a drink at the gaming table, you can buy yourself a rabbit's foot for a lucky charm!

Dean behaved like a perfect gentleman. He ushered Sarah into a rather quiet room clearly for the more serious gamblers. There were no cargo shorts and Hawaiian shirts in here. The people inside this room were dressed a bit better than the average Las Vegas tourist. The gamblers at the tables were quiet and every one appeared serious and focused on the game they played.

Dean held a seat out for her and then ordered drinks for both of them. When she pulled out a cigarette, he lit it. She watched carefully, and tried to hide her admiration as Dean played with hundred dollar chips then moved up to thousand dollar chips.

~~~

It's only been an hour and a half and this guy is up by eight, nine, ten grand. Yikes! Maybe I am lucky.

As the clock approached ten pm, Dean finished his drink. He turned to her with his bright blue eyes full of merriment. "Sarah, my dear, you've been a fine lucky charm. I've got to go meet my wife for dinner and drinks, but I have thoroughly enjoyed your company. Thank you."

He slid a thousand dollar chip across the table to her and smiled.

A thrill jolted her as she looked at the chip in front of her.

"There's a little something for you." He stood up and touched her shoulder. "Have some fun at the tables. You're definitely lucky tonight."

Lucky? Are you kidding me? This is the luckiest night of my life.

Stunned by his kindness and with all the charm she could muster, Sarah patted Dean's hand gently resting on her shoulder. "It was my pleasure, Dean. Good night."

Dean left the room and Sarah stared at the chip in front of her. One chip represented about a month's worth of her Air Force salary.

The dealer cocked his eyebrow at Sarah, obviously waiting to see if she would play.

Sarah grinned at him before she picked up her chip. "Good night."

With a lighter step, Sarah strolled to the cashier's cage and cashed in her chip.

I'm cashing out while I'm still ahead of the game.

Ten

Energized by her newfound powers of attraction, Sarah decided to see how she'd fare at a nightclub if she even made it past the door.

She stepped into the nearest ladies room to check her hair and lipstick before going to *Pure*. She still didn't recognize the woman in the mirror but smiled and threw her a wink before straightening her shoulders a little more and turning to strut out of the ladies room.

Pure was *the* club at Caesar's Palace. Sarah expected a long wait since this was one of the best nightclubs in the country.

She took her place at the end of the twenty-person deep line. She peered toward the door to see which fabulous people were being admitted to the club tonight. That's when the doorman stared in her direction and motioned for someone to move up to the door.

Unaccustomed to special treatment, Sarah instinctively turned around to see who he had signaled to behind her.

No one is behind me.

A tingle ran through her from her feet to the top of her head.

Can it be this easy?

When she turned back toward the doorman, he pointed at her and waved her up.

Sarah's palms grew sweaty. She smoothed her skirt in an effort to wipe her palms without seeming too obvious.

Stay cool, girl. This is it. You're about to see how the sexy half lives.

Every man in line looked her over. The women either smiled or turned their backs as she walked by them.

She took a deep breath and tried to control her racing heartbeat.

Calm down, loser. It's just a club for Pete's sake!

Sarah never had this kind of attention before, but now that she did, she craved more.

The doorman unclipped the velvet rope as she approached. He reached gently around her waist to reattach the rope and whispered in her ear. "Don't ever go to the end of the line again."

Sarah caught her breath and then exhaled with a light giggle. She mustered all of her confidence and smiled at the doorman. "I'll remember that."

No more second fiddle for me. It all seems so surreal since only a few months ago I was rejected for my looks. Now I'm a frigging goddess. I could so get used to this.

Free drinks, compliments, high rollers, lucky charms, skipping lines into exclusive clubs... Sarah drank it all in and grew giddy.

Act confident even if you don't feel it yet. Own it.

As Sarah stepped through the entrance to *Pure,* she stepped into a bold and luxurious new world. Old insecurities nipped at her newfound confidence. She considered turning around and walking out, but her desire to explore this exciting new world was too strong.

If I can get into a joint like this, then I'm going to stay long enough to see what all the fuss is about.

She strode straight toward the bar for more liquid courage. The air was electric as Sarah passed through the white room. She surveyed the area slowly, half expecting to see her old comrades from Nellis partying there.

It isn't likely military cops would ever make it through the door, and even if they did, they'd never recognize me. All the better.

Sarah sipped her Margarita and drank in the beauty of the club. To her right, a woman's voice cut across the crowd, a bit louder than appropriate.

Sarah glanced over to see what the fuss was about. A large man wearing a blue silk suit had his back to Sarah and a very attractive blond stood nearly toe-to-toe with him.

Well, aren't you the stereotypical Vegas bimbo? Strappy sandals, surgically enhanced figure, bleached blond hair and a sugar daddy by the look of those diamond earrings.

Sarah wondered if the woman had been beautiful all her life. It was a simple enough question. Women who have been beautiful all their lives learn to take everything for granted. These dolls assume they're due more of everything and better than the rest. Better treatment becomes expected simply because it is always given. Of course nobody bothers to correct these beautiful girls. Resentment rose in Sarah as she studied the woman's body language.

Oh, yeah. Clearly you've never known an ugly day in your life. You probably don't even get premenstrual bloat.

The woman continued to make a scene. "Look, I don't care! After all those nights of wondering where you are, I deserve the house, the car and some alimony. You can afford it and it's the least you can do for me after not even being there during our marriage."

Sarah stifled a chuckle in her drink. The blond pointed her fingers and made large gestures with her hands, but the hair stayed perfect.

Okay, sounds like she has a good case. I might as well have another cigarette and enjoy the rest of the show.

Then the man spoke. He had a deep, baritone voice that caught Sarah completely off guard. His voice was so smooth and warm she had difficulty remembering where she was. "The least I can do? You knew what it was going to be like going in." He didn't have to raise his voice. It carried like a warm breeze.

Isn't that just like a man? You're probably the kind of guy that likes to have a wife at home while you're out with your girlfriend. Silk suit, buff body, smooth voice¾you've got "bastard" written all over you.

Then came the whammy. "Let's not forget, sweetheart, you were the one who decided to sleep around on me."

Sarah was stunned and disappointed in womankind. For a woman to cheat on a man and then demand everything in the divorce settlement was completely beyond her comprehension.

Whoa! Quite the plot twist. This bimbo has balls!

Sarah had never cheated on a man in her life. She'd been every man's doormat.

It's one thing for a woman to honestly let men know they're being used for sex, but another thing altogether to commit to one and then cheat on him.

Sarah glanced at her cigarette, finally realizing she'd been so intent on staring at the woman and watching the unfolding drama that the ash on her cigarette was about to drop off the tip. She dropped the ash into an ash tray and turned back to watch the scene.

The blond's furious gaze met Sarah's. "What the hell do you want?"

I want to kick your ass for being born beautiful and thinking the world is supposed to hand you everything you want on a silver platter, bitch!

Sarah stood a head taller than the woman and wasn't at all used to being yelled at by women she could so obviously crush into a fine powder. It took Sarah barely a moment to recover herself from the surprise, then she looked down at the bimbo and said, matter-of-factly, "Margarita on the rocks, no salt, please."

The blond gave Sarah the once over. "Screw you. I don't work here. Now turn around and mind your own business."

Sarah's temperature rose. She clenched her fists so tight her nails dug into the palms of her hands.

Clearly this broad is in need of having her teeth handed to her! Okay, Stevens, consider your options. You're a civilian now, so there won't be any problem with Uncle Sam if you take this tart to task. Of course, mixing it up means the possibility of missing your ride to camp. Option two, diffuse the situation.

Sarah couldn't resist one final jab. "There's hardly any need to be so rude. After all, you do look like you're on the job." Sarah turned back to her drink.

"What the hell is that supposed to mean?" trilled the tramp as she pushed past the man and moved into Sarah's personal space.

Nothing would have pleased Sarah more at that moment than to blacken this woman's perfect blue eyes, bloody her pouty, pink lips and leave her for dead in a Las Vegas alley.

Get a grip, Stevens. Don't let this trash and your short fuse ruin what has so far been a fantastic night. She's not worth it.

Sarah took a deep breath, put on her best game face and said innocently, "I'm so sorry! Oh, you're just so pretty I assumed you worked here."

The blond seemed completely taken in by the sugary-sweet diversion, glanced at the man with a "see, I'm beautiful and you don't stand a chance" smile, turned on her stiletto heel and strutted away.

Note to self¾one of these days I'll clean that bitch's clock!

The man who'd taken a verbal beating from the bimbo turned to face Sarah. He wore a dark blue, double-breasted silk suit and a white collarless silk shirt. He had skin the color of dark, rich honey. Like a caramel that makes your mouth water at the very thought of a taste. He didn't have traditional good looks, but was magnetic nonetheless.

As though he couldn't be bothered with hair, his head was shaved, leaving him nothing to hide behind, nothing to distract the eye from the man himself. He clearly took great care of his body. His physical presence overpowered. Sarah had only seen one man built so perfectly, but he would never be in a place like this.

As the man took a drink, she caught the faintest hint of a scent, smooth and musky. Sarah found the scent so compelling she couldn't help but breathe deeply to draw as much of it in as possible.

He smiled at her with eyes that drew her in as though she were entering a softly lit room furnished with overstuffed velvet chairs in front of a crackling fire. Eyes that took her somewhere she could finally relax, forget the world, and be at ease after a long day. His dark brown eyebrows only accentuated and punctuated the effect of those fawn colored eyes.

Broad shoulders so amassed with muscle that the weight of the world shouldn't make them stoop. His chest appeared chiseled from granite, rock hard with edges yet to be sanded and filed. Her eyes trailed lower to his legs, like tree trunks, they were solid and well defined. So well defined that even the drape of a finely tailored silk suit couldn't hide the power contained within. No, he wasn't pretty, but he was a man so completely male, so absolutely masculine that she couldn't help but be totally drawn to him.

Sarah felt a growing warmth inside that confirmed her immediate sexual attraction to the man. She snapped out of the trance and realized this was the point where she usually fell for the guy, leaving herself open to more pain when he dumped her for a bimbo just like the one she'd just exchanged words with.

No, thank you very much. I don't care how hot you are, how great you smell or how much I'd like to hear your voice in the dark. Men like you are bad news for me.

"Thanks," he said with a smile that made her knees tremble. "I thought you might make my dreams come true and actually smack her for being so rude." He held out his hand. "I'm Vince."

Sarah didn't shake his hand. "I'm, uh, sorry. I have to go," she said hurriedly as she tipped the bartender and took her drink to a corner table well away from what had to be the sexiest man on the frigging planet.

I'm a blubbering idiot. Oh, I'd be happy to make your dreams come true, and then some, but you are just too much. Too hot. Too smooth. Too fine. You are the kind of guy who would rock my world for about a week and then make all my nightmares come true. Nope. It's best that I just steer clear of you altogether.

Soon after Sarah sat down and lit another cigarette, she noticed a large group of people in the corner nearest her were having a fabulous time. Waitresses brought trays of champagne bottles and the people laughed and carried on as though they were having the time of their lives. At the center of all the mirth was an attractive man who must have been about fifty. He had short black hair with just a touch of gray at his temples and dark brown eyes that seemed to be constantly laughing. He had beautiful teeth and a melodic laugh. There was something about his manner that made him look like he knew how to have a good time. Just a good time was exactly what Sarah wanted for tonight.

Not another man to pull me in and break my heart, just a guy who wants to have a little fun. A guy that I'll be able to walk away from.

When the man glanced at Sarah, she didn't turn away. She simply stared into his eyes and smiled.

Not long afterward, he and what appeared to be his entourage stood and headed toward the door. As they passed Sarah's table, he stopped. "*Que bella!*" He said approvingly in a thick Italian accent.

That explains it.

Sarah nodded graciously, smiled and replied, "*Gratzi.*"

Jackpot! There's just something about Italian men. They're useless if you want a commitment, but perfect if you want a good time.

He winked. "Ah, you speak Italian, but surely you must be American?"

"Yes and yes. My name is Sarah." She reached out to shake his hand.

He gently kissed the back of her knuckles. "Call me Angelo and tonight I will call you my queen. Come with us. We are going to a party in my suite upstairs. You must come!" He continued to hold her hand.

Sounds perfect.

Eleven

Sarah accepted Angelo's offer. She joined his entourage of raucous assorted jet setters, who all looked liked they belonged on the pages of Vogue and GQ, to Caesar's Palace's finest suite. Sarah was treated like a queen, as promised. She and Angelo's entourage drank the finest champagne that room service could provide and lots of it. Sarah didn't really need the champagne. She bubbled with the excitement of how this night had evolved and how her life had turned around.

Angelo stroked Sarah's hair. "*Cara*, more champagne?"

Sarah offered her glass and smiled. "Yes, thank you."

You are just what I need¾a fling with absolutely no demands and no expectations.

Sarah and Angelo flirted shamelessly all evening.

Angelo couldn't keep his hands off her. He ran his fingers through her hair, caressed her back when she stood beside him and touched her legs, lightly but never inappropriately whenever they sat together.

Somewhere around three in the morning, Sarah snaked her arm around Angelo's shoulder and whispered that it was time for her to go to bed.

Angelo's eyes sparkled. "Yes, of course." He took Sarah's hand and stood. "*Buona notte, tutto*! Please continue to enjoy yourselves." He led Sarah through the room as he said goodnight to his guests and then opened the door to the master bedroom. As soon as he closed the door behind them, he pulled her toward him and met her with a long, slow kiss. They never spoke, but Angelo seemed to instinctively understand Sarah's needs. She truly felt like a goddess as Angelo worshipped and pleased every inch of her body.

Sarah lay in bed, physically exhausted and sated.

Closure. Scott was wrong. It isn't me. I'm attractive, sexy, men want me and want to be around me. I'm not invisible any more. I want more of this. A lot more!

~~~

Sarah had only slept about three hours when she awoke at ten the next morning, but her energy had been renewed nonetheless.

No sense letting that huge Roman tub go to waste. I might as well get that bubble bath I've been wanting and make this a winning trip all around.

Sarah filled the huge garden tub with hot water and bubbles. She stepped in, sighed and enjoyed the best soak of her life.

Her thoughts wandered back to the man she'd forced herself to walk away from the night before. The old Sarah would have stayed at the bar and talked to him all night. The old Sarah would have wasted her whole night on him and then watched him go home with somebody else.

The old Sarah was a sucker, a chump, a loser. The new Sarah needs to be the shoe instead of the doormat. I'll never let myself get into a situation where a man can hurt me again. Vince? He is too hot for any Sarah to handle¾old or new.

After about an hour, Angelo entered the master bathroom with a sleepy smile and a tray containing espresso and biscotti. He set it down on the table beside the tub. "I thought you might enjoy some breakfast."

Sarah opened her eyes and smiled at him from her cloud of bubbles. She took the small cup of espresso Angelo offered and sipped. "Thank you, it's perfect."

Now this is where I should be¾on a pedestal.

Angelo leaned against the vanity and crossed his arms with a smile. "I have business meetings all day, but you should stay. Make yourself comfortable. Order room service. We'll have dinner together tonight."

Sarah stood and wrapped one of the plush cotton towels around her body while Angelo watched.

Damn, it's nice to be looked at like that.

Sarah drank the last bit of espresso in the small cup. "That sounds wonderful, but I can't. I'm leaving town within the hour."

The last thing I'm going to tell you is I'm on a twenty-four hour pass from fat camp and have to return immediately.

Sarah caressed Angelo's unshaven cheek, sauntered into the bedroom and began to dress.

The hum of an electric razor came from within the bathroom as Sarah slid her feet into her stilettos.

Angelo, now clean-shaven, came into the bedroom. He picked up his cell phone on the bedside table and checked his messages while Sarah brushed her hair.

When he'd pocketed his phone, Sarah kissed him lightly on the lips. "Thank you for a wonderful evening."

He returned her smile. "*Prego, cara*. It was my pleasure."

I know. But it is nice to hear it anyway.

Twelve

Sarah felt quite pleased with herself when she returned to camp.

I can't wait to tell Tracey what happened. She's never going to believe this.

Sarah and Tracey had become pretty close since they'd started their programs at the camp. They encouraged each other to push past their boundaries and test their physical and mental limits. They each knew the pain of rejection and what it was like to be invisible in the world of beautiful people. Feeling that same sort of pain and fighting to overcome it had created a very strong bond between them.

Time to come out of your shell, too, Trace.

Sarah's heart rate kicked up a notch and her palms grew moist as she put on the now familiar blindfold for the final leg of the trip back to the camp.

Shawn, her trainer, drove the Suburban. "Nervous, Sarah?"

"No, just anxious to get back to my training. We gonna do some sparring this afternoon?"

Shawn chuckled. "Hey, if you're lucky, I'll let you fight Jason."

The scout named Jason piped up from the back seat. "No way man. I'm not fighting a girl. If I lose, I'm a pussy. If I win, I'm a bully. No way."

"Jason, I got news for ya," Shawn answered. "You are a pussy."

Sarah smiled but said nothing.

The vehicle stopped.

"We're here, Sarah," Shawn announced. "Go get your fighting clothes on."

Sarah left the blindfold on the front seat and stepped out of the Suburban. She took one last look at the two scouts and began the walk to her hut.

Something doesn't feel right. Those guys smiled at me like they know something I don't.

As Sarah neared her hut, a nervous sensation churned in the pit of her stomach. She flipped the latch on the hut door and walked in. Somebody was inside but it took her eyes a few seconds to adjust from bright sunlight to the dark hut interior. Two men wearing black BDUs came into focus and Tracey was nowhere to be seen.

Sarah spoke first. "Who are you?"

One of the men spoke. "Would you come with us, please?"

I knew this would happen. I have to leave eventually.

Sarah was ready. Last night only served to prove to her that her weight was no longer a liability. The only problem was that she still didn't have a plan. A sudden wave of panic threatened to drown her. Her mind raced. She had no place to go and very little money to get started.

No job. No college degree. That's okay. I'm going to make this work. I wonder if I'm too old to get into another branch of the military.

Sarah followed the men as they walked to the command hut. They escorted her to a stark waiting area that consisted of a small, unpainted room no bigger than a closet. There were two chairs that looked as though they'd been tossed around military offices since World War II.

"Knock once, and then wait," said one of the men in black BDUs before they closed the door and left her alone inside the room. She knocked once on the inner door.

A man's voice came from within the next room. "Enter."

Sarah opened the door and walked into a gorgeous office. Dark oak paneling covered the bottom three feet of the walls and then forest green paint covered the rest of the wall up to the ceiling. There was a ceiling fan that looked as though it had come out of the movie Casablanca and the room was noticeably cool. Sitting behind a large, solid oak desk, was a man with imposing dimensions.

Wow! They sure do pick the right guys for these jobs, don't they?

The man behind the desk had a dark tan and light hair cut "high and tight." He also wore black BDU trousers and a black T-shirt. In front of the desk were two red leather, wing-backed Chippendale chairs.

Sarah stood between the chairs, in front of the desk.

He gave Sarah a visual once over. "Have a nice time last night?"

It must have been a rhetorical question because he didn't wait for an answer.

No sooner had Sarah opened her mouth than he began speaking again.

"So…eight weeks in Phase I and you lost fifty pounds. After five weeks in Phase II you lost another twenty-five pounds." He opened a file folder. "I hear you've used up all your sparring partners and have to spar with instructors now. I might add that the list of volunteers to spar with you and your pal, Tracey, is getting shorter by the minute." He looked up at Sarah who remained standing in front of the desk. "You've really gone about as far as you can go here."

"I think I could really accomplish a lot more if I stayed just a bit longer." Sarah hoped to buy herself some more time at the camp to get a plan together.

Why haven't I been thinking about a plan?

He dismissed her suggestion with a wave of his hand. "Most people who've come as far as you have said the same thing. So, what will you do now?"

"I honestly don't know, sir," she replied. "I have no job, no place to live…"

"Well, you seem like the kind of woman who can get whatever she's after."

Are you judging me? Just what do you know about me?

"With all due respect, sir…"

"Spare me the righteous indignation. What you've got is a marketable skill like any other. I was merely making a statement of fact. In fact, you have quite a package of skills when it comes right down to it." He shuffled through several pages in the file folder. "Let's see here. Joined the Air Force as a Linguist. What language do you speak?"

"Spanish, French, a little Italian and some Russian."

"Where did you go to school for those?"

Pride swelled in her chest. "I didn't, sir."

"Hmm…self taught, huh? Not bad." He browsed through the file again. "Says here you were trained as a Hostage/Crisis Negotiator by the FBI. Looks like you also managed to get a BA in International Relations during your enlistment. All that and you're an expert marksman, too. Not bad."

Sarah suddenly realized how much she missed the military life. She missed feeling as though she had a mission and always being on the move to some place even more exciting than the last. "Sir, would you mind telling me where you're going with this?"

He closed the file and pushed it to the side. "Okay, Stevens, here it is." He leaned back and looked her in the eye. The full breadth of his shoulders and chest was striking. Sarah had only ever seen guys that wide with muscle in magazines. "Have you considered putting your skills to use for another government agency?"

Sarah chuckled. "Sure, but who would take me? I've already been discharged from the Air Force and I'm thirty years old."

"Well, maybe we could help you out with that." He left the words hanging there and watched her.

She stood, not moving, hoping this guy wasn't going to jerk her around. She needed a plan and she was open to just about anything at this point. Getting back into the military would be like a second chance at her life.

A do-over?

He raised an eyebrow. "Do you have any moral reservations about clandestine operations?"

Sarah wanted more information on where this guy was going. "What do you mean? Could I kill someone?"

He watched her expectantly.

"Sure," she answered her own question. "I trained for that in the Air Force. I expected to do it during Desert Storm but ended up waiting out the war in Turkey."

Turkey. What a trip! Packed up and dressed for war and what did I get? Six months of the finest shopping and partying I've ever done. No matter how prepared I was and no matter how good a shot I was, nobody ever wanted to send chicks into war zones back then.

He interrupted her thoughts. "Yeah, I saw that. M-60 gunner. You're pretty hot shit on heavy weapons from what I hear." He straightened in his chair. "No, what I'm talking about is something more along the lines of what you did last night."

What is he talking about? It isn't against the law to get laid in Vegas. Hell, it's the rule!

"Excuse me?" she asked. "What are you talking about?"

He replied matter-of-factly. "You go to Vegas, party at one of the finest clubs, spend the night in a high roller's suite and come back with your bank account untouched and nine-hundred some odd dollars stuffed in your bra."

How the hell do you know what's in my bank account or how much money is in my bra for that matter? What is this place and who the hell are you?

She stood and glared at the man. This guy knew too much about the contents of her undergarments and her hackles were up.

He continued. "That sounds like prostitution to me."

That's it. You're way over the line, asshole!

Sarah switched in to fight mode. Her blood boiled at this guy's nerve.

Screw it! They're going to send me away anyway. This guy is just getting off on jerking me around. Big deal, so you followed me.

Sarah was careful to keep her voice low so he wouldn't mistake her angry tone for hysterics. "Well, it would be if I got the money from the guy I slept with, but I didn't, and I don't appreciate your implying I'm out turning tricks in Vegas. That's just bad form."

Sarah's hands made fists and she leaned forward with her knuckles braced on the man's desk. "I don't care who you are. I don't have to take this shit from anybody so check yourself before you continue. What's the bottom line here? I don't know what your game is, nor do I care, so why don't you just skip the bullshit and get to the point?"

Is this guy just pushing me to see when I'll push back or is he really just an asshole?

The big man smiled a satisfied smile, leaned his elbow on the desk and locked his gaze onto Sarah's. "Point taken. You're absolutely right and I apologize. I wondered how long it would take to get your hackles up. I could break you like a twig, but you're confident enough to stand up for yourself. That's good." He motioned to a chair and smiled. "Sit down, Stevens. You're not going anywhere."

Sarah juggled intrigued, confused, pissed off and a multitude of other emotions, but what mattered most was the relief that coursed through her.

She was staying.

These guys are spooks of some sort. I knew there had to be an angle to this place. That's why it's free. This has got to be a government operation.

He cracked his knuckles and took a sip from the coffee mug on his desk. "Here's what we're talking about. HUMINT. Human intelligence. Real people dealing with real people to get the information our government needs. The CIA was great at it during the cold war, but the Clinton Administration with their kind and gentle philosophy put an end to all of that and got rid of those agents that specialized in HUMINT."

Sarah crossed her ankles. "Why would they do that?"

"Seems they were under the impression we could do the same thing for less with electronic intelligence. Now we're fighting a different sort of war¾the war on terror¾and we need HUMINT agents again. Problem is the cold war agents are all collecting Social Security so we need to train a whole new group of operators."

Sarah looked around the room. "So, is that what all this is about?"

"It takes ten years for the CIA to produce a good field agent America just doesn't have that kind of time. We need people with specific skills now. People who can speak several languages fluently with military experience and who understand national security issues. We need people of high intelligence who can work independently as well as with a team. We need people who can handle themselves. I'm beginning to see why you came so highly recommended."

Sarah didn't let her face register the excitement pulsing through her veins.

Highly recommended? Holy crap! Now it all makes sense!

"This camp is a recruitment center. We use it to recover and then recruit ex military personnel for Black World Operations. 'Black Ops' can't be a foreign term to a former Security Specialist."

Sarah nodded as he continued. She knew all about Black Ops and how it was the dirty work everyone knew had to be done but nobody wanted to acknowledge.

"Anyway, this camp is an effective cover. We select quality people who are on their way out of the military and then give them additional physical training while our scouts monitor progress and performance. I'm sure you've seen our talent scouts. They're the ones wearing all black. Do you remember how you found out about this place?"

Sarah remembered the simple white business card her Commander had given to her. "Yes, of course."

"Our officers on the inside, in the services, only refer the finest recruits for our operations."

Sarah's head reeled. What this guy was talking about was the kind of job she'd wanted to do when she first joined the Air Force. Things changed and she'd ended up in the mainstream with a million other Security Specialists and she'd had to revise her plans.

Am I actually getting a second chance? To hell with caution!

"Okay, I'm in. What's the deal?"

His eyes sparkled as he beamed a wide grin that showed off a perfect set of ultra-white teeth. This was clearly a man who enjoyed his job. "Everyone who is referred here has certain skills that the government would like to recover for its own use. You speak several languages, have specialized training in negotiation, you spent eight years immersed in national security issues, you're no dummy and, as evidenced by your recent trip to Vegas, you have a particular skill set that we were unaware of but one of our teams needs immediately."

He leaned back in his chair. "You'll stay here at the camp and continue your training with a few modifications. Shawn will continue to train you. You'll have a final test in about two weeks. Providing you pass, you'll be assigned to a special task force team and given your first assignment immediately thereafter."

"What kind of test? What if I don't pass?"

"If you don't pass the test, you'll be escorted back to your vehicle free to do whatever you like with the rest of your life."

No pressure, huh?

Sarah grew anxious at the "all or nothing" nature of this deal but felt up to the challenge. She smiled. "Sounds fair."

"Okay, get back to your training and I'll talk to you again after you take the test."

Sarah left the office in a daze and almost tripped over someone on her way out.

"Tracey! What are you doing here?"

The voice of the man she'd just spoken to came booming from behind her. "Same as you. Carry on, Stevens."

Thirteen

For the next two weeks, Sarah had way too many things going through her mind as she trained. This was a great opportunity not to be missed.

No slacking off, Stevens. You need this shot. This is everything you ever wanted. Failure is not an option.

Training was modified significantly and demanded a great deal more energy than the previous phases, but there were times when the body was engaged in running or lifting and the mind took the opportunity to wander. She couldn't help but wonder what the final test would be like. They hadn't given her anything to study, so she assumed it would be a board style test where they would analyze responses to various scenarios. She'd been through plenty of those tests in the Air Force and was comfortable with the drill.

When she wasn't wondering about the job or the test, like in the shower or lying in her bunk at night, Sarah's mind would wander to something else entirely. The idea of Vince, the guy she had walked away from at *Pure*, haunted her. Her instant attraction to him was so powerful it was dangerous. He had the kind of voice a woman wants to hear in the dark from the pillow next to her. He was twisted steel and sex appeal. He was too much to let in and way too much to forget, try as she might.

The usual training schedule of running, weight training, and martial arts continued, but Shawn introduced another element to it that took up an additional two hours every day. Martial arts training was stepped up to include weapons training. When Shawn announced they'd begin training with weapons, Sarah was thrilled.

"I love guns, what kind are we using?" she asked anxiously.

"No guns." Shawn shook his head. "You know enough about firearms. You need close quarters weapons training. Now you'll learn how to effectively use every blade we've got."

That's a switch. I'm intrigued.

For two hours every day, Sarah trained with blades. From machetes to tiny throwing knives, she learned how to use them all and how to inflict the most possible damage with each one. The work exhausted her, but with each new skill learned, she felt more and more powerful.

Sarah spent so much time, every day, just practicing and sparring that her fighting skills improved to a point she'd never believed possible. She found when she fought, she could focus so completely that her mind only focused on the fight. The rest of the world would disappear into a blur and time seemed to slow to a crawl. With or without knives, she felt ready to take on the world.

One thought rarely left her mind. Just a few months ago she'd hit absolute rock bottom because she'd focused her energies on a relationship with a man and let herself go to the point where she was so fat she was invisible.

I will never do that again. My needs come first now. I'll fight tooth and nail to stay in control this time.

Fourteen

Ten days after being called to the command hut and offered a job, Shawn stopped Sarah's training at noon. "Go get cleaned up, Stevens. You're going to take your test the day after tomorrow and you need to have a clear head. You've got twenty-four hours liberty in Vegas starting tonight."

Sarah stretched from the long hike they'd just taken over several miles of dunes. "Great. I could use a little rest and relaxation after the way you've been driving me."

"You think I'm tough?" Shawn laughed. "Just wait until you pass the test. You don't know tough yet. Now hit the shower. We leave at eight tonight."

~~~

Sarah took a long, hot shower and then napped for several hours. Since she had nothing else to wear, she put on her black outfit and carefully placed the money from Dean in her bra so she could buy a few civilian clothes once she got into town.

No wild night tonight. There is too much at stake. I'll get a room, order some room service and relax. Then tomorrow I'll do a little shopping.

The Suburban waited outside her hut with the back, passenger side door open. Shawn sat in the driver's seat.

The scout in the other back seat had been one of the guys who had escorted her to the command hut the day she was offered the job. He had short dark hair with a touch of gray and mesmerizing blue eyes.

The shoulders on the man sitting in front of her were unmistakable. It was the hot scout that always showed up in her fantasies and was showing up in person more and more during her training every day. This was the man she liked to think about when she lay in her bunk at night.

When they reached the ridge where Sarah usually had to put on the blindfold, Shawn didn't stop the Suburban but kept on driving.

"Shawn, do I need the blindfold?"

"Not tonight, Sarah. Stay alert."

Sarah looked for every landmark and terrain change she could find. She watched the stars and made mental notes of the positions of constellations.

Once, Shawn looked over at the mystery scout and broke the silence in the Suburban. "Man, I'm telling you, this one is going to be good. Fight of the century, brother!"

The mystery scout never spoke. He merely shook his head and shrugged, as though he weren't impressed.

Sarah assumed they were going to a fight at the MGM Grand or Caesar's. There were major boxing matches in Las Vegas all the time.

When they reached the city limits, Shawn announced, "Okay, rendezvous point this trip is the Stratosphere at sixteen-hundred tomorrow."

Sarah noticed the drive into town was different this time. They were driving through the seediest part of the city.

Shawn pulled over. "This is your stop." He turned in his seat and looked back at Sarah.

"No, that's okay. You can just drop me at the strip." She peered out the window and winced. "There isn't anything I want to do in this part of town."

"No, you don't understand." His voice took on more of an edge. "This is your stop. Rendezvous the Stratosphere, sixteen-hundred tomorrow. You're on your own until then."

Did he just stress the words "on your own?"

Sarah glanced at the guy in black in the other back seat.

"Time to bounce, pork chop." He wasn't looking at her, but she could see a smile curl at the corner of his mouth before he turned and stared out his window.

She had no sooner stepped out of the SUV than they sped off. Sarah looked around and assessed her surroundings.

Now this is messed up. I'm not anywhere near the strip. In fact, I'm in a section of town that no white girl has any business being in during the light of day¾never mind the dark of night.

No good could come of this.

Okay, Stevens, recon. No weapons, no phone. Bars on all the windows and not a light to be seen. Shit, even the streetlights are out!

Anger began to rise within her like magma.

I'm dressed to the nines in a mini and three-inch stiletto heels. Somebody is going to pay for this. I'm so going to kick Shawn's ass.

Before she could move out of the way an older model Cadillac screeched to a halt cutting off her path as she crossed an empty lot.

Four men jumped out of the car and ran toward her.

Oh, hell no!

There was no time for flight. The only option was to fight. Something ugly was about to go down. Sarah braced herself for a fight. Adrenaline kicked in hard and time was marked by the heartbeats that reverberated inside her ears.

Sarah scanned the area quickly for anything she could use as a weapon.

Nothing. Not even a rock!

Sarah eyed the biggest guy there. "You might take me down, but I guarantee I'll take at least two of you down with me."

It all happened in the blink of an eye, but it seemed like slow motion for Sarah.

She was surrounded.

Someone grabbed her around the waist from behind.

She jammed her heel as hard as she could into the arch of his foot. Her attacker screamed and let go.

Another man lunged at her from the side and grabbed her arm.

She reacted automatically and threw him to the ground.

He landed flat on his back and groaned as the breath was knocked out of him.

Another one jumped behind her and grabbed her around the waist while the fourth came at her from the front.

The flash of a blade registered in Sarah's mind.

Knife. Kill or be killed.

Muscle memory and instinct took over and Sarah high-kicked the one with the blade, catching the knife as it was thrown from his hand.

The man behind her let go. Sarah took advantage of the moment and turned on him with the knife in hand, ready to pounce.

He threw up his arms and shrieked like a little girl. "This isn't worth a hundred bucks!" He ran into the alley and disappeared, leaving the car behind with the engine still running.

Three on the ground. One hoofed it.

Sarah made a dash for the driver's side of the Cadillac and hopped in.

What are they going to do? Tell the cops? Yeah, we tried to mug a chick but she beat us up and stole our car?

She put the car in gear and was about to drive away when she realized she was missing a shoe.

Sarah put the car back in park and stepped out, with the knife still in her hand.

She watched the guys lying on the ground. Waiting for one of them to blink wrong and give her another reason to kick their asses.

No one moved enough to pose a threat.

She walked toward the guy she'd high-kicked and picked up her shoe. As she slid the shoe on, she caught a broken nail on her nylons.

She stared at the nail. "Damnit!" Sarah glared at the guy on the ground, who held a very bloody nose. "You made me break a nail and now my nylons are ruined. You son of a bitch!"

She kicked the guy hard in the side. The perfect toe point of her patent leather stiletto made hard contact with a rib. A loud *crack* mixed with the sound of the man's groan as she walked back to the car and sat in the driver's seat.

If they wanted a second round, they'd have started it before now.

Sarah had no idea where she was, but she could see one landmark. She drove toward the light at the top of the Luxor hotel.

I need a drink.

Once she found herself on the strip, she pulled into the parking garage of Caesar's Palace, wiped her prints from the steering wheel and gearshift and left the keys inside the car.

She strode with purpose to the front desk and asked for a room.

When she arrived at her room, she stared at herself in the mirror and saw exactly why the desk clerk and everyone else in the lobby had gawked at her.

I'm a mess!

Torn skirt, blood on her right shoe and calf, not to mention her hair was a total wreck. She had just survived an attack by four men and should have been hysterical, but all she could muster was anger.

She picked up the phone by the bed and called room service. "This is room three-eighteen. I'd like a pitcher of Margaritas, on the rocks, immediately, please. One glass and don't salt it."

I sure as hell don't feel like shopping tonight, but I am definitely going to have a few drinks and listen to some loud music!

Then she called the concierge. "I need a dress appropriate for *Pure*, preferably black, in a size eight. I'll also need a pair of shoes to match. Three-inch heels, size ten. Oh, and some nylons. Tan."

Sarah had just finished with the call to the concierge when room service arrived.

The waiter appeared stunned when Sarah opened the door. "Ma'am, are you okay?" He leaned toward her, looking around the room for anyone else and whispered, "I can call the police."

Sarah laughed. "I know. I look like hell. No, there won't be any need for the police. This happened before I got here. I had a fight with a flat tire and lost." Sarah paid him for the pitcher and tipped him twenty dollars. His concern touched her.

"Thank you very much, ma'am. Are you sure you're all right?"

Sarah nodded. "A shower and a drink will have me feeling just fine in no time at all. Thank you."

Sometime between her first and second Margarita, she had a chance to wind down from the adrenaline high and think.

"This isn't worth a hundred bucks!" Is that what he said?

Sarah breathed a sigh of relief as she realized she must have just passed the final test.

Ha, ha! Surprise attack on the street or a board question and review session? I've been through board reviews. I'd rather have the surprise attack on the street any day!

A knock on the door pulled her from her thoughts.

Sarah set her drink on the bedside table and answered the door.

A well-dressed young woman carrying a Versace garment bag and a shoebox stood in the hall. The woman gasped at the sight of Sarah. She stepped just inside the doorway then whispered, "I can call the police for you."

"No, that won't be necessary, thank you. My car broke down and I tried to fix it myself. I should have known better."

Sarah signed for the dress, shoes and nylons and tipped the woman before ushering her out the door. She laid the clothes on the bed.

After a hot shower and another Margarita, Sarah decided a change in plans was in order. She wanted to celebrate her new job.

She walked straight past the line at *Pure* and directly up to the same doorman who'd been so nice to her last time. He had the velvet rope opened by the time she got to him. He placed his hand on the small of her back again, and this time, she kissed him on the cheek, slipped a twenty into his breast pocket, smiled and said, "Thank you."

I'm living large now. Rock bottom is moving further away and my life is finally looking up.

A part of Sarah hoped she'd see Vince in the club again, but her mind told her he probably wouldn't be there and that would be for the best.

Now that I have my life together, the last thing I need is an emotional entanglement. This infatuation needs to be squashed.

Sarah quickly scanned the white room as she walked in and her eyes stopped at the end of the bar as she caught her breath reflexively.

There he was.

Sarah, get a grip! Men are nothing but trouble for you and any man that has this sort of an effect on you is definitely more trouble than you can handle.

She watched him for a moment as he motioned to the bartender and then said something to him. The bartender nodded and went back to mixing drinks.

Sarah spied a spot at the other end of the bar, far away from Vince and walked toward it.

The bartender brought her a Margarita, just the way she liked it, as she arrived and sat. "From the gentleman in black at the end of the bar," he said in answer to her quizzical look.

She already knew who the gentleman was, but when she turned, he was gone.

Who is this guy and why does he have such an effect on me? Worse yet, why couldn't he just do me a favor and ignore me since I'm clearly incapable of ignoring him?

~~~

The next day, after a good night's sleep and a little shopping, Sarah took a taxi to the Stratosphere to catch her ride back to camp.

The black Suburban pulled up right on time. Shawn and the other two guys were already seated and ready to go.

Shawn nodded toward the Versace garment bag. "Do a little shopping?"

"Among other things," Sarah replied confidently. She wore a pair of hiking boots, jeans and an AC/DC T-shirt she had picked up at the Boulevard Mall that morning. The clothes and shoes she'd worn into town last night had been trashed. Sarah slid forward until her head and shoulders were between the two front seats. "Shawn, you pull a stunt like that on me again and I *will* kick your ass."

The mystery scout in the other front seat started to smile and turned away, before she could get a good look at him.

The blue-eyed guy who had told her to bounce gave a hearty laugh.

"Easy, Killer," Shawn said jovially. "Don't bite the hand that feeds you. Besides, it had to be done."

"So, did I pass?"

Blue eyes nodded. "Straight A's, pork chop."

Sarah turned and scowled at the man, not sure how to take his comment.

My God, you are an attractive man.

She returned his smile. "Thanks, I think."

Shawn glanced at her in the rear view mirror. "Yeah, you passed."

Getting dropped and jumped was a setup, but what Sarah didn't understand was what the mystery scout had to do with the whole scenario.

Were you the person who has been spying on me? Is that what you do?

Upon checking back in to the camp, Sarah received a short briefing by the very well put together man in the cool office.

He stood by the door when she entered his office and shook her hand. "Nice work, Stevens." He motioned for her to sit in one of the Chippendale chairs as he moved around to sit behind the desk.

"Okay, you've been chosen specifically for assignment to a team within Task Force 125. It's a special task force created for clandestine counter-terrorism operations. Few people know about this task force and that is how we'd like to keep it. As long you all fly under the radar of the press, your missions will never be compromised. You can expect to spend extensive periods of time abroad and under deep cover. It isn't an easy job."

I came here to escape my troubles in the real world. What better way to escape than deep cover? Long live the new Sarah!

He pulled a folder out of the top drawer of his desk, laid it carefully on the desk and opened it. The first item on top of the pile of papers was a blue credit card. He handed the piece of plastic to Sarah.

It read, "Credit Suisse" along the top and had a Master Card logo. "A Swiss account?" Her eyes widened.

He pointed to the card. "This is attached to a numbered Swiss bank account. It's the account we'll deposit your monthly pay in as well as any extra money you'll need for job-related expenses. This account can't be traced back to the U.S. government, but if you ever go rogue on us, we'll kill the account quicker than you can say *oops*."

Sarah had seen enough movies and read enough to know that she'd signed on for life. "Okay. Since we're talking about money, what am I looking at for pay?"

He handed her a small slip of paper. "The first number is your pin. Memorize it. The second is the pay amount your particular job earns."

Sarah stared at the small five-digit figure.

This is ridiculous!

She placed her elbow on the desk in front of her, leaned in and glared at the man. "Are you kidding me? A GS-1 starting out with a federal job makes more than this every year!"

"Uh…Stevens." He smiled. "That's monthly."

Sarah suppressed a nervous giggle. Excitement threatened to bubble out her ears. She took a deep breath to calm herself, sank in her chair, crossed her legs and leaned on one of the armrests. She stared at the toe of her boot and blinked several times while she wrapped her brain around the math. After a few moments, she looked up at the man and smiled sweetly. "That'll be just fine."

He smirked. "Okay, now that we have that out of the way, we'll need to take care of the formalities."

Sarah spent at least forty-five minutes reading and signing a slew of nondisclosure, personal risk, health insurance and life insurance papers. When she made it to the final document and signed her name, she dropped the pen on the desk and let out a sigh. "Is that it?"

He shook his head. "Do you have any civilian clothes in your storage unit that fit you?"

Her answer was easy. "Nope."

He gestured to the door. Jeff is outside my office. He'll take you into town so you can pick up a few things. Your mission orientation briefing is tomorrow at o-seven-hundred in building one-twenty-five. Wear casual attire."

~~~

As per her instructions, Sarah arrived wearing civilian clothes. She wore leather hiking shoes, black canvas shorts and a black tank top. For some reason she still couldn't manage to shake the military look, even in civis. Two guards stood outside the door when she arrived ten minutes early at building one-twenty-five.

"Name?" one of them asked.

"Stevens, Sarah M."

He looked her up and down. "If you have a cell phone, leave it with us."

Sarah shook her head. "I don't have one."

"Go ahead." One of the guards stepped aside as another guard opened the door.

Sarah counted six men already in the room and seated at a large table. She recognized several of them. One was her fantasy man with the massive shoulders and a second was the handsome blue-eyed guy who'd told her to "bounce." Two others she recognized as the ones she'd rode into town with her on her first liberty.

This should be interesting…

A man at the far end of the room stood. "Okay, let's get started."

She found the nearest empty chair and sat.

"Welcome to Task Force 125. Take a look around the room. These people are going to be your family until you either die or retire."

Family, huh? Holy moly! I've got one seriously buff family! Look at these guys...you'd think I'd died and gone to heaven! Pecs and biceps and delts, oh my!

"I'm Colonel Young. I'm the handler for Task Force 125, which is the special unit you now belong to. This task force is a special counter-terrorism unit. We receive information from the U.S. intelligence community and act upon that information. Generally we add to that information and share our findings with them. At least that's how it's supposed to work."

"Yeah, sometimes we have to give them the information," someone mumbled.

Young continued, ignoring the side comment. "You're in 'Black World' now. You're spooks and you don't exist. You are part of the Central Intelligence Agency's Special Activities Staff. The Special Activities Division is divided into Air, Maritime and Ground branches, but you folks are going to have to be a little more versatile. We need a team in the Mediterranean AOR that can work both land and sea. You may also need to work with operators from coalition nations. Between the six of you, we believe you've got the skills necessary to do all of that."

"Flatterer," mumbled the guy sitting to Sarah's right.

"Your primary mission is to acquire the necessary intelligence on high value targets to remove them and their organizations from circulation. That means you'll be doing a lot of undercover work, some snatch and grab, interrogations and a lot of link analysis. In particular, you'll deal with the people who are financing and supplying terrorists. The regular military is doing what they can, but your job is a bit more delicate.

Young stopped and looked out the window as he spoke. "You have to do things that Congress doesn't really want to know about. You operate outside the Geneva Convention and although that means you have more freedom to get the job done, you're also going to encounter more risks to meet your objective." He looked around the table. "Before we go too far, let's get one thing out on the table now. If any of you get captured or killed, the government will not negotiate for your release. In fact, here's the official statement that will be issued:

U.S. citizen, John Doe, has allegedly represented himself as an American government and/or military official. The public should be aware that Doe does not represent the American government and we do not employ him."

"That's love," said the jokester sitting beside Sarah.

Young looked directly at the jokester. "The people in this room are all you'll have. You will be equipped as necessary and have at your disposal anything the Agency can muster. You are your primary support unit. You'll have a contact within the Sixth Fleet, but you'll be expected to accomplish your missions on your own. Seated in this room are people from diverse military and paramilitary backgrounds. We've got Marines, Air Force, Army, Navy, CIA and FBI. The fact is we need the experience and expertise that each of you has in order to create a team that will be equipped to fight terrorism from a very unique angle."

Just the people in this room against all the terrorists in the world?

The puzzlement must have registered on Sarah's face.

Young pointed at her. "You got a question, Stevens?"

Sarah took a deep breath as she prepared to ask the question on her mind. "Yeah. Is this the only team that does this sort of thing?"

"No. We currently have nine other teams on this task force doing missions similar to yours. Your particular area of responsibility will be the Mediterranean and the surrounding area. This, like everything else about your job, could change at a moment's notice. Stay flexible."

Sarah nodded her understanding.

"The code name for your team is American Swift. In our branch of operations, secrecy is a matter of life and death. If the media gets wind of what you're doing or who you are, there will be a veritable shitstorm from the White House on down and we'll have an even bigger handicap in the war on terror. Bottom line, stay under the radar at all times. Your primary mission is to gather as much intelligence as possible, any way you can, without being detected. We don't do assassinations. The Clinton Administration made that illegal. However if a terrorist or financier dies in one of your operations, well that's unlucky for him. You'll be expected to either clean up the mess or make sure it looks like somebody else did it. I shouldn't have to explain that to any of you."

Sarah glanced around the table and saw a few barely hidden smiles.

Colonel Young stood. "Okay, you've got fifteen minutes. There's a smoking area behind the building. If anybody is too squeamish to deal with what we do, report to the command hut now for debrief and you can do the duffel bag drag back to your civilian life."

The guys in the room exited through a back door and into what looked like an office.

Squeamish? Nope. This is my chance to do something big. I'm staying.

Sarah decided to go have a cigarette. She exited the door she'd come in through and walked around back to the smoking area.

I don't have a problem beating terrorists at their own game, but where exactly do I come into the equation?

As Sarah rounded the first corner of the building, she reached into her cargo pocket and removed a box of cigarettes. She tapped out a cigarette and placed it between her lips. She dug into her front pocket for the lighter. As she rounded the second corner of the building, voices in the smoking area caught her attention and she glanced up. There was the mystery scout she'd been admiring for weeks and it hit her like a brick as she realized who he was.

She stopped short, cigarette still unlit between her lips.

He wore the black BDU cap and the dark glasses, but Vince's voice came from the mystery scout. There was simply no mistaking that voice. The two men she'd fantasized about were the same guy.

Oh, dear God!

"Morning," he said with a wide, brilliant smile. "I guess this means you're going through with it? Welcome to the team. Nice work on your final test, by the way. I lost fifty bucks to Shawn on that fight."

Just hearing his voice makes me weak in the knees! Okay, check yourself. There are four other guys here and not one of them will admire your ability to get stupid at the sound of one man's voice. Be tough, be cool and for God's sake don't drool.

Sarah regained her composure, cigarette still unlit. "That'll teach you to bet against me."

She broke off her stare when the familiar *clink* of a Zippo lighter sounded to her right. She turned toward the source and recognized the guy who had whistled at her before her first trip to Vegas from the camp. He looked to be in his mid twenties.

He lit her cigarette and said, "I made two hundred on that fight, thank you very much. I'm Jason. Hey, did you keep the knife?"

Sarah took a drag from her cigarette and smiled. "You're welcome. Sarah Stevens and yes, I did. Do I get a cut of the take?"

He smiled a devilishly crooked smile and looked her up and down. "I'm sure we could work something out."

Cute. I'm flattered, but we both know the first rule for anyone in a military operation is not to sleep with the people you work with.

The guy that Vince had been talking to when Sarah rounded the corner reached out to shake her hand. "I'm Chris. I didn't take the bet, but I'll be happy to lay money down on you any time," he said with a wink.

More cute. What a bunch of flirts.

Sarah chuckled under her breath and nodded. "Thanks, I'll remember that."

The tall, lean drink of water with brown hair dying to have fingers run through it had brown eyes to match his hair. He raised a hand nonchalantly and introduced himself. "I'm Brian. Nice touch taking the car. Took balls. I like that." He sat at a picnic table while keeping eye contact with Sarah. "What would you have done if the Caddy had been reported stolen and the cops stopped you?"

Sarah was interrupted before she could answer. "Balls or just plain necessity? Did you see the shoes the car thief was wearing? Figure the odds of her hoofin' it in those!" The guy with a touch of gray and stunning blue eyes smiled at Sarah. "Hey, pork chop. I'm Will."

"Hi, Will. We're gonna chat about that pet name." Sarah looked at Brian to answer his question. "Cops? Hot girl, blood on her face, miniskirt…I've done plenty of speeding and never got a ticket when I wore a mini. You do the math." Sarah looked around at the guys she'd been talking to. "Wait a minute here…were you all watching or what?"

Will, the guy who liked to call her "pork chop," answered. "Well, you know Vince and I were there. Shawn drove the truck around the corner and we filmed the whole fight. The rest of the guys here saw the film."

"Yeah, it's in my home video collection entitled 'Black Betty and her Stupendous Stilettos.'" Brian grinned. "Too bad it's not porn. It's an awesome title for one. Hey, still not too late to add a little…"

"Let me get to know you a little better first, stud. Black Betty?" Sarah frowned.

"Yeah. You didn't happen to notice the song playing on the car radio as you kicked ass, did you? 'Black Betty' made an excellent soundtrack for the video." Brian laughed.

Then the smooth baritone that made Sarah's insides tremble and her breath come a little faster said, "All right ladies, enough bullshitting. We've got work to do. Get your asses back inside." He took a drag off the cigarette he'd been holding, then flicked the cigarette into the butt can and started back inside while the other guys followed.

Sarah took a long drag off her own cigarette.

Okay, Stevens. Whatever you do, do not look at his ass. Damn! Too late. Hmm…I hate to see you leave, but I love to watch you go. That ought to be illegal.

After the last guy rounded the corner, she put out her cigarette, took a deep breath and returned to the briefing room.

When the door closed, Colonel Young spoke. "Okay, everybody's here. Let's get started. We've taken your individual specialties into consideration in creating this team. I'll let your tactical commander, Major Hennessee, explain your duties and brief you on your next mission. Vince, they're all yours."

Colonel Young stepped through a door in the front of the room and Sarah turned her attention toward the end of the table where Vince sat. Dread rose inside her, tightening her chest. Her fantasy man was her boss, married, and a Major no less!

Oh man, there are so many degrees of uncool here. I've got to get over this ridiculous infatuation. I guess this explains why he was watching me during training. He's got to have some input on who he gets on his team. But why me?

Vince stood and moved away from his chair. As he walked around the table, he stopped behind each team member whose job he described.

"Listen up. Chris is communications. Radios, phones, bugs and translation, he's our man."

Sarah glanced at Chris.

He raised an eyebrow, winked at Sarah and said in an exaggerated voice-over voice, "I'm here if you need to talk."

Sarah smiled. Chris appeared to be too pretty to be a technical wonk and interpreter.

Jason rolled his eyes as he mumbled, "Frigging geek."

Sarah stifled a laugh.

Chris pointed at Jason. "Hey, Jase, you're just jealous you can't chat up the ladies in seven different languages. Hell man, you're lucky if you can stammer it out in English!"

"Lock it up, girls." Vince stood still, arms crossed over his massive chest. "Jason is our weapons guy. He'll equip us for this job. Sarah." Her heart jumped when he said her name. "You'll get your knives from him." Vince paused for a moment and held Sarah's gaze.

Beefcake like you and knives, too? Sweet. I certainly wouldn't mind knowing exactly what I'm supposed to do with those knives. Is it just me or is he staring?

Vince broke eye contact and stepped behind the blue-eyed wonder who kept calling her "pork chop." "Will is our supply guy and medic. Let's hope we don't need his medical skills." Vince pointed to the hottie with the hair. "Last is Brian, our explosives man."

Brian ran his fingers through his hair and sat back confidently. "We always need those skills."

Another man Sarah didn't know walked through the door.

"Sorry, man," he said distractedly to Vince as he flopped down in the empty chair next to Sarah.

"You're late again, Tony." Vince's voice was stern. "Getting a little too accustomed to civilian life, eh, trust fund?"

Vince glanced at Sarah again and spoke directly to her. "Tony is a floater. We bring him in on special jobs. He's the inside guy who will make the introductions."

Tony flashed a friendly smile at Sarah and whispered, "Hi."

Vince peeked at the clock on the wall and then turned to the table. "Any questions about your duties?"

Sarah tentatively raised one hand.

"Oh, yeah, this is Sarah. She'll be our inside operative and our main source of information on the target. You're all familiar with her handiwork." He smiled as his eyes met hers and then quickly looked away.

A barrage of questions surged through Sarah's mind at that moment, but she didn't have time to ask as Vince continued his briefing.

"Okay, here's the deal. Our task force has been created to deal with those very special people obsessed with power and money who finance and supply terrorist groups. Gun runners, drug runners, slave traders and other scumbag types are the folks we'll be dealing with. This is not a short assignment, but an ongoing program that will most likely include several missions each year with little downtime."

What the hell would I do with downtime anyway?

"The ops tempo will be high out of necessity. It'll take time and energy to find out where our targets are and then even more time and energy to get inside. Once we're inside, we'll need to get close enough for link analysis. We have to become a part of the inner circle. We have to find out who they know, who their relatives and associates are and then we start tactically removing all of those people from circulation."

Sarah's eyes widened with surprise as the true purpose of their mission hit her. A shiver ran up her spine.

We find them, bleed them of information and kill them?

Vince paced at the front of the room. "Nothing will blow the mission faster than a team member breaking cover and being involved in an embarrassing news story. Everyone needs to keep their mouth shut and lay as low as possible if anything goes sideways. If anybody here gets into a sticky situation, there had better damned well be five others ready to facilitate an emergency egress because we're all we've got."

He went on to describe how with the war on terror, satellite photos were next to useless while spies inside the targets' organizations were invaluable. "Our team uses any means necessary to get inside terrorist organizations, determine the chain of command and then eliminate it. We're not only cutting off the snake's head, but we're expected to chop up the body and dispose of it to completely eliminate any future threat."

Everyone wants terrorism to go away but nobody wants to know how far the front line has to go to make it happen.

Reality settled in Sarah's stomach like a small stone.

It makes sense to do it this way and use the terrorists' own tactics.

Sarah understood as far as Congress and the public went, Black World didn't exist, therefore anything a Black World operator did didn't actually happen. It was all about plausible deniability. If the media found out anything, the government could deny it all since Black Ops never left trails. As for the public, well, they'd never figure it out. After all, they thought "Men in Black" was just a funny movie.

Sarah's thoughts were interrupted when Will spoke up. "So, we're still on the money trail, right, boss?"

Vince turned to Will. "That's right. The cash sources and credit lines for supporting terrorism are still out there and as long as the money is there, these groups will still be dangerous."

Jason leaned back in his chair. "But I thought the Saudis were cracking down on that crap?"

Chris answered his question. "The financiers are getting more creative. The Saudis slowed the process for a while, but recent intel suggests it's on an upswing."

"That's right," Vince agreed. "There is a growing group of younger men in their thirties and forties whose access to unguarded terrorist cash has corrupted them and addicted them to a much more luxurious life than the more idealistic Muslims who were involved for principle rather than profit. These profiteers are more dangerous than anyone else because their motives don't include religion."

Will interrupted again. "That's our opening, right?"

"Exactly. These guys are easily accessible by westerners if approached properly, preferably with the sale of guns or drugs or through social connections. Just like the IRA and South American Marxists turned their organizations into drug cartels, there are Islamic radicals who are starting to freelance. Since they maintain their connections to their terrorist organizations, they provide an excellent opening for groups like us to get inside." Vince rubbed the back of his neck. "Anybody need a break before we go into mission details?"

Sarah scanned the table and memorized every face.

"No." Will sat back in his chair and cracked his knuckles. "Let's get to it, boss."

Vince picked up a file folder off the table. "Our target for this operation is Sheikh Hassan Abdullah Mohammed al-Rashid, a Saudi with considerable holdings in Syria and North Africa. He started his career as a grunt for Al Qaeda, but he made and used enough political connections to get himself in tight with Osama."

Sarah watched Vince as he spoke. When his eyes met hers, she held his stare.

Vince looked back down at the file. "A couple years ago, he and Osama had a difference of opinion and decided to part ways. That's when he began operating independently as a major smuggler and financier of radical Islamic terrorism. Smugglers like this guy have been making a killing since the war on terror began because they can move items like drugs, munitions, large sums of money and even people quickly while also making the trail difficult to trace. Because these guys are shadows, police organizations can't do a thing about them. And that's where we come in."

The cop in Sarah had to ask, "So, if police organizations can't get anything on guys like this, what evidence have we got?"

Vince's eyes twinkled as he met Sarah's gaze.

Sarah instinctively took a deep breath as her blood began to race through her veins.

"Hassan has been buying and selling a lot of ships lately and we have good intel that these ships are not empty and they're being sold to individuals or relatives of individuals with connections to specific terrorist groups operating in the Mediterranean, Africa, and the Indian Ocean."

Brian spoke for the first time since they'd entered the briefing room. "So, how are we taking this guy down?"

Vince glanced at his watch. "Our mission is to infiltrate Hassan's inner circle and figure out who's who in the organization, and who the links to other organizations are. We have to map out as much of his organization, family and associates as possible. Once we do that, we eliminate the problem through apprehension and turning individuals over to the appropriate agencies."

"And if things go tactical?" Brian asked.

Vince laced his hands together and leaned forward. "Then we eliminate the threat by any means necessary with little regard for collateral damage."

"I'm guessing Tony has something to do with getting us in?" Will asked.

Vince smiled at Tony. "That's right. Tony has a small but significant role in this job. Hassan is a notorious womanizer and enjoys a life of conspicuous consumption."

Vince's eyes met Sarah's again. "Sarah is going to pose as a socialite and get as close as possible to Hassan. If she can move in his circle, she'll be the primary source of information on him and his associates. This will be deep cover. Tony is only going to be able to get Sarah into Hassan's orbit. The rest is gonna be up to her. I'll be working undercover on this one as an arms supplier, but my contact with Sarah will be limited and unpredictable, so her primary point of contact will be Chris."

Deep cover? A socialite? Me? You gotta be kidding. What the hell do I know about being a socialite?

Vince's voice broke through Sarah's panicked thoughts. "Okay, people, we've got four weeks to prepare for this mission. Sarah and Tony, you need to report to Forum Tower Suite one-twenty-five at Caesar's Palace at o-nine-hundred tomorrow. You'll receive further instructions on mission preparation at that time. Until then, we've got twenty-four hours mandatory R&R and an icebreaker at Brian's place."

Everyone stood to leave, but Sarah remained seated a moment to let it all soak in. She had so many questions that she couldn't put anything into words.

The room emptied except for Sarah and one other person.

Fifteen

Sarah rubbed her eyes as she tried to wrap her mind around her new job.

"Hey, Stevens, you all right?" Vince's hand rested on her shoulder as he sat beside her.

His touch distracted her reeling mind. "Uh, no. I don't think so."

Vince crossed his arms on the table and stared into Sarah's eyes. "Listen, if you don't think you can do this, it's not too late to back out. You can still debrief and forget you were ever offered the job."

"No, oh, no! I want the job. I definitely want the job. I've wanted this for a long time."

"Well, then what's the problem?"

Sarah spoke to herself as much as to Vince. "A person goes through life wishing for something, trying everything they can to make it happen. They push and push but never quite get there. They get close enough to see it but it's always just out of reach. Then one day the bottom falls out and the world is pitch-black. When the lights come up, there are five guys standing there handing you that life you've wanted on a silver platter. I don't know if I should jump up and down, cry or laugh."

Vince smiled. "Okay, babe. If you're going to jump up and down, give us fair warning 'cause I think we'd like to watch. If you're going to cry, don't do it in front of the boys 'cause they just don't know what to do around weepy women. As for laughing, you can do as much of that as you like, whenever you want."

As Vince stood, Sarah gazed up into his smiling face and caught her breath.

Vince pulled a pack of cigarettes out of his pocket. "Now why don't you go pack your gear and meet me back here in five? I'll start answering some questions for you on the ride into town. You got a vehicle at the airport?"

"Yeah, I do." Sarah stood. "Thanks. I'll be right back." Sarah walked to her hut to throw her few belongings into her duffel bag.

Tracey was on her way out as Sarah opened the door. "Catch you later, loser!"

Sarah held out a hand to stop her. "You made it, right?"

"Oh, hell, yeah!"

"What unit are you with?"

"White Wolf. We work the stans." Tracey smiled wide.

Sarah thought about the crime in that particular area of the world. "All the stans? What's that? Pakistan, Afghanistan, Uzbekistan, Tajikistan, Kyrgyzstan, Turkmenistan, Kazakhstan?"

"Hey, you passed sixth grade geography." Tracey dropped her duffel bag on the floor and leaned against the wall as she spoke to Sarah.

Sarah thought about her friend's safety. "Damn, girl. That's a rough neighborhood."

"Yeah, no shit." Tracey pushed a stray blond lock of hair out of her eye. "Beats being homeless in Florida though. What about you?"

"American Swift. We'll be in the Med."

"Score for you, loser." Tracey shook her head. "I'll be freezing my ta-tas off in a yurt in the Tien Shans and you'll be working on your tan in Greece."

"Hey, look on the bright side. I hear mink is cheap in that part of the world." Sarah winked.

"Yeah, that's a comfort." Tracey laughed as she picked up her duffel bag.

"Watch your ass, Trace."

"You, too. I'll see you when I see you." With a smile and one last "L" on her forehead, Tracey walked out the door.

Sarah packed the rest of her things and returned to the briefing hut. When she arrived, Vince was waiting outside in a Black Dodge Ram pickup truck. "Hey, this thing got a Hemi?" she asked jokingly.

"Yeah, as a matter of fact it does," Vince deadpanned. "It's the only thing the wife hasn't taken...yet. You do remember my estranged and soon to be ex wife?"

"Oh, yeah," Sarah said nonchalantly, trying to be polite.

"Cut the crap." Vince shrugged. "She's a hell-bitch."

"Well, now that you mention it, she was a little unpleasant." Sarah smiled tentatively. Anxious to change the subject, she had dozens of questions and needed answers. Since Vince was smoking, she pulled out a cigarette, too. He flipped open a Zippo and Sarah took a long drag as she tried to gather her thoughts enough to form coherent questions.

"So, those times I saw you at *Pure*, you were on the job, following me?"

"Nope. Just lucky. My team needs the kind of woman who can walk into the best club in town like she owns the place¾and then you walked in. The fact that you stood up to Lori put you over the top in the interview process. Honestly, I didn't even recognize you at the club. You clean up pretty good. After that, we checked out your background and decided we wanted to take you on if you could pass the final test."

"The dump and jump."

"Yeah, that's what it was, too." Vince gave a deep chuckle. "You were great though. I've got to admit I was pretty impressed that you pulled it together and went clubbing afterwards."

Sarah thrilled at the praise laid on her by Vince but did her best to appear cool. She flicked an ash out the truck window. "Hey, thanks for the drink, by the way."

"You earned it."

"So, what exactly am I going to be doing on this mission?" Sarah finally asked.

"This op is what we call a Honey Pot operation. You're going to go in as Tony's girlfriend, make nice with Hassan and get names and faces so we can map out the organization."

Sarah turned and stared at Vince. "Honey Pot sounds like I'm expected to make extremely nice. Is that about right?"

They came to the end of the dirt road and were about to turn onto the highway toward Vegas. Vince stopped the truck and put it in park. He turned sideways in the seat and stared at her. "Only as nice as you're comfortable with, but making real nice helps. You're a bright babe. You know damned well why it's called a Honey Pot. We wanted you on our team because you came highly recommended as a good soldier, a negotiator and a linguist and, quite frankly, we all agreed you're damned easy on the eyes. But if we'd wanted a hooker, we'd have hired a professional. That being said, there are just some secrets a man will spill easier under the spell of a beautiful woman than looking down the barrel of a gun." Vince straightened in his seat, stared down the empty highway, put the truck in gear and drove.

Sarah cheeks warmed. "It's been a while since I've been accused of being beautiful. It still sounds funny."

"Well, get used to it because you are a stone-cold hottie. On that note…you're not going to get special treatment just because you're a woman. We expect you to pull your share. As you've seen, the guys aren't exactly the most politically correct lot. Will was Navy, Brian was a SEAL, Jason was in the Army and Chris is on loan from the FBI. If you're the type that offends easily, you'll never make it in this business."

"And what are you?"

"Marines. Force Recon until the Agency recruited me."

"Well, I don't mind a little joking around. I usually give as good as I get. As for everybody's background, I'm feeling a little out of my league amidst so many heroes."

"Hey, hold on a sec. You don't have to be spec ops to be a hero. Anybody can be a hero, but few ever choose to do so. Being a hero means sticking your neck out for a good cause and standing for what you believe in. Everyone we have fighting in this war is a hero, whether they're on the front lines or in the rear with the gear. They're a part of it just like you are now. Everyone has their own calling, their own skills. It's the ones who choose to take those skills and use them to make this world a safer place that are the heroes. Now what are you going to be?"

Nobody ever expected me to do anything great. This could be just that.

Sarah came back to reality and realized Vince was watching her expectantly. "I'm with you guys."

He chuckled and pointed to the rows of cars. "Okay, hero. Now which car is yours?"

Sarah turned away from Vince for the first time since they'd left the camp and realized they were already at the airport. "White Wrangler at the end of this row."

Vince turned to smile at Sarah and then nodded toward the Jeep. "Cute. You know if you feed it well and give it plenty of water it just might grow up to be a real truck."

Sarah smiled at Vince. "Hey, it's not the size of the truck but the skills of the driver that count."

His eyebrows furrowed. "You really believe that?"

Sarah nodded. "Absolutely."

Vince took the bait. "I'm a firm believer in size backed up with plenty of skill."

Sarah was getting way too turned on by the innuendo, she took a deep breath. "I'm sure you are." As she climbed out of Vince's truck, he handed her a business card. It had a printed phone number on one side and an address written on the back.

"Don't lose that. You run into trouble anywhere or anytime, you call me at that number. Brian's address is on the back. Show up around fifteen-hundred. We're going to barbeque and have a few drinks. I'll give you a chance to get to know the boys a little before we start working together. Bring a suit. He's got a great pool."

"Okay, will do. Thanks for the ride." Sarah grinned and started folding the soft top down on her Jeep. It was looking like it would be a really nice day. Then, his last words rang inside her mind and made her blood run cold.

Me in a bathing suit in front of all those gorgeous men? Oh, God. I think I'm going to be sick!

Sarah spent four hours shopping for a bathing suit. It took her two hours to muster the courage to walk into a dressing room and try one on. When she tried on her usual size eighteen in a one-piece, it suddenly hit her she wasn't "Fat Sarah" anymore. She kept trying smaller sizes until she finally found one that fit. It was a size eight. Then, emboldered by the single digits, she started trying on bikinis. She finally settled on a bikini from Victoria's Secret. She felt goose bumps rise in a wave up her arms. She covered her mouth to muffle a gasp as she looked at herself in the mirror.

I'm gorgeous!

By the time she'd finished at Victoria's Secret, it was already two-thirty in the afternoon. She stopped at a liquor store on the way and then drove to Brian's house. Lesson number one from her Air Force days was to never show up at a barbeque without booze.

Sixteen

Sarah pulled into the driveway of the address Vince had given her. The driveway represented every testosterone junky's dream. There was Vince's truck, a red BMW coupe, a Harley V-Rod that looked to be more chrome than anything, a forest green Range Rover and a silver Corvette convertible.

Oh, yeah, I've definitely got the right house.

The house itself was very nice by Vegas standards. A huge two-story, sand-colored, Mediterranean style home with an attached three-car garage on a double lot. As though Sarah wasn't intimidated enough by the fact that most of them were seasoned soldiers and agents, the house and the cars made her feel way out of her element.

After all, she was still homeless and lucky to be making her Jeep payments. The depressing thoughts weighed heavy on her. She had no idea where she'd sleep at night until they left on the mission.

I got a good pay advance. I can always stay at a hotel for a few weeks. Oh well, I'll think about that later. I've got a house full of men waiting for me.

Sarah shouldered the case of Corona and grabbed her bag complete with bathing suit and a bottle of Jose Cuervo and walked up to the front door. She knocked but there was no answer. She tried the bell and heard it ring. This time voices inside shouted, "Come in!" in unison, so she opened the door.

"Hello?" She peeked inside to see five grown men surrounding a massive flat screen television, playing a video game.

"Hey! Sarah's here."

"'Sup, girl."

"Come on in."

"Hiya."

The one voice she could place rumbled a simple, "Hey, babe, beer's in the fridge. Get me one while you're up?"

Any woman who hadn't spent the last eight years with Air Force cops would have been offended, but that sort of talk just made Sarah feel welcome. "Rank has its privileges. Anybody else want one?" She placed the case and the bottle of tequila on the bar that separated the kitchen from the living room area.

"Nah, I'm good."

"Me, too."

"No takers. Thanks."

She rounded the bar and removed two cold beers from the refrigerator and popped the caps. She took a swig out of one and handed the other to Vince. She watched the carnage on the television. They played a battle game. The scene was reminiscent of a street in the Middle East and they were tearing it up.

Big boys and their big toys. They're not much different than Air Force cops after all.

The tall, dark haired one that had introduced himself as Brian glanced over quickly. "Come on in and have a seat. Sorry, I don't have any fruit for the beer."

"You don't put floaters in your Budweiser, why would you do it to a Corona?"

She didn't see who said it, but somebody mumbled, "She knows the Man Laws. I'm definitely warming up to the girl."

Sarah smiled and took a seat on the couch near Brian. She picked up the game box on the coffee table and read it.

She laughed out loud. "Task Force 121? Oh, you have got to be kidding me!"

Will responded but never took his eyes off the television. "Yeah, I know. Funny, huh? At least in this game we can kill indiscriminately. Check this out."

"God damnit, Will." Brian threw himself backwards onto the overstuffed couch as his player died from not so friendly fire.

"Isn't it time you got the grill going?" Will asked pointedly.

Brian got over his disappointment. "Yeah, I am pretty hungry."

The blond who had flirted with Sarah during the briefing turned to Brian. "Yeah, get in the kitchen and cook me some food, bitch."

Jason, the weapons guy, spoke up. "All right, that's all I can take of this game. These weapons suck. A real Mark-19 gets 350 rounds a minute. I'm lucky to get forty on this piece of shit. I've seen better graphics, too."

"Yeah, I'm out," Vince said. "Got that grill going yet?"

"Hey, I don't see you doing anything, leatherneck," Brian retorted.

Sarah turned to Brian. "I didn't know if I should bring anything. Should I make a salad or something?"

Brian stared at her and smiled as he stood. "Salad's what food eats. You're always welcome with beef or alcohol." He pointed to the case of beer she left on the bar. "And a case of Corona with a bottle of tequila on top will buy you a bed in this house. There's room in the fridge if you want to chill that beer."

Vince piped up. "Hey now, don't be giving my bed away."

Sarah started emptying the case and put the Coronas in the refrigerator, which contained several cases of assorted beers, a few fifths of tequila and several packages of steaks.

"Okay, half a bed." Brian winked at Sarah. "I'll share mine. It's a nice big one. You'll love it."

Will turned to Sarah and rolled his eyes. "Don't pay any attention to him. It's his nature to try to score with every female he comes in contact with. Nature of the beast. You'll be staying in my room. Jason and I will bunk up in his room tonight."

Sarah wasn't quite sure what was going on. "Oh, that's okay, I saw a hotel just a couple miles back."

Will wagged his index finger at Sarah. "No, no, no. We're drinking tonight. You aren't going anywhere. Brian has got more beds in this place than the Chicken Ranch. My room is clean. I even changed the sheets for you."

Sarah gave Will a nod. "Well, thanks." She glanced around the room. "Do you all live here?"

Vince turned his head to face Sarah as he finished his beer. "Brian owns the house. Will and Jason rent the spare bedrooms. I've got the couch on a temporary basis thanks to my currently inhospitable home life. Chris has an apartment on a golf course somewhere. Where is that place, Chris?"

"Players Club. In Henderson."

Vince took a swig of his beer. "We all stay here when we drink. It's safer that way. We don't need anybody getting picked up by the local cops. It just pisses them off when they can't touch us."

"What do you mean?" Sarah made her way back to the couch and sat.

"You're invisible now, babe. Sure, you've still got ID but when the cops run it through the National Crime Information Center, like they do all traffic stops, they get a Do Not Detain order, a phone number and a code to call with. They hate that shit."

"Yeah, they do." Jason giggled, flashing his wicked grin.

"Yeah, you need to stop provoking those guys with your bike, man," Will said sternly. "One of these days a bunch of off duty cops are going to kick your ass. And then we're going to have to take care of them. You know how I hate digging holes in the desert, man."

What?

Chris walked out of the kitchen with two bottles of cold Corona from the refrigerator. He swapped one for the empty bottle in Sarah's hand. "He's just kidding, Sarah."

"Am I?" The dark eyebrows over Will's stunning blue eyes were raised in question. He really was a handsome man, but there was something very dangerous about him.

Chris changed the subject. "So, Sarah, did you bring a suit or are we skinny-dipping?"

Sarah's cheeks warmed. "I've got a suit."

"Bummer. Well, go put it on, girl." Chris pointed down the hallway. "Let's see what Hassan's going to come up against on that yacht of his."

Sarah was afraid she might have faded out during the morning briefing. "What yacht?"

Chris scowled. "Guess I didn't brief you on that yet. You're going to be a guest on Hassan's yacht. Tony's social secretary is working out the details now. We'll get you all the pertinent information when we nail it down."

"Oh, okay." Sarah took a drink from her beer. "Where can I change?"

"Down the hall. First door on the right. That's your room. Don't mind the camera. The green light means it's off." Will's blue eyes glimmered with mischief.

Dangerous but charming.

"I'll be sure to give it my best side."

"I don't know, honey, they all look pretty good to me."

Sarah grabbed her bag off the bar and walked into Will's room to change. She couldn't help but be impressed. A valet stand with a pant presser stood between the walk in closet and the bathroom. The jacket and tie that obviously went with the slacks and shirt he currently wore hung from the stand.

Few men take such good care of their clothes. Much less an obviously straight guy.

Sarah put on her bathing suit and peered at herself in the full-length mirror. It was a beautiful dust-free mahogany mirror but more noticeable was the reflection staring back at her. She felt extremely self conscious in her bathing suit and second guessed her impulse to buy the bikini. The sarong didn't cover or help much either.

Well, I guess it's time to have my first public showing.

She downed the rest of her beer and placed the bottle in the nearby trash can that contained a dry cleaner's receipt and some collar stays. She steeled herself and walked out to the living room where several of the guys already had their shirts off and were packing a cooler to keep by the pool.

Brian stood at the bar seasoning steaks for the grill and let out a long low wolf whistle as she walked out.

Jason stood from where he was hunched over the cooler. "Oh, damn me straight to hell!"

Vince turned around and his jaw dropped.

Chris stretched his arms out wide. "Come to papa."

Sarah felt on edge now and tried to cover herself. "You guys are fucking with me, right? What's wrong?"

"I can't find one thing wrong with that picture." Chris leaned against the wall and stared at Sarah. "Turn around. I'll keep looking for it if you like."

Will hadn't moved from the easy chair he'd been in when Sarah arrived. He continued to puff on his cigar and appeared the picture of cool. "Now, boys." He stood and punctuated by pointing his cigar at Sarah. "This is definitely the camp's finest production yet." Then he walked back toward his bedroom. "Nice work, pork chop. Very nice."

Vince shook his head. "Poor bastard. Hassan doesn't stand a chance." He immediately turned and headed out the sliding glass door to the pool area. Over his shoulder, he yelled, "Brian, I hope that pool is cold."

"Oh, hell yeah!" Jason said as he and Chris quickly followed Vince out the door, loaded cooler in tow between them.

Will came out of his room with swim shorts on and walked straight out the door to the pool.

Sarah stared at Brian who still worked in the kitchen. "They're messing with me, right?"

Brian looked up at Sarah and tilted his head. "We're going to be working pretty closely together. Can I be honest with you?"

Sarah leaned on the bar. "I wish you would."

I knew I should have bought the one piece.

"Darlin', let me save you the trouble of looking in the mirror. You are F-I-N-E, fine. If you weren't already on this team, every guy here would be all over you. We'd be pooling money for the first to score. Matter of fact, you're the sweetest piece of eye candy this house has ever seen¾and I don't mind saying that it has seen a lot."

Sarah sighed.

I've got to get over myself. I'm not fat Sarah any more.

She was so relieved that she walked up to Brian and kissed him on the cheek. "That's the nicest thing anybody ever said to me." She grabbed the tequila bottle and walked toward the sliding glass door. Some of the finest men she'd ever seen were already topless out there.

Oh, yeah. This is definitely going to be a good night. All this and a big fat paycheck, too. When life is good, it is very good.

As an afterthought, Brian called after her. "Hey, I can be even more honest if it'll get me some more of that."

Sarah was feeling really good about herself now, so she turned her head toward Brian, smiled and then took off her sarong and walked out the door.

"That'll work, too." Brian said as she stepped outside.

Seventeen

Vince listened to the gurgle and drip of the coffee maker. After years of running ops where hot coffee and dry socks were a luxury, he appreciated his job as a paramilitary operations officer with the CIA.

Sure, there are bad days, but being based out of Las Vegas and running missions in the Mediterranean is pretty sweet duty.

Vince tapped in the login and password for his Cayman Islands account and checked the balance.

Hmm. Gun running has its perks.

The coffee maker went silent.

Vince logged out and closed the laptop before going to the cupboard for two coffee mugs. He poured fresh coffee into both of them and then reached into the freezer for four ice cubes.

Who knew she'd take her coffee like I do?

He dropped two ice cubes into each cup and brought them outside to the patio. Vince stood beside the chaise where Sarah slept and watched her sleep for a moment.

My God, she's gorgeous. Everything a man could want¾rockin' bod, great personality, holds her liquor like a guy and tough enough to defend herself against four men. Too bad her being on the team completely eliminates her from the dating pool.

Eighteen

Sarah was on a warm beach, in the sun. She heard him breathing next to her.

"Good morning," he said in a low, sexy rumble.

"Mmm…good morning." She purred as she rolled toward him and stretched.

Sarah opened her eyes and realized she'd been dreaming. She was lying on a double chaise by Brian's pool and staring into Vince's light brown eyes. He grinned back at her.

Am I still dreaming? Am I dead? That's the only explanation. I've died and gone to heaven.

"Oh! Good morning," she said in a less provocative tone once she realized where she was.

"Make a note. I definitely prefer the first greeting." He smiled a perfect smile and handed her a big mug of black coffee.

Sarah took a sip. "Mmm… You bring me a big cup of strong coffee every morning and I'll keep that in mind." She returned his smile and scanned the patio. "Where is everybody?"

"They're still sleeping. I thought you might enjoy a quiet cup of coffee before the animals wake up and drink it all."

"Ah, you remembered. Thanks. That was really thoughtful of you."

Vince sat on the other side of the chaise and drank his own coffee.

She had learned a great deal about each of the guys last night.

There was Chris with his blond hair, blue eyes and charisma for days. He was so tanned he looked like a typical California boy. He'd blend well on the beaches of Greece. What people outside the team didn't know was that Chris was a wizard with languages. He spoke Spanish, Portuguese, Arabic, Farsi, Russian, Kyrgyz and Uzbek. For a guy who described himself as a geek, he sure seemed pretty self-confident.

Then there was Jason with his short brown hair, hazel eyes and crooked grin that made him always appear to be up to something. Sarah guessed most of the time he probably was. He seemed like the typical boy next door and joked around like nothing else mattered. He never made a big deal about the fact that he had been a prisoner of war in Desert Storm I, and Sarah had a great deal of respect for what he'd gone through.

Will was very serious about enjoying the finer things in life like silk shirts and Cuban cigars. He had short, black hair with a touch of gray at the temples and dreamy Caribbean-blue eyes. He joined the Navy at seventeen as a corpsman and spent most of his career in the Middle East doing surgery in the sand, patching up soldiers before they were shipped home. Sarah could only imagine what horrors he'd seen there.

The amazing thing about Will was that he appeared about ten years younger than he was. When Sarah asked him why he hadn't retired, he said it was because he wanted to keep doing the job as long as he could. He'd seen firsthand what terrorist attacks could accomplish and he remained passionate about being a part of stopping terrorism.

Brian had brown hair, dark brown eyes and a phenomenal tan. He was lean, long legged and seemed like he belonged on an Italian soccer team. His father served as a Navy SEAL in Vietnam and was still MIA. Brian fought his demons by also becoming a SEAL. When an operation went sour and the other members of his team were killed in action, he was recruited as an original member of Task Force 125 for his expertise in explosives. He lived hard. His motto was "Live fast, die young and leave a good looking corpse." He was a man who liked hard liquor, lots of women and risky work. When he wasn't on the job, he was either in or near water. He gave the term "frogman" a whole new meaning.

The last thing I want to do is let these guys down. How I perform on this mission will define me. I have an obligation to do the best job possible, no matter how difficult it may be.

Sarah really enjoyed talking to all the guys, but when everybody else had drunk their fill and wandered off to bed, she and Vince stayed awake. They sat in the double chaise by the pool and talked well into the morning. To Sarah, the time spent with Vince was worth every moment of lost sleep.

Vince was an amazing mass of striated muscle that appeared as though he could crush anyone and would on a bad day. Sarah discovered underneath the rough and gruff exterior he was actually a very sensitive guy. Sensitivity is frowned upon in the military, so he hid it well.

Everyone in his family had served in some branch of the military, including his sister and two brothers. His sister retired from the Army, one brother was killed in action in Baghdad, and his other brother was currently serving in the Marines at an undisclosed location in Iraq.

Vince had been Force Recon in the Marines and was then recruited by the CIA to take on some particularly sensitive assignments that were mostly arms deals. When he got wind that Task Force 125 was being created, he'd volunteered immediately. His family had already invested so much in the war on terror that it had become their personal war and Vince wanted to do his part.

After talking about everyone's background, Sarah and Vince discussed many other things. She'd hoped getting to know him better would help kill her infatuation with him but it did just the opposite. The more she knew, the more she liked.

Vince's wife had been a showgirl. They hadn't lived together in over a year. She'd wanted diamonds, a Jaguar and the freedom to sleep around with whomever she liked while Vince was out on missions. He gave her the diamonds and the Jag. She took the rest.

Vince had fallen asleep by the pool at about o-three-hundred. Sarah spent the night on the chaise, enjoying the night air and drinking in all the amazing changes in her life. She must have fallen asleep shortly after Vince did.

And here you are waking me with that dead sexy voice and a cup of coffee. Add some hot sex and it's a storybook romance. And there's the rub. There will be no sex. There's one rule even a dog won't break. You don't shit where you eat.

Will appeared at the sliding glass door wearing nothing but baggy pajama pants. "Well, isn't this cozy. Mata Hari and Captain America sipping coffee by the pool."

"That's Major America to you, mop jockey."

Sarah smiled at their casual banter. "Good morning, Will."

"Morning, gorgeous. Sleep all right out here?"

"Just great. Thanks anyway for the room."

"Any time." Will winked a dreamy blue eye at her.

"Morning, jarhead. Brian is cooking this morning. Eggs are up."

Vince turned to Sarah. "You're probably the first woman in history Brian has ever made breakfast for. You don't want to miss his scrambled eggs."

Sarah and Vince crossed the patio to the chaotic mess hall that Brian's kitchen had become.

Jason stood in front of the coffee maker. His hair hadn't decided which way it wanted to go so it just stuck out everywhere. The bare chest and ripped abs were an interesting complement to his frazzled hair and flannel pajama pants. Coffee grounds were scattered all over the countertop in front of him.

"Morning, guys," Jason mumbled as Sarah and Vince stepped inside. "Coffee's empty, I'm making another pot."

A commanding voice boomed from behind Sarah. "Step away from the coffee pot."

Sarah's feet left the ground and she instantly found herself set down two feet to the right of where she'd been. Will ran into the kitchen and relegated Jason to a seat at the table.

"What was that about?" Sarah asked Chris, who sat at the table, reading the Wall Street Journal.

"Jason loves coffee but can't make a decent pot to save his life. We only let him make a pot when we need gun cleaner." Chris winced. "Nasty stuff."

Brian passed Sarah a plate of scrambled eggs as she sat at the table.

"Thanks, Brian." She smiled at him as she set the plate in front of her.

Jason turned toward Brian. "So, Bri, this would probably make Sarah the first woman you've ever let stay for breakfast, huh?"

"Yep." Brian winked at Sarah. "If she plays her cards right, she can be the first one I serve breakfast in bed to as well."

"Where were you guys two years ago? My ego could have used you back then."

"Classified." Vince replied almost automatically as he set his coffee mug on the table.

"Same," Brian and Will said at the same time.

"Fort Bragg," Jason said between mouthfuls of scrambled egg.

"Quantico." Chris shrugged.

Sarah smirked and turned her focus back to her breakfast.

Damn! Real live heroes with humor. I think I'm going to like working with this crew.

Nineteen

As instructed, Tony and Sarah reported to the suite at Caesar's Palace.

Young, the team's handler was waiting inside. "Morning." He opened the door to let them into the suite.

Sarah marveled at the main room of the suite. "This place is beautiful."

"Glad you like it." Young sat and poured himself a cup of coffee from the silver service on the coffee table in the parlor area. "You and Tony have to create your cover as a couple, so you'll be staying here together until you depart for your mission. There are two bedrooms." He nodded toward both ends of the suite between sips of coffee. "You two will be posing as a couple for Hassan so this will give you a chance to get to know each other and establish your story. Your team will be based out of this suite and receive all further briefings here."

Sarah's mouth dropped in shock. "But this is Caesar's Palace. Shouldn't we be concerned about security and bugs? Anybody could get in here and plant something."

Young took a big gulp of coffee and set the mug down on the table in front of him. "No. We've had this set up with Caesar's for years now. Nobody else uses this room but us, and we have certain electronic security measures in place that eliminate the threat of bugs. It's perfectly secure so long as all the windows stay closed. Any questions?"

Sarah helped herself to a cup of coffee. "Yeah, who pays for room service?"

Young gave a half laugh, half snort. "I see you're already playing the part you've been assigned. The Agency covers it. You can charge your meals to the room, too. We need you to establish a good cover in case you meet people Hassan knows. Everything you do in public from here on out has to be in character. That means first class. Got it?"

Sarah beamed. "Not a problem."

Sarah and Tony spent their first morning together getting to know one another and going over their back-story. Tony had spent the past several years becoming known as a jet setting party boy. He was in a position now where he was a welcome guest at everybody's party, vacation house or yacht. To Sarah's surprise, he spoke of it all as very hard work.

"It really is quite a pain in the ass," he explained. "I have a whole staff of people that work full time just to keep me popular. I have a stylist who makes sure I'm wearing all the appropriate clothes, a hairdresser I see every week and a personal secretary who handles my mail and my schedule.

My secretary answers RSVPs, sends birthday and wedding gifts for me and keeps me up to date on who is having what party and what new club is opening. Thankfully, she's brilliant with my schedule and always ensures I'm making the most of my time in any given city. Then, of course, I have a public relations firm that works closely with my secretary to schedule my own parties and charity events."

"You host charity events?" Sarah couldn't hide the incredulous tone of her voice.

"Oh, yes, it is absolutely necessary." Tony picked a practically invisible bit of thread from his white silk shirt. "It's all about noblesse oblige. When you have a lot, you're expected to give a lot. Every year I host a charity polo event in West Palm. It's great fun." He gave Sarah a thoughtful glance. "You should come this year. I'll make sure my secretary sends you an invitation." He pulled a buzzing Blackberry out of his breast pocket and shut it off before continuing. "Then I generally host at least ten to twenty luncheons, brunches and dinners each year. So, you see, being a free and easy party boy isn't free or easy."

The door opened and Vince strode into the suite wearing a black ribbed sweater and jeans. He carried a briefcase. "Sorry, kids. I didn't mean to interrupt. I need to use the computer." He sat at the desk, pulled a laptop from the briefcase and started typing. Without turning around, he asked, "You two getting comfortable?"

Tony turned in his seat to see Vince. "Hey, you're welcome for drinks after four, but surfing porn isn't cool, man."

Vince turned around in his chair and faced Tony. He lifted his chin slightly toward Sarah. "Who needs porn when you're in her company?"

Sarah noticed he held her gaze just a little longer than was comfortable. Her cheeks warmed.

Damnit. I've never blushed a day in my life then this guy shows up and I'm an apple-faced fool.

Sarah could have sat there all day and watched Vince, but she was still curious and needed to know more about Tony. After all, they were going to be posing as lovers. After that last comment, watching Vince made her temperature rise anyway. She turned back to Tony. "So, how did you get involved in all of this?"

Tony chuckled softly. "Oh, this?" He waved his hand nonchalantly. "I wanted to prove to my parents and myself that I could do more than just tap a trust fund, so I joined the Air Force after high school. I completed a bachelor's degree during my first enlistment and wanted to study international law, so I started out in the Security Police field and then cross-trained over to the Office of Special Investigations.

After eight years, I decided it was time for law school and more advanced studies, so I got out and went to Harvard. Since I had a large circle of social and political connections, I was asked to occasionally assist the NSA with certain operations that were vital to national security. This is just one of those operations."

Vince jumped into the conversation from where he was seated at the desk. "Don't let him whitewash the story. Tony is laying a lot on the line to get us in. If anything ever got traced back to him, he and his very well-known family would be in serious trouble. Tony opens doors for us that would take forever for agents to get through on their own." Vince turned back to his computer and began typing.

Sarah poured herself another cup of coffee. "So, Tony, how do you know Hassan?"

"Oh, we were roommates at Harvard," he replied indifferently.

Sarah nearly choked on her coffee. "Knowing the purpose of our mission, this must be very difficult for you."

Tony tilted his head and replied as though to a child. "A great many people attend good schools together, but that doesn't make them good people or good friends."

Sarah gazed out the window beside her to the strip below and tried to process everything going through her head. This man in the chair across from her had everything money and good breeding could buy, and, yet, he laid it all on the line to fight terrorism.

Sarah realized what she had wasn't just a job. This was a real war and too many people depended on her for her to not take it seriously. She wiped her damp palms on her jeans. What she had was a mission and she had to be ready to lay everything, including her life, on the line in order to ensure its success. Sarah's thoughts were interrupted by the door to the suite opening.

Chris stepped into the room with someone Sarah hadn't met yet. "Sarah, Tony, Vince, may I present Hamza Abbas of the Defense Language Institute. Hamza will be tutoring Sarah in Arabic."

Sarah stood and shook his hand. "Hello, Mr. Abbas. I'm very happy to be working with you."

"It's my pleasure." He shook her hand lightly. "The classrooms at DLI get pretty boring. A paid trip to Las Vegas to work with a beautiful woman will be a welcome change." He pulled a folder out from under his arm. "I've taken a look at your DLAB scores from the test you took when you enlisted and I don't think you'll have any trouble learning enough Arabic to be effective."

Tony stood and shook Hamza's hand. "It's very nice to meet you. I'm sure we'll be seeing a lot of each other over the next few weeks. If you'll all excuse me, I have some phone calls to make." Tony disappeared into the bedroom he'd claimed as his own.

Sarah spent the next eight hours going over Arabic books with Hamza and getting acquainted with the DLI method of language immersion.

Preparation for her first mission involved much more than Arabic lessons. They were turning her into two completely different people and it was her job to not only become both, but to find a way to make them come together seamlessly. She had to be a glamorous, sexy socialite and have all the accouterments to go along with that lifestyle. She also needed the skills and accouterments necessary for a spy dealing with dangerous people.

Creating the socialite was the easiest part. It involved shopping on a nearly unlimited expense account. "V" became Sarah's favorite letter. Louis Vuitton luggage, Valentino and Versace dresses, and a full complement of the best of Victoria's Secret underneath. There was something about dressing in only the best that made Sarah feel the part.

She'd never had the money to buy such extravagant clothing and accessories. She'd always dreamed of someday having thousand-dollar handbags but never truly believed it could happen. Now she had five. When she put on the clothes, she became the glamorous, sexy socialite and started to fall in love with the part she would play. Sarah's life was truly becoming larger than any life she'd ever known, and she loved every minute of it.

The difficult part of the transformation was becoming the spy. She had basic skills in the Arabic language that had to be built upon quickly. She had to know much more than how to locate a bathroom and buy a cup of coffee. She was immersed in Arabic with Hamza for eight hours every day while every night was spent at the best restaurants and nightclubs, being seen and getting to know the real jet setters and socialites.

Outside of her lessons in Arabic and social graces, she made sure to work in a very serious exercise routine every day. A swim every morning and weight training every afternoon. After her lifting session, she'd get Jason to go out to the desert and spar with her. He still didn't like the idea of fighting a girl but who better to train with than a Green Beret?

Simply showing up on Hassan's yacht with Tony wouldn't be enough. Sarah had to be seen with Tony in Vegas, and she had to be seen by the sort of people who would get the gossip mill going and reinforce her cover as a sexy "it girl." That meant going to and being seen at the hottest clubs. Every night became a new lifestyle lesson.

Though she was busy preparing for her part in this assignment nearly twenty-four hours a day, her infatuation for Vince still raged. When she found herself daydreaming about him, she would fight it by delving deeper into her studies. She had a complete dossier on Hassan that she had practically memorized just to keep her mind off Vince.

"Studying Hassan's dossier again?"

Sarah set the dossier down on the couch beside her. "Oh, hi, Tony. Yeah. He's got a huge family."

Tony sat in the chair across from Sarah. "Hassan comes from a very wealthy Saudi family. The larger the family, the more rank conscious they are. The first born son usually holds all the power among the siblings, but siblings in the wealthy families generally do a lot of political maneuvering. If the eldest son falls out of favor, the next in line holds the power and so on."

Sarah winced. "Seems like a hell of a way to go through life."

"Yeah." Tony nodded. "As the youngest son of a man with nine wives and thirty-two children, Hassan had to work hard to stand out. His mother, having only one son, doted upon him in an attempt to make up for his father's lack of interest."

"He got the best education money could buy, didn't he?" Sarah picked up the dossier and pulled out a sheet of paper and read from it. "Eton, undergrad degree from Cambridge, Masters from Georgetown and then, of course, Harvard."

"Excellent education," Tony answered. "His grades were always exceptional, but he was also very well known as a ladies man. He speaks fluent English and Arabic."

Sarah turned to the next page in the dossier. "It says here he joined Al Qaeda at twenty-five."

"He couldn't get his father's attention so he worked on his eldest brother," Tony added. "His association with Osama Bin Laden's organization earned him his eldest brother's favor and moved him up in family rank. However, just as quickly as he'd gained favor, he lost it again when he fell out with Osama."

Sarah understood even more about Hassan now. "So, rather than continuing in the family political games, he took the trust fund he received from his father and built a successful shipping business. It was when he added smuggling to his business that he really struck it rich."

"Correct." Tony nodded. "And after several hefty donations to Al Qaeda, he found favor once again with Osama as well as his own eldest brother, thus buying himself back into the family political scene. Hassan then leveraged his business and school networks to create a brilliant social network. Through his networking, he proved himself an able fundraiser for Al Qaeda and quickly became one of the few primary financiers for the organization. With all the income from the shipping, smuggling and fundraising activities passing through his hands, Hassan soon became a connoisseur of fine things and grew to enjoy a lifestyle of conspicuous consumption complete with large estates, expensive toys and priceless collections of art and horses."

Will and Brian walked into the suite.

"'Sup kids?" Brian walked straight to the bar and poured himself a drink.

"Ah, Brian. I see how it is. You only visit me for the booze," Sarah joked.

"Hey, Uncle Sam pays for it when I drink here and until you start putting out, this is going to be the big attraction." He raised a glass to Sarah and took a drink.

Will sat on the other chair across from Sarah and lit a cigar. "While you're there, Bri, pour me two fingers of Scotch."

Brian pulled a crystal glass from the bar and poured Will's Scotch. "Anybody else?"

Tony turned his wrist and glanced at his watch. "Eight-o-clock already. Yeah, I'll have a gin and tonic."

Brian looked at Sarah. "Sarah, the usual?"

"Sure. Thanks." Sarah lit a cigarette. After taking a drag from her cigarette, Sarah tapped the dossier. "Says here he likes American women. What's that about?"

"Yeah." Tony grinned. "He never cared much for Middle Eastern women. He goes for the tall, athletic type. Just the opposite of his mother."

Sarah raised an eyebrow at Tony. "So, I just endear myself to him and then get him to spill his secrets?"

"Sweetheart," Will interjected. "You are what we spooks call a swallow. Swallows use sex to get secrets. You know what the name American Swift is about, right? It's a sort of swallow. The success of our mission is resting on your sex appeal."

No pressure, huh?

~~~

A week into her preparation for the mission, Sarah was enjoying a fabulous evening on the terrace at *Pure* with Tony and several of his friends when she literally bumped into Vince. She was returning from the ladies room when she saw Chris lounging with a group of people. Just as she smiled at Chris, Vince, who was seated with his back to her, stood and turned right into her. Sarah stumbled backwards but Vince quickly wrapped his arms around her and caught her before she fell.

Sarah gasped as lightning ripped through her body.

Control yourself, Sarah. He's still married! He's a co-worker! He outranks you! He's your boss!

"Excuse me. I'm sorry," he whispered with his lips only inches from hers.

Feeling him holding her and having the opportunity to wrap her own arms around him emboldened her. Her blood was racing and every cell of her body was screaming for more of him.

Oh, don't be sorry!

Sarah snaked her hands over his shoulders as she righted herself and whispered seductively into his ear, "It's okay. I'm sure I'm not the first woman who's fallen for you."

And by the look and feel of things, you've got a whole lot going on here. I'm sure I won't be the last to fall for you!

Something in his eyes seemed to soften, but it disappeared as quickly as it appeared. Vince slid his hands from around her waist and let go of her. "Are you all right?"

You're my boss and make me weak in the knees. No, I'm definitely a frigging mess but you're the last person I'm going to tell!

Sarah's socialite smile shined at Vince. Playfully, and loud enough so his party could hear her, she sighed and feigned a swoon. "I'll never be the same again."

She then strutted back to her table to join Tony and the others. Sarah curled up near Tony on a banquette and gazed around the terrace at all the beautiful people, hoping Vince still watched her. Her eyes eventually returned to Vince. He sat with Chris, Brian and Will…and they were all watching her.

If he had any idea how serious I was, he'd throw me off the team in a heartbeat!

~~~

The next day, Sarah awoke to Jason tromping into her room and demanding with a rather affected English accent and a very wicked smile. "Okay, love, show me your knickers!"

After seeing Vince at the club the night before, Sarah had been so distracted she drank a few too many glasses of champagne. Tequila, no problem, but champagne never failed to go straight to her head. The first

111

thing she realized after Jason's voice boomed through the room, was that her robe sat several feet away from the bed.

Great. I'm in the raw and he wants to see my underwear. I don't even want to think what he might be up to.

Sarah pulled the sheet up around her naked body as she sat up in the bed. The room spun in slow circles.

She groaned, slumped back down on the pillows and closed her eyes. "I'm not wearing any, but you just may see my birthday suit right before I kick your ass."

Of course, I'm in no shape to kick anyone's ass because the tiny bubbles from last night have banded together and decided their mission is to kill me. But if I could kick an ass, yours would be at the top of the list.

"Hey, sorry. Boss's orders. He was adamant we outfit you with a few weapons for your own safety. It's important you get used to wearing them now so you can act natural when you go in. I'm definitely up for the birthday suit thing though." He flashed a wicked smile. "If you're going to be wearing the kind of clothes we've seen you around in lately, the best place to pack heat is going to be in your undergarments. So, let's see what you've got here."

Jason began opening and closing dresser drawers. Whenever he closed a drawer, he seemed to take particular joy in slamming it closed.

She snarled and willed daggers from her eyes.

Jason, I will find a way to pay you back for this.

Sarah wrapped her sheet around herself and walked carefully over to her robe on the back of the chaise. Even the plush carpet seemed to make noise this morning. When she finally reached her robe, she wrapped it around herself and dropped the sheet where she stood. Let the maid get it. Bending over to lift something, even as light as a sheet, may just be too taxing at this point. The light sound of the silk robe sliding over her shoulders sounded more like a belt sander than the whisper it was. Sarah slowly turned around to watch Jason exploring her dresser.

Holding her head, just in case it might fall off, Sarah made her way to the dresser to open the appropriate drawer for Jason. The sooner she did, the sooner he'd stop slamming drawers and making her feel as though concussion grenades were going off inside her head.

"Hot dog!" he shouted as she opened the drawer containing all of Victoria's best secrets. Jason turned to her and smiled his crooked, Cheshire cat grin. "I just love my job."

"That's super," she deadpanned. "Can I trust you in here alone while I get some coffee?"

Jason held up a violet embroidered garter belt. "Yeah, sure. I'm not going anywhere." Then he added, "Hey. You always look like this when you wake up hung over?"

Sarah's head throbbed and threatened to split open at any minute. "I don't need any shit from you this morning."

He raised his hands in surrender. "No, hey, I've seen hung over chicks in my time…usually helps to get them drunk before I sleep with them…but you look pretty damned good for all the booze you put down."

I'm pretty messed up, but I think that's a bit of a backhanded compliment. I can't bear to think with all this drumming inside my head.

"Charming," she mumbled, walking into the other room to get a cup of coffee from the pot Tony always had delivered bright and early. She poured herself a cup of black coffee, lit a cigarette and returned to her room where Jason had spread a collection of small knives on the bed. The previous conversation finally settled into Sarah's head.

"Wait a minute. When have you seen me lately, other than last night, and how do you know how much I drank?"

"Listen, Sarah," he began. "First of all, sit down, you silly, hung-over bitch."

Sarah was in too much pain to deal with hurt feelings. "Hey…" She sat on the edge of the bed with Jason's assistance.

"Do you have any idea how hard it is to find a chick that will do this kind of job? We had one before you but she just didn't have what it took. When you go out, we will never be far behind. When you go in, we'll be even closer. Not only do we know how much you drink, but we know the average amount of time you spend in the ladies room."

Sarah tried to focus through the headache.

"Seriously, Sarah. A lot depends on how you perform. If you get the info we need, we can put this bastard and quite a few others out of business and that's going to save the lives of a lot of uniforms on the ground." Jason suddenly seemed very serious. "This isn't an easy job, but a lot of troops and their families are depending on us to shorten this war. Putting Hassan out of business could help do that. Every six dollars we stop is one less AK-47 in a terrorist's hands."

Only six bucks for an AK-47? Can that be right?

Jason gave a little tug on the collar of Sarah's robe. "Now cover up some of that cleavage before you drive me completely nuts and let's check out the blades I brought for you."

Sarah became quite sober after hearing this from Jason. Nobody had ever actually described this job to her that way before. This assignment was her chance at redemption. This was her chance to do something big. She wouldn't let them down.

Sarah pulled her robe a bit tighter and cinched the belt. She stubbed out her cigarette in the ashtray on the dresser and then watched as Jason tapped out two cigarettes from his own pack, lit them and handed one to her.

Sarah took the cigarette. "Thanks, man."

"Hey, we take care of each other."

Sarah and Jason spent the rest of the morning fitting some of the finest small knives she'd ever laid eyes on into her wildly expensive undergarments and footwear.

I had no idea you could hide knives in places like these.

"Jason, what did you do before you were recruited for this job?"

Jason took a drag of his cigarette and puffed out a perfect O. "Well, you know I was a Green Beret. Joined up straight out of high school and had some crazy dreams about Delta Force. After training, I went straight to the sandbox for Desert Storm."

"I'm guessing you saw some action?"

"Little bit." He nodded. "Got caught painting a skiff for the bombers and spent forty-nine days as a guest of Saddam's Republican Guard."

Sarah had never known a prisoner of war. "Oh my God!"

Jason's expression turned dark. "They weren't as friendly as you might think." He shook his head as if to shake off the memories. "The fuckers left me on the side of the road when they ran out of food and water. Too busy worrying about their own asses to deal with POWs. I took a cushy job teaching survival school at Fort Bragg after that. That's where the task force picked me up."

"Wow." Sarah ran her hand through her hair and tried to wrap her mind around the idea of being a POW.

"Hey, we all have stories," he said coolly. "You'll have a few of your own before it's all said and done." Jason stood. "I gotta get going. Chris should be here any minute to go over the com equipment you're gonna use."

Twenty

Sarah had enough time to shower, dress and drink some more coffee before Chris arrived.

Chris waltzed into the room with his wavy blond hair shining and his blue eyes sparkling. "Jason says you've got some hot lingerie. What say you slip into something and model it for Big Daddy?"

"I've got a better idea." After a pot of coffee, Sarah was a bit more up to speed and ready for Chris's flirty banter. She lit a cigarette and eyed him provocatively. "Why don't you model it for me?"

"Ooh, kink. I like that in a woman."

Sarah was ready to get down to business. She had some shopping to do before they left for this mission. "Why don't we get the serious stuff out of the way first?"

Adopting a look of dejection, Chris pouted. "Killjoy." He sat and opened his briefcase. "Okay, you and Vince are our eyes and ears. We're counting on you guys, especially you, to get the goods on this dirtball. If you can get the intel to me, I'll report it so we, and anyone else we need for backup, can act. Understood?"

So far, Sarah thought it sounded pretty easy. "Yeah, sure, but I'm guessing a cellular phone isn't the way we're going to go. So, how do I get you the information?"

"Well, you'll have this cell as part of your cover. Load it up with party people. If anybody ever checks it, they shouldn't be able to connect you to any of us." Chris then pulled three Mikimoto jewelry boxes out of his briefcase. He opened the largest box to expose an exquisite four strand, pearl choker.

She had always wanted fine jewelry, but this was well beyond her dreams. "Oh, it's beautiful!"

"Hmm." He shook his head. "I'll be damned."

"What?"

"Oh, I just figured you for diamonds. Vince picked them out and said it had to be pearls. He wouldn't even discuss it. Are you sure you wouldn't prefer diamonds?"

Sarah picked up the choker and ran her fingers lovingly over the pearls.

I've always wanted pearls…

"No." She sighed. "These are perfect." She wondered how somebody like Vince could possibly know to buy her pearls instead of diamonds. "Vince has impeccable taste."

Chris laughed. "You'll never hear his ex-wife say that. Don't tell him I told you, but every time that poor bastard gave her a gift, she'd return it within twenty-four hours for something bigger and flashier. I'll let him know you like the pearls. It'll be a pleasant change for him."

He opened the other two boxes to reveal three similar strands of pearls for her wrist and two perfect pearl stud earrings.

While Sarah tried them all on and marveled at their beauty in the nearby mirror, Chris explained. "Each piece has a transmitter and the earrings have receivers as well." He handed her a small, flesh colored ball, no larger than a pencil eraser. "Put this in your ear. The earrings will pick up my transmissions but this is what you'll hear them through. I'll monitor everything, so if you hear it, I'll hear it."

"Whoa." Sarah's eyes opened wide. Knots tied and untied themselves in her stomach. "You'll be listening to everything I do?"

Chris eyed Sarah sternly. "Get over it. I've heard chicks fart and I've heard them in the sack. I'm a professional and so are you."

This job leaves no room for modesty.

Chris helped Sarah with the clasp on the choker as she tried it on. "Now if we need to get a message or instructions to you and we can't do it in person, we'll do it through the earrings. One word of warning though, when you want to talk, turn on some music or water just in case there are bugs in the room. Oh, and here's a little something just to pass the time and help you mix with the rich and famous." He pulled a small Rolex box out of his briefcase and handed her a sleek gold watch. The face was Mother of Pearl with diamonds where each hour should be. More diamonds encircled the entire face and trailed in two twinkling lines along the perimeter of the band.

How exquisite. With jewelry like this, who needs time?

The watch alone had to be worth more than the value of all her worldly possessions added together. "It's beautiful, Chris."

"I know. I picked this one out. Glad you approve." He closed his briefcase. "Okay, I shouldn't have to tell you how important it is you wear at least one piece of jewelry at all times and always wear the earrings. You never know when you're going to catch something good." He stood. "You should probably start making a habit of wearing them all the time now so it becomes second nature by show time."

Sarah stood and stared at herself in the mirror.

I am dripping with pearls!

"That is not going to be a problem." Sarah stared at the pearls at her ears and around her neck and stifled a giggle. The watch was spectacular in a very flashy sort of way, but the pearls were what really impressed Sarah.

The watch says "I've arrived," but the pearls say, "I've always been here."

Wait a minute...

She turned toward Chris. "Are you the only one who will be monitoring these?"

He nodded. "Yeah, it all comes through my receiver." He tapped a tiny Bluetooth earpiece. "If you run into anything you can't handle, you let me know and I'll send the cavalry." His blue eyes flashed and the corner of his mouth lifted in a crooked grin. "Well, us and the Sixth Fleet, but that ought to cover any trouble you could possibly get yourself into."

"Nice." Sarah smiled as she realized who had her back. "So, how did you get on this team?" Sarah was anxious to know as much about all of her teammates as possible.

"It's a common story actually." He shrugged. "I was a geek. I learned Spanish in grade school, Portuguese in high school, studied Russian in college and picked up Kyrgyz and Uzbek during spring and summer breaks. When I graduated with a degree in communications, the FBI offered me a job. That's where I picked up Arabic and Farsi. When the bureau got overwhelmed with requests for linguistic assistance for Task Force 125, I was permanently assigned."

"You hardly strike me as a geek." Sarah chuckled.

He laughed. "Contact lenses, a personal trainer, a tan, haircut and a nice car can make for quite a metamorphosis."

"Yeah, I know what you mean." Sarah thought about her own recent changes. "How long have you been working on this team?"

"Oh, this is only our second assignment together. We're a pretty new team. We had our first assignment together about six months ago."

"But you all seem so close. Like you'd been together for years. Did you work with any of these guys before then?"

"No." He shook his head. "This team is really new. The reason we all seem so close is because we're all we've got. None of us are married. A couple of the guys are divorced. Well, Vince's divorce isn't final yet but they haven't been together for well over a year now. Long-term relationships don't work out so well when you're incommunicado for months on end. So, when we're not working together, we're usually hanging out together. You get to be really tight if your whole life revolves around the same four people, well, now five. It isn't bad though. We've got a good crew here. You'll see."

Sounds more like a family. All the more reason to get over this stupid infatuation with Vince.

Twenty-One

Sarah lounged on the couch in the suite's sitting room as she drank her morning coffee. It was an added bonus to be able to watch Vince as he worked with his back to her from the desk in the sitting room. She listened as he spoke on his cell phone.

"Yeah, that's right, two tons of AKs and five tons of 7.62. Deliver to my warehouse in Dubai. Always a pleasure, Nikolai." Vince bent over his paperwork and wrote something.

Did he just do what I think he did?

Sarah knew what AKs and 7.62 were. "So, you're really a gun runner, too?"

Vince rolled his chair away from the desk and turned to face Sarah. He leaned back, laced his fingers together over his belt buckle and rested his right ankle on his left knee.

He just bought two tons of AK-47s and five tons of ammunition for them, yet he looks so relaxed.

Vince looked into Sarah's eyes and half smiled. "You know what we do is on the edge, Sarah. We work in an industry where ends justify means, no matter what those means may be. Yeah, I'm an arms dealer. I've been doing it for about a year and a half now. It's my cover, not who I am, just like your cover isn't who you are."

Why do I always melt when he looks into my eyes?

"Well, I don't know," Sarah protested. "Maybe I am this person we've created."

Vince stood and crossed to where Sarah sat. He lifted her chin and looked deep into her eyes. "You're not a bimbo, Sarah. You're an intelligent, strong and beautiful woman. Don't ever forget that."

The rest of the world disappeared and Sarah allowed herself to get lost in Vince's eyes. Her whole body warmed at his touch.

The spell broke as Tony came into the suite beaming. "Hey, great, you're both here. I just got a call from Hassan. Sarah and I have been invited to cruise the Greek Islands with him for a weekend."

"That's good, Tony. You couldn't get a week?" Vince strode back to the desk and placed his papers and laptop into his briefcase.

Tony's smile deflated. "Hardass as always, eh, Vince?" He turned to Sarah. "I get a weekend on a yacht with a terrorist and he wants to know why I couldn't get a whole week?"

Vince picked up his briefcase. "Well, if anyone can get an invitation from Hassan to stay longer, it's Sarah." He nodded at her and turned to open the door. "Between that and the arms deal I'm putting together with him, our mission will work. Text me the details. I'm on my way to the camp to brief Young and get the green light." Vince walked out and closed the door without another word.

It is almost scary how he can switch from caring and sensitive to all business. I could learn a few things from him.

Tony sat next to Sarah and spoke as he started texting Vince. "He's right, you know. You'll do great."

Sarah placed her coffee cup on the silver tray on the table and stood. "Well, I guess I'd better get ready."

"For what?" Tony gazed up at her.

"I need to go work out, get a mani/pedi, micro-dermabrasion deep condition the hair and tan. Beauty like this doesn't just happen, you know."

Whatever we have to do to sweeten the pot, right? These guys are counting on me to charm the secrets out of Hassan and that is exactly what I intend to do.

Sarah reclined in the comfortable chair as her hairdresser applied a deep conditioner and wrapped her head in a plastic turban. She couldn't stop her mind from wandering to Vince and how it had felt to be touched by him.

The jingle of her new cell phone interrupted her thoughts.

She flipped the tiny phone open. "Yes?"

"Sarah, its Vince."

The sound of his voice sent a jolt through her body like lightning.

"Yes, I know the voice."

"We leave Wednesday."

"So soon?" Sarah's nerves suddenly kicked into overdrive.

Vince's voice softened. "Take it easy."

The sound of his voice calmed her nerves but every inch of her skin begged to feel his touch again.

How does he know just how to talk to me?

"We fly out Wednesday and then we'll spend a week cruising the Med. I've got some business to attend to out there and Chris will need to set up his toys."

Sarah gave in to her urge to be flirtatious. "Oh, so we have to bring him, too?"

Vince paused at the other end of the line.

Sarah rolled her eyes and smacked her forehead with her fist for acting so impulsively.

"Yeah, we have to bring all the boys, but next time it'll be just the two of us."

Ooh, I like your tone.

Sarah inhaled deeply as she envisioned it. "I'll hold you to that."

"Do."

Sarah's heartbeat raced and her fingers trembled as she closed her phone. The thought of being anywhere alone with Vince made her hot. She grabbed a tissue and patted the sweat on her forehead.

Early Wednesday morning, Sarah packed her Louis Vuitton luggage into her Jeep and drove the dusty road to the camp. She chuckled to herself as she pulled out of the garage at Caesar's Palace. It might have been more in keeping with her cover to have a driver and a Town Car but blindfolding a driver never goes over well. There were more important things to worry about anyway¾like surviving her first mission as a secret agent. She pulled into hangar one, where she was told departing teams always parked their personal vehicles, and saw Vince and Will standing by Will's Range Rover drinking coffee.

She stepped out of the Jeep and opened the back door. "Morning, guys."

Will raised his cup. "Mornin', pork chop."

"Here, have some coffee." Vince's voice behind her sent a charge up her spine and she smiled automatically as she turned to see him. He stood with one cup of coffee to his lips and another in his outstretched hand.

Sarah took the cup and drank. "Thank you."

Gorgeous, smart, considerate and completely off limits. This would be easier if you were an asshole.

The hanger filled with the roar of engines as three black Suburbans, being driven by Brian, Jason and Chris, rolled into the hangar.

Vince was back to business. "Okay, Sarah, Brian and I are in number one. Will and Jason, load your gear in number two, Chris you take number three."

Sarah loaded her luggage into the first Suburban and scanned the hangar. "Where's Tony?"

Vince kept loading gear into the truck. "He had some prior engagements. He'll join us in a week."

Sarah climbed into the back seat of the Suburban to finish her coffee. Within moments, everyone was loaded up and they were on the road to the airport.

Man, this is the life. VIP convoy to the airport.

Sarah pulled a book out of her bag and lost track of time as they drove.

"This is it," Vince said from the front seat. "Last chance to back out, Sarah."

"Not a chance." Sarah stuffed her book back in her bag and realized they were at Henderson Executive Airport. "Vince, how are we going to get all that stuff through customs?"

"We aren't." Vince pointed to a gate. "That one, Brian. We're taking a private jet. We'll stop over briefly in New York for fuel then overnight to London where MI-5 will put us up for a night and then we'll continue to Souda Air Base in Crete. From there we convoy to the dock."

A sliver of sunlight peeked up over the horizon. They drove toward a shiny, white jet that was well lit and had two men moving around it. Six portholes glowed with golden light. Sarah's stomach flip-flopped with excitement.

"Holy shit." The whispered words escaped Sarah's mouth before she realized it. "Oh my God, is that our plane?"

Brian parked the Suburban and opened his door before turning to grin at Sarah. "Nothing but the best, darlin'."

After Sarah finally calmed her flip-flopping stomach and adjusted to the luxury and comfort of the jet's main cabin, she visually assessed the men with whom she now worked. At first glance, they appeared to be your average American guys. It would have been so easy to underestimate them. Lucky for Sarah, she'd had the opportunity to get to know each one of them as she prepared for this assignment.

Once everyone settled in and the jet took off, Vince tapped Sarah's shoe with his and then tipped his chin motioning for her to join him at the back of the plane. Sarah followed as Vince led the way through the back door of the main cabin that led into a luxurious bedroom.

Oh, howdy.

"What's up?" She tried to stay calm while her pulse raced.

"Listen, we need to talk about something." Vince closed the door behind them. "Have a seat."

Sarah was acutely aware that they were alone in a bedroom together.

Does he know? Oh yeah, you're going to make a great spy, Stevens! You can't even hide an infatuation, you loser.

Sarah sat on the edge of the bed awaiting the inevitable while Vince leaned against the door and crossed his arms over his massive chest.

After a long tense silence, Sarah couldn't stand it anymore. "Okay, what's going on?"

"Look, this mission isn't like anything you've ever done as a Security Specialist. That was flat out defensive and impersonal stuff. What we're about to do is strictly covert, offensive and very personal. Although you've been trained well in tactics and fighting techniques, there is no training for what you're about to do. You either can or you can't."

Phew! Maybe he doesn't know?

"Look, Vince, I understand your concerns but a roll in the hay to work over a terrorist is nothing compared to the soldiers giving their lives every day in this war. Besides, I've been with bastards before, so what's one more?"

Working over a jerk is just what I need after all those jerks who have worked me over in one way or another all my life. Hell, it might even be fun.

"Only a strong woman can do what you're about to, and we need to know now if you can handle it or not."

Sarah stared up into Vince's eyes and tried to reassure him. "I wouldn't have come this far if I couldn't. I can do this, Vince."

"When you were in the Security Police, it was all black and white. You're deep in the gray area now and the success of this mission depends on how convincing you can be."

Sarah fixed her eyes on his. "Vince...I can do it."

Vince uncrossed his arms and slid his hands into the pockets of his jeans. "We're all getting our hands dirty in this war. Nobody on this team is going to judge you, but no matter what, at the end of the day, you have to be able to live with yourself. We can't put you in there and then have you melt down over a moral dilemma."

How am I going to convince this guy I can handle this? Once I convince him, the rest of the team will be onboard.

There's only one way...

Sarah smiled a thoughtful smile.

Sarah locked her gaze onto Vince's and stood. She took a deep breath and exhaled with a soft sigh. "Oh, Vince." She couldn't believe the seductive purr of her own voice as she ran her hands slowly over her hips and down the length of her mini-skirt to straighten the creases that had formed from sitting. Still maintaining eye contact, she took two slow steps toward Vince until she stood about six inches away from him.

"Did I ever thank you for the pearls?" She raised her right hand to her neck, gently caressing the pearl choker from left to right.

"They're so beautiful," she whispered as she trailed her fingertips slowly down the edge of the v-neck blouse she wore until they rested on her ample cleavage.

His gaze dropped from hers to follow the path of her fingers to her full breasts as she breathed slowly and deeply, but she continued to stare directly at him. With her left hand, she gently touched his right shoulder and trailed her hand seductively down his muscular arm. Liberated by the charade of playing a part, she drank in his scent, the texture of his skin, the form of his muscular arms.

"Mmm...so strong."

When she reached his hand, she gently placed it on her left hip, holding it there with her left hand. Her body burned for him and she thrilled at his touch.

His gaze dropped to where she had placed his hand, and he took a deep breath before pulling her close and looking into her eyes once again.

The heat between them was unmistakable to Sarah. She could have him now or make her point. What she wanted to do and what she needed to do would lead to two distinctly different paths in life. The importance of her new job was far greater than the momentary satisfaction a roll in the hay might bring.

She caressed his neck just below his left ear. Her fingertips told her his heartbeat was fast and strong. She skimmed her fingertips along the line of his jaw and down his neck to his shoulder where she rested her hand. Then she whispered, "So hard."

She pressed against him, closing the space between them. Her body was full against his and she could feel his interest rising, a hard length against her stomach.

The power she had in this situation was better than any buzz she'd ever felt. Every cell in her body was yearning for him but she fought it and stayed in control.

She led his right hand around her waist and then let her left hand creep up his strong, solid chest and around to the back of his neck.

His mouth opened slightly and she knew he was ready to kiss her, so she sighed meaningfully and moved to within a breath of his lips with hers. Dark desire filled his eyes.

Sarah let her own eyes reflect what her body was feeling. Her mind maintained true control.

Vince's left arm tightened around her waist and held her close while his right hand slowly caressed her hip and began to travel slowly up her waist.

When he moved to kiss her, she very gently moved her head to the side and whispered sensuously in his ear, "I am going to make him an offer no man could refuse, and then, I'm going to rock the bastard's world."

It took every ounce of strength she had to step out of Vince's embrace and pretend it was all an act.

He can never know exactly how much I wanted to finish that!

Sarah allowed herself the luxury of looking Vince over slowly, from head to toe, as though he were dinner and she hadn't eaten in, well, she'd never eaten a dinner like that.

Her gaze paused at the impressive and telling bulge below his waistline.

Such a shame we have to let that go to waste.

Her body screamed at her own betrayal. He was a sexual electromagnet switched on. Her mind fought to keep control of her body.

Walk out of the room, Sarah.

Walk out of the room, Sarah.

Walk out of the room, Sarah.

When she met his gaze again, she nodded to his apparent arousal. She barely managed to control her urge to pounce.

He couldn't tell her in any more obvious a way that he wanted her.

She took a deep breath and appeared all business when she spoke. "Sorry about that, but I needed you to understand I can do this. By the look of things, I'd say I have you fairly well convinced." She straightened her skirt and tossed her hair back over her right shoulder. "Now you guys need to back me up and make sure I don't get left hanging in the warm Mediterranean breeze."

Vince smirked and nodded. "Good enough." His breaths were heavy and fast.

Sarah watched the telling rise and fall of his chest as she remembered what it was like to be held close to him. "Now I'll leave you with your, uh, thoughts and see you out in the cabin in a few minutes." Sarah slid her hand behind Vince to reach the doorknob as he stepped aside.

Before she left, she turned back to take a long look at Vince. "By the way, I'll take that as a compliment. Thank you very much."

Vince grinned. "You should, but the pleasure was all mine, babe. You really had me going."

Stay cool, Stevens. He's off limits. That was just to prove a point. Well, maybe a couple of points.

She walked out, closed the door and strutted back to her seat with a confident chuckle

He may be off limits, but it sure is nice to feel wanted.

Chris grinned at her, pointed to his earpiece and whispered, "Nice. You can rock my world any time. Don't you worry. We've got your six, babe."

Sarah was relieved Chris received the message she meant to send. "I'm counting on it, Big Daddy."

Vince entered the cabin with a grin and sat back in his seat.

When Sarah glanced at him, he smiled, blushed slightly and nodded his head.

The team was finally ready to go.

~~~

The captain announced their approach to New York. "We should be on the ground at JFK in twenty minutes. We're going to fuel up and grab a meal before the overnight trip to London. We're cleared for a nineteen-hundred departure so you've got a few hours to stretch your legs and grab some chow."

Jason stretched in his seat. "Great, I'm starving."

Sarah quickly put a brush through her hair. "Should one of us stay with the gear?"

"No need," Vince answered. "Jim's got it covered."

Sarah checked her lipstick. "Who's Jim?"

A rather well equipped man stepped out of the cockpit. The boys Sarah was working with were well equipped in a physical sort of way, but this guy had loaded holsters on each thigh and two shoulder holsters equally packed.

"Hey, Jim. How have you been?" Jason waved nonchalantly, then nodded at Sarah.

Sarah smiled at Jason and then at Jim. "Yeah, I guess he doesn't need us hanging around."

Brian cracked his knuckles and sat back in his seat. "Thank you for flying Air America. Please be sure your seats, tray tables and firearms are in their upright and locked positions."

Twenty-Two

As they landed in London, Sarah checked her watch. Eight in the morning. She peered out the window to see an unseasonably clear day. They weren't anywhere near the terminal and two black Range Rovers converged to the left of the aircraft.

The vehicles parked beside the plane and the drivers stepped out onto the tarmac.

Vince rose from his seat and stretched. "These should be our spook escorts. You all chill while I coordinate." Vince opened the hatch that doubled as stairs and disembarked the jet.

Sarah watched as he shook hands with the two men and spoke to them.

The guys seemed to be collecting their personal gear.

Vince bounded back into the jet. "Overnight gear only, girls. No weapons." Then he disappeared into the cockpit.

Sarah picked up her overnight bag and her leather handbag.

Get a look at me. A Rolex, matching Luis Vuitton luggage, handbag and designer clothes. Who knew?

Jason let out a sigh as he sat beside Sarah and pulled up his pant leg. He removed the Beretta that had been safely tucked inside an ankle holster. Next he pulled a Gerber boot knife out of his hiking boot. Then he opened his denim shirt and removed the sidearm from his shoulder holster.

Brian slapped Jason on the shoulder. "Jesus, man. Sarah and Vince are the ones going in on this op. What the hell are you so loaded for? This is London, man, not frigging Baghdad."

Jason tilted his head and shrugged. "Habit?"

Will eyed Jason as he passed him on the way to the door. "A dangerous habit you got there, brother."

Sarah leaned over and whispered in Jason's ear, "I think it's hot."

"See, chicks like it," Jason yelled to Will and Brian who were disembarking.

Sarah was the last to leave the plane and found the guys being greeted by one of the drivers.

The first driver greeted Will with a handshake. "Jim Lloyd, MI-5."

"Will Adams. Good to meet you. This is Sarah, Brian, Chris, you've met Vince and that's Jason."

"Cheers, lads." Jim reached out to shake Sarah's hand. "I wish MI-5 had agents that look like you."

Sarah gave the fellow a once-over and although he had a smaller build than the guys she was with, he was about six feet tall, built nicely, and there was something about his blue-gray eyes and bright smile that was very attractive.

You aren't so bad on the eyes either.

Sarah had forgotten how much she enjoyed hearing English accents and smiled. "Thanks very much."

Vince's voice came from behind her. "Sarah, Jason, you're with me and Jim. Will, Brian and Chris, you ride with Ian."

Sarah carefully placed her bags in the back of the shiny, new Range Rover and sat in the back with Jason. She watched the city go by as Jim drove them to a gorgeous home in Chelsea.

~~~

Sarah tried to control her enthusiasm as she marveled at the exterior of the building. She walked inside and halted in her tracks when she noticed the security panel inside the door.

Chris paused for a moment on his way in. "Completely secure. It's a Safe House. What's said here stays here. No signals going in or out. It's a smaller version of the Pentagon's electronic security system."

Jim stood in the middle of the luxurious living room. "Right, lads. You'll find bedrooms for each of you upstairs along with three bathrooms. The house is fully equipped with a kitchen, dining room, exercise room, parlor and living room. You'll also find a big screen television in there and this fireplace works, too. Make yourselves at home."

Vince shook Jim's hand. "Thanks, Jim."

"No worries. We'll pick you up tomorrow." He waved a hand on his way out. "Cheers."

"Okay, girls. Go claim your rooms." Vince pointed up the stairs. "We've got twenty-four hours."

Sarah walked upstairs and unpacked her overnight case. Then she followed her nose to the kitchen where she found Will cooking something that smelled wonderful. She pulled up a bar stool and watched as Will continued chopping vegetables and sautéing chicken.

Will glanced up and grinned.

"It smells delicious. What is it?"

"Chicken Tava," Will answered. "It's a Middle Eastern dish."

"This whole past month we've been together, I've never seen you cook, Will. That's a very attractive quality in a man."

He continued chopping. "There are a lot of things we don't know about each other, but I guarantee you, after a year or two of working with us, you'll know every attractive and unattractive quality about each of us and we'll know the same about you. You think you can handle that?"

"You'd be surprised at how much I can handle. So, what's with the secret cooking skills?"

"I only cook when I have the right ingredients. Cooking or eating any old slop is a waste of time and energy."

Sarah considered the man standing in front of her. He wore Armani slacks and a silk shirt open at the neck. His tie was carefully folded and laid on the counter by the sink. His Armani jacket hung over the other barstool. "That policy seems to have worked pretty well for you. So, can I eat this, too?"

"Yeah, pork chop." He winked. "It's safe. Just lean meat and vegetables with a little olive oil and spices. Guaranteed to skip the hips."

"Excellent. I'll be back after I clean up." Sarah walked back upstairs to take a bath and refresh herself after the long transatlantic flight. She strolled through the living room to see Jason and Chris hooking up a Play Station III to the big screen television. She noticed that Vince and Brian had already started their workouts in the fully equipped gym.

They never miss a workout and it shows.

Sarah lingered a while at the door to enjoy the view.

"Hey, this isn't a peep show, girl. You lifting or leaving?"

Sarah raised her hands and smiled at Brian. "You got me. Can't blame a girl for wanting to watch."

Sarah headed to her room and grabbed her toiletry case before going to the bathroom down the hall.

Oh, wow. This is huge. Enclosed shower and a garden tub in addition to a double vanity and toilet. Very nice.

Sarah filled the large tub with hot water and bubbles and settled in for a relaxing bath. She must have dozed off because she awoke when she heard the shower running. Unsure if she should leave or not, she decided to enjoy her bath.

Hey, I was here first.

Sarah opened her eyes when she heard the shower stop.

This should be interesting.

Brian stepped out of the shower and reached for a towel on the warming rack.

"Go, Navy," Sarah said appreciatively.

"Hey!" Brian turned around and wrapped the towel around his waist. "When did you come in?"

"Been here the whole time." Sarah was completely impressed with what she saw, but was determined to stay cool.

I guess Will wasn't kidding about us getting to know everything about each other.

"You know, for somebody who was so modest in the gym, I'm a little surprised to see so much of you now."

Brian squinted at Sarah and looked like he was trying not to smile. "Yeah, how do you like it?"

"Not bad."

"Not bad? Girl, you know you want some of this."

"Yep. Just as badly as you want to get into this tub, but we both know it isn't happening. Now get your fine ass out of here."

"All right, all right," Brian said as he walked out.

Sarah stood up to dry off.

Almost immediately, the door to the bathroom opened and Vince walked in. He stopped just inside the door, hand still on the doorknob. "Hey there." He smiled a wide, perfect smile.

The sound of his voice and the look in his eyes caused an instant sexual need in Sarah. She had the presence of mind to not let it show. She feigned outrage. "Hey, nothing. This isn't a peep show. Get out!"

Vince laughed. "Okay, okay. I'm going." The door almost closed before he popped his head back in. "Can you pass me the soap?"

"Get out!" Sarah threw a bar of soap at him but he closed the door before it hit him.

Sarah could hear him laughing all the way down the hall as she dried off. By the time she dressed and made it back down to the dining room, the guys were already seated and digging in. She sat in the empty chair near Jason and helped herself.

Vince was the first to speak. "So, Brian. You want to tell me what you and Sarah were doing in the bathroom together?"

"Hey! I was in there first." Sarah jumped in before Brian could say anything. "He snuck in when I dozed off in the tub."

"Oh, Brian. That's a new low for you," Will chided. "Taking advantage of a sleeping woman? See what I meant about all of our unattractive traits? Lock your doors, kid. Always lock your doors with this guy around."

Brian kept a straight face as he continued eating. "Hey, it was an honest mistake. It's not like I walked in knowing she was naked in there, Vince."

A thrill ran up Sarah's spine when she realized Vince's intrusion was intentional.

You were looking for a chance to check me out, you dog!

"Hey, you can't blame a guy for wanting to watch."

Sarah didn't miss the reference. She figured she had it coming after watching them work out.

"I thought we were a team," Jason blurted out in a hurt tone.

"Yeah, what's the big idea? What ever happened to all for one and one for all?" Chris whined.

"Hey, we're five soldiers." Vince scowled at Chris. "Well, four soldiers and a geek, not the three frigging musketeers. If you want to see a naked woman, you're gonna to have to do your own recon, boys."

Sarah shook her head and drank a sip of the wine that had been poured. "Will, this is an excellent meal. Thanks for cooking."

Vince swallowed a forkful of the chicken dish. "Yeah, thanks, man."

Will looked up at Vince. "Don't thank me, leatherneck. Just take a picture next time."

Sometimes a girl just needs to be objectified.

Twenty-Three

A knock sounded on Sarah's door and she rolled over. "Yeah?"

"Hey, Sarah, we're going down to the pub. Are you coming?"

"Yeah, Jason, just give me a minute to get dressed."

Sarah glanced at her watch and realized she'd slept about eight hours and it was already ten pm. She dressed in a short, red plaid skirt, tucked in a white shirt and draped on her pearls before slipping into her shoes. She ran a brush through her hair and let it fall over her shoulders.

Hmm…add some pigtails and I'd have the schoolgirl thing going. Oh well, I look pretty damned good if I say so myself!

Sarah strutted to the living room where the guys were waiting for her. They all wore T-shirts and jeans except for Will who wore a button down shirt the same dreamy blue as his eyes and black dress pants.

~~~

Sarah gazed at the photographs behind the bar of the pub as she waited for the bartender to pour their second round of drinks.

"Well, looks like they'll let any old loser into this place."

At the sound of the familiar voice behind her, Sarah spun around to see Tracey smiling back at her. "I'll be damned! I never thought I'd see you again." Delight filled her at having another woman to talk to, especially one that was in the same situation she was.

Tracey hugged Sarah. "Lucky you, huh? So, are you on R&R or enroute?"

"Enroute. You?"

"Yep. Let's drink." Tracey pointed to the bartender. "Four shots of Cuervo. Hold the fruit."

Sarah and Tracey each picked up a shot and drank.

"It's good to see you, Trace."

Tracey slapped her empty shot glass on the bar. "You, too. Nervous?"

"As hell! Bottoms up." Sarah handed Tracey the last shot as she drank her own.

Tracey took a look around the pub. "Is it just the tequila or are there some fine looking boys over there?"

Sarah sighed. "Yeah, tell me about it. They're my team."

"No shit? Those are mine over there. Not bad, but not as easy on the eyes as yours."

"Ah, well…somebody's got to be second place." Sarah nudged Tracey. "It might as well be you. Four more, barkeep."

Brian stood and started toward Sarah and Tracey.

Tracey's eyes opened wide. "Ooh, tell me about that tall drink of water."

Sarah remembered her first lusty response to seeing Brian and grinned. "His name is Brian. He was with the SEAL teams until he was recruited. Ladies flock to him. He's got a house, a pool, and a boat. He's a solid guy and great on paper but never sleeps with the same woman twice."

Tracey raised an eyebrow. "Once would be just fine with me."

Brian put his arm around Sarah's waist. "Hey, girl, we were a little ticked that you were taking so long with the drinks until we realized you were pulling chicks for us." He nodded toward Tracey. "Is this one for me?"

"You can have her when I'm done. You can take the drinks back with you now though."

Brian took the bait. "Oh, so it's like that is it? How about the three of us go talk about it?"

"Brian, this is Tracey, a fellow pork chop."

Tracey mumbled, "Thanks, loser." Then flashed Brian a winning smile. "Hi, Brian."

"Don't sweat it, Tracey. I don't discriminate. Besides, we consider 'pork chop' to be a term of endearment. You here on business?"

"We're passing through on our way to Uncle Stan's."

"No kidding? Where's your crew?"

"They're over there, with the redhead in the corner."

"No shit! Don and I went through SEAL training together. I'd better go say hello. Good to meet you, Tracey. Any friend of Sarah's is a friend of ours."

"You, too." Tracey watched as Brian walked over to the group of guys in the corner. "Oh my God!" She whispered to Sarah. "I've got to run my fingers through that hair!"

"I know. It's got a pull like gravity, doesn't it? Have another drink."

Sarah and Tracey tossed back another shot and watched four of Tracey's crew jump into fighting positions as Brian slapped Don on the back of the head. Don didn't move.

"There's only one guy in the world dumb enough to do something like that. How you been, Bri?" Don stood, turned around and shook Brian's hand with a smile as his crew sat and returned to their drinks.

Brian was introduced to everyone at the table and sat down for a drink with them.

Sarah brought the long awaited tray of drinks to the boys, introduced Tracey to them and then walked with Tracey over to meet her crew.

As Sarah and Tracey approached the table, one very attractive guy who looked like he was born and bred on a Pacific island spoke up. "Hey, look. Ballantine brought us a woman. Nice one, Trace. Thanks!"

"Hold on there, troop." Brian spoke up as he pulled Sarah onto his lap. "My boys and I have first dibs on this one. She's ours."

"Get off me, Brian." Sarah lightly pushed herself off him.

"Hey, what's the big idea, cramping my style in front of the boys here?"

"Brian," Sarah crooned, "How can I ever get another man to take me home when they think I'm with you? We all know no man can handle that kind of comparison."

He grinned, dignity in tact. "Yeah, I guess you're right."

Tracey made the introductions. "Sarah, this is Don, Mike, Will, Tom and Doug, otherwise known as The Wolf Pack."

"Nice to meet you guys. You'd better take good care of my girl here."

"No worries there," the redheaded Tom said. "She takes pretty good care of herself."

Don nodded to Brian. "She broke a guy's femur during her test."

The news didn't surprise Sarah, Tracey definitely had it in her. They'd sparred with each other enough for Sarah to know that Tracey always went for the legs. "Nice one, Trace."

Tracey proudly nodded her acceptance of the compliment.

"That's good," Brian said. "This one got pissed because she broke a nail kicking four guys' asses and actually turned back to kick the last guys ribs in for it. Then, adding insult to injury, she stole their car and played the club scene afterwards."

They all laughed.

Don shook his head. "No way!"

Brian threw his shoulders back and seemed proud of Sarah. "Oh, yeah. Walked right into *Pure* like she owned the joint."

Tracey slapped Sarah on the shoulder. "That's my girl."

"Well, as much as we'd love to talk shop with you guys, Tracey and I are going to go find some ugly men to buy us drinks. Later, Bri. Nice meeting you guys."

Sarah and Tracey left the pub and walked back to the house where American Swift was staying. They spent the whole night drinking and talking. After the way the year started for each of them, they were both equally excited and nervous about their new careers. Neither had planned it this way, but they both thrived on adventure and agreed that working for the Agency would be the ultimate adventure.

Will and Vince wandered in at around two am.

Sarah stubbed out a cigarette in the ash tray. "Where are the others?"

"They met up with some babes and followed them home," Will answered.

"Those three goofballs got laid and you guys didn't?" Sarah was shocked. "Damn. Tough crowd tonight, huh? "

Vince smiled. "There's still time. Sun's not up yet and you two seem to be pretty available."

"Tempting." Tracey pointed to Vince. "But I have a rule against fishing off the company pier."

Will yawned. "Good rule. Too bad for us, but a good rule nonetheless. And on that note, I'm going to hit the hay. Goodnight all."

"Yeah, me, too. I'm beat," Vince mumbled on his way upstairs.

"Nice guys," Tracey whispered to Sarah. "Still got a thing for Vince?"

"Can you blame me?" Sarah lit another cigarette and took a long thoughtful drag. "I'll get over it."

"Do they know about Scott?"

Sarah had finally let go of her desire to hide the Scott incident while she and Tracey were in Phase II together. "If they do, they haven't said anything about him."

"What are you going to say if they ask?"

"Trace, we're in the big leagues now. These guys can get any information they want. I guess I'll just have to tell them the truth and take the crap they'll give me over it."

"Hey, they might surprise you. They seem like good guys." Tracey shook her head. "Damned shame they're all so frigging gorgeous."

Tracey left just before dawn after they'd exchanged cell phone numbers and promised to keep in touch. Sarah and Tracey both knew keeping in touch was unlikely considering their missions, but hoped to meet again someday.

~~~

Sarah woke to a knock on her door.

She wasn't in the mood for much besides breakfast. "What?"

"Hey, Brian is making breakfast before we take off. You up for some eggs?"

"Jason, you gotta stop waking me up. What time is it?"

"Sorry, rank has its privileges so I always get the short straw. It's fifteen-hundred hours."

"Okay, I'll be down after I shower."

Sarah showered and dressed then joined the guys in the dining room where Brian had laid out a huge breakfast of eggs, bacon, fruit, biscuits and coffee. Sarah sat at the table and poured herself a cup of black coffee.

Chris was the first to speak. "So, Sarah. Who's Scott?"

Sarah took a deep breath and exhaled before shooting Chris a very evil eye. "What? No good morning? Scott is an ex."

Vince buttered a biscuit. "A serious one?"

Sarah was still groggy from jet lag and tequila, but she realized then that Chris had heard her conversation with Tracey.

So much for that whole "safe house" thing. Crap.

That meant he knew all about her feelings for Vince, too. Damned earrings. Sarah gave up trying to hide anything from these guys. Being a spy would be difficult enough. There just wasn't any sense in trying to have any personal secrets so she resigned herself to her fate.

138

She tried to maintain her composure even though she knew she'd take a hellacious ribbing when it was all said. "A couple years, long distance."

These guys are going to chew me up when they find out that I got jilted for a guy.

Jason sat back in his chair. "So, what's the story?"

"No story. I caught him cheating and left."

Will smiled. "Caught him in the act, huh. So, what did the girl do?"

Sarah tilted her head. "The girl?"

"Yeah, the girl he was with."

It's time to bite the bullet. They might as well get it from me.

"No girl. She was a he. *He* ran into the bathroom and hid until I left."

Chris's fork clanged to the table. "Oh, snap!"

Brian laughed. "What did you do?"

"Left, got kicked out of the Air Force, went to fat camp and became an ass-kicking hottie. Any more questions or are you guys going to let me have a cup of coffee while it is still hot?" Sarah stared into her coffee and prepared for the jokes.

None came.

Vince took a bite of his biscuit and drank some coffee. "Well, I guess we should send the fudge packer a thank you note, boys. Chris, add that to my list of things to do."

"Will do, boss. I'd love to help you with the delivery, too."

Sarah gave a small smile of thanks across the table to Vince. His eyes were soft and she felt safe.

What does that mean?

Vince nodded and returned to his eggs.

Twenty-Four

Sarah couldn't believe her luck. She was stuck on a yacht in the Mediterranean with five of the coolest and absolute hottest men she'd ever met, and every one of them was off limits. Still, a bad day here easily blew away even the best day of her life before she was kicked out of the Air Force.

Pork chop, indeed!

The six of them spent the entire week in their bathing suits, in and out of the water and the boys were quite liberal with their compliments.

They might be trying to build up my confidence since they all know I'm still a bit insecure, but I don't care.

Sarah thrived on the attention and did a lot of flirting back. The boost to her ego was just what the doctor ordered.

It had been a while since Sarah had gotten laid and she was pretty hungry for sex at this point. There were times when she couldn't deal with another buff body and simply had to go to her cabin for a cold shower.

Will gazed up from his magazine as Sarah returned from her cabin after yet another cold shower. "I've never seen a woman take so many showers in a day. Why don't you just jump in? What's with all the showers?"

Chris was driving golf balls into the sea while the others were lounging in chaises with beers in their hands.

They all watched Sarah expectantly.

"The salt is very damaging to my hair. I can't show up on Hassan's yacht with split ends, can I?" Sarah averted her eyes and stared at an empty chaise.

As she sat, her eyes met Will's and he raised an eyebrow.

He doesn't believe me.

Vince flashed his perfect white teeth. "Really? Is that all?"

"Aw, shit, guys. I'm like a diabetic kid in a candy store. Do you have any idea how long it's been since I've been good and properly laid?"

Will raised an index finger. "That Angelo guy, about six weeks ago."

Sarah glared at him. "And before that? Any idea?"

"At least a couple of years." Chris chuckled as he drove another golf ball far off into the sea.

They all stared at Sarah and smiled with the ridiculousness of it all.

"Yeah. What the hell am I supposed to do?" Sarah raised her hands to emphasize the question. "Look at you. There isn't a beer belly in the bunch and you all have that three day beard thing going on." Sarah was on a rant now. All the sexual frustration she had came out in a verbal tirade. "Why couldn't I be on a team with a bunch of ugly guys? Seriously. You have no idea how tough this is on me." She glared at each of them and the abundance of rippled abs overwhelmed her. She picked up a liter of cold water near the chair, closed her eyes and poured the entire bottle out over her bikini-clad body to make her point.

The boys burst out laughing.

"You know, boys," Vince deadpanned. "We're pretty lucky there isn't a hottie running around here in a bikini all day."

Sarah opened her eyes in time to see them all staring at her.

Jason stood and walked toward Sarah. "Okay, I'll do it. If none of you are man enough, I'll take one for the team."

Sarah rubbed her face and seriously considered taking a header off the deck just to escape the embarrassment she felt. "Jason, that's very generous of you, but I don't think…"

"Oh, shut up. Get your mind out of the gutter. Jeez!" He grabbed her hand and led her up to the fly deck.

Sarah stared at what Jason had on the fly deck and realized the solution to her problem.

Perfect.

"Ah, Jason. You shouldn't have."

Jason picked up one of the many shotguns laid out. "Which one do you want to try first?"

Sarah pointed to one that caught her eye. "Benelli Supernova with the eighteen and a half inch tactical barrel and tac pistol grip."

"The lady knows her firearms." Jason loaded the black Benelli twenty gauge shotgun and handed it to her.

"You ready, Chris?" he called down to the lower deck.

Chris' voice sounded from below. "Hold on…yeah, go for it."

Sarah smiled a wide grin at Jason. "Baby, you're the best."

"Sadly, you can never know."

"Mmm-hmm…take one for the team, indeed." Sarah took aim just above Chris' head. "Pull!"

Chris swung and a golf ball flew out onto the horizon.

Sarah took aim and decimated it.

Sarah spent the rest of the afternoon on the fly deck taking out her frustrations on golf balls. When Chris got tired of driving doomed golf balls into the ocean, Jason took over and taught her some trick shooting.

Sarah spent the next two days learning how to pump and shoot a shotgun single handed. She was pretty sloppy at first but after two full days on it, she'd completely forgotten about her sexual frustrations and became totally focused on her new weapons skills.

Early on the evening of the second day, Sarah finally got it right. The shotgun dropped like a pendulum. She caught the pump between her upper arm and torso, pumped it with a flick of her wrist and then let it swing back before taking aim and shooting.

"Well, I'll be damned," Will muttered from the deck below. "Hey, Vince, check out Gattman and Robin up there."

Jason handed her a second shotgun. "All right, hot stuff. Do it with two."

They all watched now, but she kept her focus and did it on the first try.

"Now that's what I'm talkin' about. A babe with brains who can pump and fire two shotguns at once. That's hot. God, help me. I'm in love." Brian raised a beer to his lips and chugged it.

Jason nodded his approval. "You go, girl."

"So, how's that little problem of yours, Sarah?" Vince called up from the sun deck.

"Sufficiently repressed, smartass. Thanks for asking." She could laugh about it now.

The next afternoon, Sarah stood on the fly deck cleaning guns while the guys examined their maps and charts to see where the best spot would be to drop anchor and monitor Hassan.

As Sarah finished wiping down the last shotgun, she glanced up to see a Zodiac-type inflatable boat on the horizon that appeared to be coming toward their yacht.

"Hey, guys," she shouted down to the deck below. "Are we expecting company?"

Vince straightened up, stared in the direction of the oncoming boat and put a set of binoculars up to his eyes. "Sarah, stay out of sight."

The urgency in his voice startled her and she dropped to the deck instinctively, heart thumping.

Within less than a minute, Sarah heard the small boat approach the yacht. She kept her head down and tried to listen for voices.

Brian's voice carried. "Oh, hell. Incoming!"

A *whoosh* and a flash about eight feet over her head caused Sarah to drop back into a prone position on the deck.

Holy shit! Pirates. And I'm up here with all the guns!

Sarah scrambled to load two shotguns. The sounds of men boarding the boat on the port side ratcheted her fear. A guttural voice shouted to keep their hands up.

Sarah carefully peeked over the rail to see how many pirates there were so she could pinpoint her targets.

Okay, Stevens, this is it. Time to rise to the occasion and be a hero, baby!

Sarah pulled off her T-shirt to reveal her skimpy bikini top and took one tactical shotgun in each hand.

And this is why they make pistol grips!

Sarah stood, careful to keep her hands and the shotguns behind the rail and out of sight from below.

"Sarah, get down!" Vince ordered.

The two pirates stared up at her admiringly and that moment was all she needed.

With a flick of her wrists, Sarah brought the shotguns to bear on the two pirates.

Both guns fired true and the pirates fell overboard. One hit the Zodiac on his way into the water while the other one fell straight in.

With steady hands, she brought both guns to bear on the one man left in the Zodiac. She fired both guns on him at the same time. He cried out in pain just before turning his boat around and taking off, dragging his buddies in the water as they hung on to the boats' ropes.

"Get your ass down here, Stevens," Vince boomed.

Sarah was riding high on an adrenaline rush and happily bounded down the stairway to the deck below.

Somebody said, "Uh, oh."

Vince's face was red and his eyes filled with rage. "Just what the hell was that Annie Oakley shit?" He shook his index finger at her. "Didn't I tell you to stay out of sight? Just what the hell were you trying to do?"

"I wasn't trying anything. I was succeeding at saving your ass! They fired an RPG over the fly deck for Christ's sake!"

Vince grabbed Sarah's elbow and fumed. "Do you know who we are? Do you have any idea how many people I've killed with my bare hands? I don't need some girl to save my ass with her latest party trick!"

Sarah shook off Vince's grip. "Trick? You want to see a trick? I'll show you a fucking trick. You get over your macho, pig attitude and accept the fact that somebody with *huevos* just saved your *cojones* or for my next trick I'm going to disappear and you can go fuck Hassan yourself!"

"Oh, no, she didn't," Jason mumbled.

Sarah wasn't about to back down to Vince. "You know, if Jason or Brian or Will had done it, you'd be cracking open the beers and toasting them, but since it was me, I get bitched out? No, thank you. You told me I wouldn't get preferential treatment and had to pull my weight. Now I see that was a load of shit. Stevens stay down? I had guns and ammo up there while you guys stood here with your dicks in your hands. You'd better get over yourself and accept the fact that I can take care of myself and you if I have to, or else this operation isn't happening. You decide."

Sarah walked over to the bar, pulled out a bottle of tequila and took a long swig. "I'll be right here when you're done thinking about it."

Oh my God. Did I just say what I think I said? Oh, shit!

Will was calm. "Hey, Vince. Take it easy on the girl. Those guys had guns and we were unarmed. She did what she felt was the best thing for the team. Any one of us would have done the same thing, man."

Vince spun around to face Will. "How many times have you been unarmed and stared down the barrel of a gun?"

"A couple."

"And yet here you are." Vince pointed at Brian. "Brian, what about you?"

"A few more than I care to recall." Brian scratched the back of his head.

"But both of you are here in perfect health to tell about it. Jason?"

Jason shrugged. "Once or twice."

Vince threw his arms up. "Am I the only one seeing a pattern here?" He paced the deck as her roared on. "There were five of us and three of them. We'd have had them disarmed and down in no time. There was no reason for her to compromise her cover!"

Brian draped his arm protectively around Sarah's shoulders and spoke up. "True, but with all due respect, boss, she doesn't have that kind of operational experience. She saved our asses and I, for one, am happy she pumped those guys full of lead rather than risking one of us having to have Will patch up a bullet wound."

Vince glared at Brian and stormed into the main salon. "Stevens, I want to see you in my cabin. Right now!"

Sarah peeked up at Brian and took a deep breath. Her voice cracked as she set the tequila bottle on the bar. "Thanks, Bri."

"Hold your ground, girl. They don't call them Devil Dogs for nothing. He can smell fear."

Sarah followed Vince into the salon and down to his cabin.

Vince slammed the door closed behind them. "Where do you get off talking to me like that?"

Sarah felt righteous indignation rising in her throat. "The same place you get off talking to me like that!"

Oh, man. I'm in some deep, deep shit now. Why can't I shut up?

Vince pointed at her and she saw every muscle and sinew in his arm tense. "I gave you a direct order. This isn't a game you know."

She slapped his hand away. "Get that finger out of my face. I know damned well this isn't a game. Your order was bullshit and you know it."

Vince took a step toward Sarah. Nobody had been so in her face since basic training. "Who the fuck are you to tell me that?"

Sarah wasn't about to back down now. She moved forward. "I was there. It was a bad call. We could have lost somebody if I had followed your orders."

Vince glared at her in silence.

"Think with your big head, Marine. I'm not some ditzy girly-girl you need to protect. I'm a member of this team. I'm just another one of the boys."

"The hell you are."

"Well then this isn't going to work."

"You're right. It isn't going to work. I've got personal issues with this and they're clouding my judgment."

"Well, maybe this will help clear things up." Sarah slapped Vince across the face.

Vince slowly cracked his neck and rubbed the side of his face before turning back to look at Sarah. He stood stock still and glared at her.

Sarah lowered her voice. If she raged, she'd sound hysterical and she didn't want her tone to be mistaken. "Don't you ever talk to me like that in front of the team again. It undermines my position in this unit." She poked his shoulder to punctuate her next point. "If you don't think I can handle this then what the hell are they going to think? If the team has no confidence in me then this operation is destined to fail and somebody could get killed. Now I don't know about you but I'm not ready to put any one of those guys out there at risk. That's reason enough to set aside your personal issues, so cowboy up."

In a flash, Sarah found herself on her back, on the bed. Vince had thrown her there and pinned her arms and legs with his.

She could feel his breath on her lips.

Vince stared into her eyes. "I had that coming but so help me God, don't you ever slap me again."

Vince dropped to his elbows and kissed Sarah.

Oh, God, yes.

His kiss was hard and demanding and Sarah responded in kind. She wanted it every bit as much as he did.

The press of his hips against hers made her wet with anticipation. Every breath he took brought his body closer to hers until they were a tangle of arms and legs.

After the longest, most passionate kiss she'd ever experienced, Vince pulled away.

"Thanks for saving my ass and my team. Now let's go have a drink and forget this ever happened."

Sarah did her best to remember where she was, who was listening and just how bad it was to be in this position. She took a deep breath to feel his chest on hers one last time. "Okay, but when this is done…"

"Oh, yeah," he answered with a nod.

Sarah walked out onto the sun deck and what just happened hit her as quickly as the bright sunlight. She walked straight to the bar, picked up the bottle of Jose Cuervo she'd opened and commenced to drink it.

Will walked up and kissed her on the forehead. "You did good, kid."

Brian followed with another kiss on her forehead. "It gets easier after this."

Killing, maybe, but not being with Vince.

Chris wrapped his arms around her and beamed. "You saved my ass, you know. I don't know shit about combat. They might have taken those guys down, but I'd have been the one to take the bullet."

Sarah hugged him. "I know."

Jason followed, smiling his wicked smile, and wrapped his arms around her. He dipped her backwards and his lips were just centimeters away from hers. He looked into her eyes and whispered, "You are so frigging sexy when you kick ass like that."

Sarah giggled as he helped her stand.

Jason took the bottle from her hand and took a swig of tequila for himself.

Yeah, I guess that was pretty cool, huh? You taught me everything I know.

"I love you guys."

Sarah felt a jolt as Vince's hands gently touched her shoulders "Have a few more drinks," he whispered in her ear. "You'll get over it. That's what we do."

There are some things I'll never get over. No matter how much I drink, I'll never get over that kiss or stop wanting more.

"Hey, Chris," Brian called. "Can your boys get us a satellite video of that? We could add it to the Black Betty DVD. That was good stuff."

"Sure, but do you all want to spend the rest of your lives explaining how a chick with no operational experience saved a SEAL, a Marine, a Green Beret, a Corpsman and a Federal Agent?"

"Yeah, you're right." Brian nodded. "Maybe we should just keep this amongst ourselves."

Sarah smiled to herself and took another swig.

I really do love you guys.

Twenty-Five

Sarah checked her gear one more time to be sure she had everything. Pulse racing, she did a final sound check of her pearls with Chris and then checked her luggage with slightly shaking hands to be sure all her knives were secured in the false bottom of the Louis Vuitton case.

Jason came to her cabin and checked her knives as well. "If you run into trouble, just slice and dice. I've seen you do it in training. You can be a butcher when you want to be."

Sarah tried to hide her nervousness. "Aw, Jase. What a sweet thing to say."

Jason took her hands in his and looked dead serious when he warned, "No rings. Keep these babies free."

Sarah laughed at the thought. "It's a weekend trip, Jase. Who's gonna give me rings? Jeez! You'd think I was going away for a month."

With that, Sarah grabbed her bags and strolled up to the helipad.

Will nodded to Sarah as she walked toward the helicopter. "Stay cool, kid. Hey, see if you can snag me some cigars. We'll see you on the other side."

"Count on it."

Be brave. Be brave.

Brian loaded Sarah's luggage onto the helicopter.

As he passed Sarah, he smiled. "You've got more guts than any chick I know. I've got a nice bottle of tequila for us when this is all over."

Sarah smiled bravely and mustered all the bravado she could. "I'll hold you to that."

After everyone else had said their goodbyes, Vince strolled over to Sarah. "This is a simple mission. Charm him, get close and let him spill whatever he will. We'll put it together from there. We'll do the link analysis. You just position yourself and your jewelry so we can get the raw data. It shouldn't take more than a week or two to blow his organization wide open if you use what you used on me." He gently placed his hands on her shoulders.

Sarah wanted to melt as she fell under the spell of his touch.

Vince's features softened. "Listen to me. If it goes tactical and bullets fly, don't be a hero. Do whatever you've got to do to get yourself off the boat. Don't worry about anyone else. Just get off that boat. We won't leave you in the water for long."

Sarah's heart beat loudly in her ears. "Got it, boss."

Vince gave her a wink. "Remember, you're a stone-cold hottie. Rock his world."

Sarah touched the pearls at her neck and gazed into Vince's eyes one last time before she turned to join Tony in the waiting helicopter for the short trip to Hassan's yacht.

I can do this. I can do this. I can do this.

Twenty-Six

Sarah watched out the window as they landed on Hassan's yacht.

My God, what did I get myself into?

She and Tony waited for the rotors to stop and the crew to tie them down before they disembarked the helicopter on Hassan's helipad.

During the few moments they had before they started their show for Hassan, Tony leaned toward Sarah. "Remember, he loves stealing women from other men. As far as he's concerned, we should appear to be very happy lovers. He can be extremely charming when he wants something, but he enjoys a good challenge. If you rebuff him a few times you should have him hooked."

"That shouldn't be a problem." Sarah chuckled.

"Don't forget about his ego. That's his biggest weakness. This party he's hosting tonight is a big deal. Nearly everyone here wants something from him. Favors, loans, business…they're all lobbying for his favor. Doing good deeds for his guests creates loyalty, good will and a willingness to do him favors in return. That's how he keeps his network growing. Just think of him as a Middle Eastern style Godfather."

Sarah blinked as the magnitude of what she was walking into weighed on her shoulders. "Yeah, no pressure, huh? Thanks for putting me at ease, Tony." Sarah had to find the strength and confidence to pull this off. She reached through her mind to a different place and time. Her Aunt Pauline had been the most magnetic woman she'd ever known. Pauline was a beautiful woman who had enthralled men her entire life. Sarah had asked her once for her secret. How had she become such a magnet to men? How could she draw them to her without speaking or even looking at them?

Pauline's answer, though it had been lost on Sarah during the past few years, suddenly came rushing back. "Enter a room like you own it and you will."

The pilot held open the door of the helicopter.

Tony kissed Sarah on the cheek for appearances. "Shall we?"

Go time.

Tony stepped out of the helicopter first and reached in for Sarah's hand.

She took it and stepped out smiling lovingly and playing her part as his girlfriend. In the instant it took her to step out of the helicopter, she became the woman she needed to be. A woman so supremely confident and desirable that nothing she wanted could possibly be denied her. She owned it.

Sarah watched the man who stepped forward to greet them. She'd studied Hassan's dossier and his photos, this man was not her target. This man was shorter than she was, probably about five-foot-six, and portly. He had light brown eyes, a full beard and wore a traditional Arab headdress.

Whoa! Thank goodness you're not Hassan! You are one cockroach-lookin' muther.

Sarah smiled serenely as he ignored her and greeted Tony.

"Good afternoon." He bowed. "I am the Sheikh's secretary, Kadeem. He sends his apologies. He has been delayed in his office and has asked me to show you to your quarters."

Tony shook his outstretched hand. "Thank you, Kadeem. May I present Sarah Stevens?"

Kadeem glared at Sarah disdainfully and nodded curtly to her. "This way, please."

Chris's voice came through Sarah's earpiece as a whisper. "Secretary and head henchman. Watch yourself with this one."

Relief washed over her at the sound of Chris' voice. It calmed her nerves to know she wasn't as on her own as she felt. She and Tony followed Kadeem from the helipad down a spiral staircase to the guest quarters. The stairs were carpeted in what had to be beige silk.

Like walking on a beige cloud.

The hallway below had beige silk on the walls and was carpeted with a beautiful and intricate oriental style runner.

My three-hundred dollar shoes are walking on a carpet that must have cost thousands. I am definitely not in South Dakota anymore!

"The Sheikh hopes you will be very comfortable here." Kadeem opened a mahogany door and ushered them into a stateroom. "He will join you shortly in the main salon, for cocktails and dinner."

152

Kadeem left as another man delivered their luggage and then disappeared as quickly and quietly as he had appeared.

Sarah stepped inside the stateroom she'd be sharing with Tony and stared in awe. The room was paneled completely in dark mahogany and carpeted in a cream-colored silk.

To the left of the door, there was a wall of closets. To the right, a queen-sized bed with a massive mirror from the top of the antique blue headboard to the ceiling. She ran her hand over the bedding. The bed was covered with a cream-colored silk duvet.

On either side of the bed were white marble vases containing at least one dozen fresh white roses each. To the right of the bed was a wall of low cupboards topped with full-sized windows. Covering the windows were cream-colored silk sliding blinds and antique blue brocade curtains. The blinds and curtains were open revealing the gemlike sparkle of the Mediterranean Sea outside.

On the far wall were more cupboards and a large plasma television directly across from the bed. The luxury of it all was quite overwhelming.

Sarah sat at the foot of the bed and gave a long contented sigh as she considered the circumstances in which she'd found herself.

All this and *a paycheck!*

Of course it wouldn't be easy. She would need to do a great deal of outstanding acting over the weekend and seem completely enamored with Tony while charming Hassan. Then there was finding a way to get this perfect stranger to want her so much that he'd offer to keep her on his boat for at least a couple weeks.

It didn't help that the most recent photo she had seen of Hassan had been taken over five years ago. Hassan didn't look repulsive, but he was no knockout either.

Adding to the pressure, Sarah would also need to act as though she didn't understand Arabic, which, thanks to her tutor, she followed quite well. But the biggest act she'd have to pull off would be to pretend not to be nervous as hell about the whole mission.

Girl, you are way out of your element and you're going to have to find a way to prove to everyone, including yourself that you can do this.

Tony's voice broke into her thoughts. "Well, darling, shall we dress for dinner?"

Tony had taken to calling her "darling" as part of the whole show. Sarah was glad he hadn't decided to call her "sugar lips" or something equally embarrassing. Tony was quite the gentleman.

Working with so many men for the past eight years, Sarah had become used to the occasional sexist remark and learned to give as good as she got. In fact, she was quite comfortable with it. Tony was different though. At first, she couldn't quite put her finger on it. Then it hit her. He was just as gay and in the closet as Scott was. The realization made her think about the final incident with Scott. To her surprise, thinking about Scott no longer bothered her as much as it used to.

Time for Sarah to go to work and she had to be at her best. She could sit around and contemplate life, liberty and covert operations when this was all over, but for now, there would be little time for reflection. Now was the time for action.

Sarah slipped into a stunning black, floor length, Roberto Cavalli gown. It had a deep V-cut in the front that allowed her to make the most of her full breasts while the wide ribbon of gold and silver wrapped around her waist and over her shoulders to accent her hourglass shape. She wore all of her pearls and pulled her hair up into a French twist to show off her shoulders and back. As she stood in front of the bathroom vanity to check her makeup, Tony knocked on the door.

"Are you decent?"

"Yes. Come in."

Tony opened the door and let out a long, low whistle.

"Darling, you are stunning. Every man up there will find you absolutely irresistible."

Sarah brushed on her lipstick. "I'll settle for one, but thanks for the compliment."

After blotting her lipstick and applying lip gloss, she turned to Tony. "Shall we?"

They climbed the single flight of stairs and found themselves at the far end of the main salon.

Sarah gently touched Tony's forearm as he led her past the dining area and the bar and into the sitting area. Sarah couldn't help but notice the tasteful décor of the room. The walls were polished mahogany with large picture windows and the upholstery done in a stunningly rich, red and gold pattern with a distinctly Middle Eastern flair.

As they entered the sitting area, Sarah counted four men and four women. A perfect complement for the table set for ten in the dining salon.

Three of the women were fairly dowdy and huddled together, chatting quietly in a corner of the couch. The fourth woman, a leggy blond appeared to be working one of the men over with a pout while the other three men enjoyed their drinks and cigars and looked on in amusement.

Sarah assessed the three men and didn't recognize any of them as Hassan. She became rather anxious to see the man and determined he had to be the tall one being worked over by the blond. The fact that he had his back to her was simply adding to the suspense and her nervousness.

Let's go, big boy. Turn around and show me what I have to work with.

"Good evening, gentlemen," Tony said to the three men standing to their left. "And ladies." He nodded to the women on the couch to their right.

Sarah turned to smile at the men, knowing full well her mission wasn't to win a popularity contest with the hens. Charming these guys would inevitably add to her value as a showpiece. As she turned back to Tony, the tall man turned around and, to her amazement, he was magnificent! She smiled broadly.

Oh, baby! Those photos didn't do you justice. This job is going to be significantly less unpleasant than I expected. We're going to hit the sheets and you're going to spill some secrets, honey!

"Tony. It is so good to see you. *Salaam Alaikum,*" he said loudly as he walked toward Sarah, eyes locked onto hers.

Oh, you have got to be one of the most attractive men I've ever seen!

He stood at least six-foot-three, had a well groomed, short haircut that could have passed for a military cut but looked stunning on him. His chiseled facial features were the kind that would make a New York modeling agent cry. He had high cheekbones and a strong rocklike jaw. The man could have been sculpture come to life.

His eyes were a dark brown and so alert and focused they brought to mind those of a predatory bird. His jet-black hair, eyebrows and trimmed three-day beard and moustache only accentuated the power of his gaze. The only thing that served to soften his face was the sensuous curve of his lips. But once he smiled, his perfect teeth proved danger lay there as well.

Sarah couldn't help but be entranced with his beauty. Were it not for the touch of gray at each temple, he would be a dead ringer for a Chippendale's dancer. His shoulders were broad and the chest under his black silk shirt and jacket, though not overly thick, was clearly well muscled. His suit jacket was unbuttoned, showing off his trim waistline. His smile captivated her like watching a cobra as it prepared to strike. So beautiful Sarah simply couldn't take her eyes away from him.

If Satan were to take a human form to sell condos in Hell, this one would do the job nicely.

Hassan took Sarah's hand while maintaining his lock on her eyes.

Sarah smiled and took a deep breath, suddenly aware of the rise of her breasts as she saw Hassan gaze appreciatively down and then back into her eyes.

He continued his gaze into Sarah's eyes as he said to Tony, "You must tell me who this beautiful woman is and why on earth she is wasting her time with you."

Chris whispered through her earrings, "Smooth. I have got to write that one down."

No shit! And I am totally digging it.

Sarah tried to remember not to let Chris's peanut gallery comments interrupt her act. She smiled as Tony said, "Sheikh Hassan Abdullah Mohammed al-Rashid, allow me to present Miss Sarah Stevens, a gem I found in my recent travels."

"Such formality, Tony. Please, call me Hassan." Gently winding her arm around his, Hassan smiled a wide, perfect smile. "Some day, my friend, you'll have to tell me where you do your shopping. A jewel like this would make any man a thief."

"The Sheikh is very generous," Sarah purred. "Thank you."

Stay cool, Stevens. Mmm… The Sheikh has got it going' on!

Sarah once again became very aware of how long it had been since she'd had sex.

"Generosity, my dear, is not one of my attributes," he whispered conspiratorially. "Come. Let us get you a drink." He led her toward the bar.

This job definitely beats twelve-hour shifts on the Law Enforcement Desk at Nellis! Ooh-ya!

The bartender stood behind the bar and seemed suddenly anxious as Hassan and Sarah approached.

Hassan leaned his elbow on the bar and gazed into Sarah's eyes. "Name your desire and it shall be yours."

You're damned right. Once this is all over, I'm going to own you, fella. Don't worry, I'm sure it'll be a hell of a ride before it's all said and done.

"White wine, please," she said to the bartender as she retrieved a gold cigarette case from her purse. "May I?" she asked Hassan.

"Of course, my dear. Allow me." He quickly produced a lighter inlaid with mother of pearl and what appeared to be diamonds. Sarah held the flame steady and drew seductively on the cigarette while looking into Hassan's eyes.

He wants me.

"What a beautiful lighter."

"I would make it a gift to you but that would deny me the pleasure of serving you."

Chris mumbled in her ear again. "I have to write this shit down."

"What does a guy have to do to get a drink around here?" Tony asked as he walked up behind Sarah and slipped his arms around her waist. "Martini, please," he said to the bartender. "Now Hassan, this one is mine. I'll not have you stealing her away like you did every woman I dated in law school."

"He exaggerates. He only dated one woman at Harvard." Hassan waved his hand dismissively, the predatory light still in his eyes. "And she was nothing like you."

The bartender handed them their drinks and nodded dutifully to Hassan. "What is the Sheikh's pleasure this evening?"

"The Sheikh's pleasure will not be found in a bottle tonight." Hassan looked hungrily at Sarah, who remembered that she was supposed to be infatuated with Tony and played the part.

The Sheikh's pleasure will not be found this evening. He's going to have to work for it.

Hassan led Sarah and Tony over to the three men and introduced them. "Gentlemen, I would like you to meet my very old and very dear friend from college, Tony Neviani and his lovely friend, Miss Sarah Stevens."

Gazing into Sarah's eyes, he said, "May I present my business associates Jaleel and Khalid, and my eldest son Khalil."

Jaleel and Khalid seemed annoyed at having been interrupted only to be introduced to a woman, but Sarah sensed a distinct deference to Hassan in their manner.

Khalil, who looked like a younger, less muscular, version of his father, smiled and held out his hand to shake Tony's and then Sarah's. He spoke with a slightly English accent. "It is a pleasure to meet you both."

"My son is visiting for the weekend before he begins his studies at Oxford University." Hassan beamed.

"A fine school. I'm sure your parents must be very proud," Sarah said brightly.

Hassan answered. "His father is simply pleased he did not pick Yale. As for my ex-wife, she knows nothing of such things and prefers it that way."

Sarah suspected his answer was to inform her not only of his pride in his son but also of his availability. She also noticed the other women in the room were not included in the introductions.

The three huddled in the corner seemed unaffected, but the blond had taken up residence at the bar and flirted shamelessly with the bartender who seemed just a little uncomfortable with the attention.

Hassan glanced toward the bar and quickly excused himself from the group. He strode over to the blond and whispered something in her ear as he unobtrusively waved his hand toward the window.

Within seconds, Kadeem, the cockroach, appeared and escorted the blond out of the room.

A small woman, dressed in kitchen whites appeared noiselessly at Hassan's right elbow.

He said something very quietly to her, then she nodded, proceeded to remove a place setting from the dining table and then disappeared quickly.

Hassan walked back over to Sarah's side and announced, "Gentlemen and ladies, let us sit for dinner." He gently took Sarah's arm to lead her into the dining salon while Tony walked quietly behind.

So far, so good.

Hassan walked to the head of the table and seated Sarah immediately to his right.

She nodded in thanks as he pulled out the chair for her.

Tony sat in the chair to her right.

As Hassan seated himself, Sarah stole a glance at Tony who smiled back and gave Sarah a conspiratorial wink.

During the course of their dinner, Hassan was the perfect host.

Had Sarah not known what she was there for, she could and would have quite easily fallen for his charms. He was everything the other men in her life hadn't been. The man was attentive, devastatingly attractive and when he turned on the charm he made her feel as though she were the only other person in the world.

But why couldn't he be Vince?

Hours later, after the final course was finished and Sarah was thoroughly intoxicated with Hassan's charms, Tony gave her the signal she'd been waiting for.

She batted her eyes at Hassan. "Thank you for a lovely evening. If you'll excuse me?"

Hassan let his hand fall gently onto Sarah's. "No, thank you for gracing my humble table." Then boisterously, he said, "These men are boors. I would leave, too, if I could." Standing, he drew her hand to his lips with a meaningful glance. "Sleep well."

Sarah stood and tried not to be surprised when the other men stood to watch her go. Out of the corner of her eye, she noticed the other women moving away from the table as she did.

Once in her cabin, Sarah unpacked the MP3 player and speaker Chris had her bring along in case Hassan had the staterooms wired. She turned it on and played it loud enough to muffle anything she might say, but not loud enough to disturb anyone outside the cabin. She then swept the cabin for bugs and cameras just as she had been trained to do during mission preparation.

Satisfied the cabin was clean, she undressed, drew a hot bath and enjoyed the luxury of the jasmine-scented bubbles.

Chris' voice interrupted her thoughts. "Are you alone?"

Sarah stretched her legs and watched the bubbles slide off. "Yep."

"I heard a bath. Are you naked?"

Sarah chuckled, closed her eyes and sighed. "Mmm-hmm."

"Oh, that's nice. I've got to remember to put a camera in the next set of jewelry I fit you with."

"You flatter me. Think Coco Chanel's early accessories. Lots of pearls."

"Noted. Did you check for cameras and sweep for bugs?"

"Yeah. All clear."

"Are you ready for the dirt on the goon squad upstairs?"

Sarah closed her eyes and laid her head back on the cool marble. "Send it."

"Okay. Kadeem is the bagman. He does the dirty work like settling up with Hassan's female friends and sending them on their way."

"Funny, I watched him do that tonight."

Chris continued. "He also handles all of Hassan's financial accounts. Jaleel is a bodyguard of sorts. He's known for being none too bright, especially with the ladies. We expect him to be the first one to spill information around you. He's quite the chauvinist, so feel free to work that handicap.

Khalid is likely to be completely unaffected by your charms. He's a Muslim extremist and wanted by the U.K. in connection with the London Underground bombings. He likely does not approve of Hassan's lifestyle, but we suspect he gets too much financing from the guy to complain.

Khalil is clean so far, except for his unfortunate relationship to Hassan. He graduated from Eaton with outstanding grades, plays soccer, visits his mother often and seems like an all around good boy. Don't underestimate his intelligence or loyalty to his father though."

Sarah sank deeper into the hot bath. "Understood."

"Hey, I'm just curious. Do his lines work on you?"

"Yeah. He's good."

160

"Of course he is. Evil bastard. There are guys kicking themselves for not thinking of using those lines on you first. Goodnight, babe."

"Goodnight, Big Daddy," she whispered in her most seductive voice.

Chris chuckled. "God, I love it when you call me that."

If only you were Vince.

Sarah reached for the thick cotton towel waiting on a warming rack. She toweled off quickly and then slipped on her robe.

A light knock sounded at the stateroom door.

Sarah tied her robe as she walked to the door.

When she opened it, Kadeem presented a folded garment to her and bowed slightly. "With the Sheikh's compliments."

"Thank you very much," she said sincerely as she took the soft, white silk bundle.

Kadeem turned and scuttled briskly away.

Sarah closed the stateroom door and brought the bundle to the bed. She unfolded a stunning white silk caftan, embroidered with gold thread.

She quickly dropped her robe and slipped the caftan on over her head. The milky white fabric slid over her skin like water. Although the embroidered hem barely touched the arches of her feet, she felt as though she were still naked as the delicate fabric cascaded from her breasts and lightly touched her hips with a gentle reminder she was indeed clothed.

I'm so in. A man doesn't give a woman a garment like this and not expect to see her in it. How convenient he should have a supply of such things. This guy is good.

The stateroom door opened.

Sarah turned around to face the door and heard a long, low whistle.

Tony's jaw dropped but he managed to say, "Well, I wasn't expecting this, but I accept."

Sarah smiled. "Flatterer. Hassan sent it. You like it?"

"Oh, baby. I don't know if I should thank him or be pissed. All I can think of is…wow." Tony growled as he rolled onto the bed and propped himself up on one elbow. Then he perked up, "Hey, with the light at this angle, I can see all your secrets."

Chris' voice sounded inside her ears again. This time he sounded urgent. "What secrets? What are you wearing? What's going on in there?

Damnit, Vince, why didn't you let me put in a camera? How come Tony always gets to bunk with the babes?"

Sarah heard Vince's unmistakable voice in the background. "Because one, a geek with a camera is a dangerous thing, my friend, and two, Tony can control himself with the ladies. We all know you'd be a blubbering idiot in that bedroom."

"And you wouldn't?" Chris accused.

"Don't go there."

I want to go there.

The sound of Vince's voice made Sarah giddy and she laughed out loud. For such a serious operation, this was becoming altogether too comical for her. If this was any indication of what working with these boys was going to be like, she was ready to sign on for the next twenty years.

If she couldn't have Vince, knowing he wanted her, too, would be enough…for a while.

When she finally managed to stop her nervous laughter, Sarah slid under the covers. "Goodnight, gentlemen," she whispered one last time. She fluffed her pillow and closed her eyes.

Twenty-Seven

Sarah woke to the sound of a motorboat moving away from the yacht. Tony was already awake, showered and dressed when she sat up and remembered where she was.

Tony stood in the bathroom doorway wearing white cotton slacks and a blue T-shirt. "Good morning. Casual cruise attire today, darling. I took the liberty of laying a few items out for you."

"Mmm, thank you." She ran her fingers through her hair.

"Hassan likes to take his breakfast on the aft deck. You should join us there when you're ready."

"Yes, of course. I'll be up as soon as I dress."

Tony left the room and Sarah began preparing for the day. She walked into the bathroom and saw the outfit Tony laid out for her.

Tony Neviani, Harvard graduate, millionaire and valet. How lucky am I?

She stepped into the white mini skirt and threw the pink, silk, short sleeved sweater on over her head. She stared at herself in the mirror

I've got to say, the Very Sexy Bra certainly is.

She brushed her long, wavy, brown hair until it shined, checked her pearls and then applied her lipstick and gloss. Sarah slipped her feet into a pair of Chanel sandals on her way out the door and made her way to the aft deck hoping there would be something akin to espresso there.

Sarah strolled through the main salon and out to the aft deck. There was a large table for ten under the shade of the upper deck, but Hassan and Tony sat at a smaller table for four in the morning sun. They drank coffee, chatted, and laughed amiably.

It's show time!

Sarah slid her sunglasses and smile in place before she sauntered over to them.

Hassan stood and smiled as soon as he saw Sarah. The man was positively stunning in a light blue silk shirt and white trousers.

"Good morning." He pulled out a chair for Sarah to sit in. She couldn't help but notice the top three buttons of his shirt were undone and revealed enough of his well-defined chest to cause her to anticipate going there. He must have noticed her staring because when she glanced up, he smiled at her.

Tempting. Very tempting.

"Good morning and thank you for the beautiful gift."

"Yes, thank you," Tony added.

Hassan sat in the chair to Sarah's right as Tony smiled at her from the chair on her left.

Sarah leaned over to kiss Tony on the cheek. "Good morning, darling."

Tony glowed. "Morning, darling."

Hassan smiled. "It was just a token to welcome you. A gift should be far more substantial for a beauty such as you."

Sarah quickly lit a cigarette. "Will the others be joining us?"

"My associates left late last night and my son left early this morning to visit some friends for the rest of the weekend." In a low almost growl, Hassan stated, "I am completely yours for the rest of the weekend."

"And she is completely mine," Tony said proprietarily as he poured her a cup of thick, black cardamom-scented coffee.

"Really?" Hassan seemed amused. "Completely?" His eyebrows rose as he glanced at Sarah.

This conversation is going into a minefield.

Sarah found Tony's foot under the table with her own and pressed her heel solidly into the toe of his soft deck shoes. "This coffee smells delicious. Is it Turkish?"

"There was a question, I believe." Hassan probed for an answer from Sarah.

Okay, you son of a bitch. I'll play your game, but I'm only going so far. After that, you're on your own. Tony is going to pay for waltzing me into this.

Sarah stared directly at Hassan and locked in on his dark brown eyes. There was no doubt in her mind as to how she had to answer the question. "Let's get something straight right now. I am not now, nor will I ever be, the possession of any man."

It was the truth and she meant every word. There was no acting involved.

"True enough. A poor choice of words. Forgive me, darling," Tony said, with a gentle touch of his hand on hers.

It is time to get this morning back on track.

Sarah dismissively waved her hand. "Forgiven." With that, she switched back to the happy beauty she was supposed to be. "Now what shall I do with two such handsome escorts today?"

"The choices are virtually endless." Hassan sounded quite satisfied and took a sip of his coffee.

Tony's cell phone rang. He pulled it out of his pocket, checked the number and frowned. "I'm sorry, I have to take this, please excuse me." He stood and walked around the corner.

Hassan leaned back in his chair. "Is the coffee to your liking, Sarah? Would you prefer something less robust?"

"No, thank you. I enjoy something robust in the morning." Sarah lifted an eyebrow and gave a slight nod.

"I see." Hassan let his left hand brush along her forearm.

The hair on the back of Sarah's neck stood up.

This guy may be a terrorist bastard, but he is one smooth, sexy, son of a bitch.

Tony returned to the table with a resigned look on his face. "Well, darling, I'm sorry but I've been called away on pressing business. I simply can't leave it to anyone else. We have to fly out this morning. Nicholas is preparing the launch and we'll need to pack."

Afraid something had gone wrong with the mission, Sarah feigned disappointment and stood. "Oh, Tony, no. We were having so much fun, and I was so looking forward to a day or two in the sun."

"I'm sorry, darling. It can't be helped." He gently took her hand.

"Thank you for your hospitality, my friend. I'm sorry we have to leave so soon." Tony apologized to Hassan.

"Of course. You are always welcome." Hassan stood as Tony ushered Sarah quickly to their stateroom.

Tony closed the door behind them and turned on some music before Sarah could ask any questions. "This is it. You've got him." He grinned. "That was Chris on the phone. I had him call me. While you were in the cabin, getting dressed, Hassan and I had quite a chat. He's very enamored with you and I think your comment about being no man's possession sealed the deal. He's all yours now. I hope you're ready for your solo."

"Well, that's all well and good, and I think he may be on the hook, but now I have to leave with you. How do we arrange for me to stay?"

"Not a problem. Hassan is nothing if not predictable when it comes to women. Just remember to thank him when we go back up on deck."

Sarah heard whispering in her ear. "Work what ya got, baby. Work it!"

Sarah packed her things and followed Tony's lead as they proceeded back to the main deck.

Hassan waited for them. "Carlos will bring your luggage shortly. Unfortunately, Nicholas is having some difficulty with the launch. I apologize for the inconvenience."

Sarah approached Hassan in all his sun-drenched glory. She gently took his hands in hers as she moved a bit closer than appropriate, kissed his soft, tanned cheek and purred in his ear, "Thank you...for everything."

Ooh, you smell good. Is that your interest rising or are you just sorry to see me go?

Hassan held on to Sarah's hands, smiled and did not let go. "Tony, surely you don't need to ruin this lovely lady's weekend simply because you can't trust your business to others. Why not let her stay and you can fly back when you've finished, or I can fly her back to you on Monday."

Tony nodded to Hassan. "As I'm sure you've guessed, the lady makes her own decisions." He smiled at Sarah. "There is no need for your weekend to be ruined on my account. I could join you later and we'll just extend our weekend a bit."

Sarah smiled and looked into Hassan's hungry eyes. "Thank you. I'd love to stay, if you're sure it isn't any trouble?"

"Trouble? Of course not. It would be my pleasure."

"Fine, it's settled then. You'll stay in Hassan's capable hands and I'll see you again just as soon as I finish up." Tony nodded to Hassan. "Thank you for your generous hospitality. I see our luggage has arrived and Nicholas has the launch ready. Goodbye, old friend." Tony and Hassan shook hands.

"*Salaam Alaikum*, my friend. I will take very good care of Sarah while you are gone."

Tony shook his head resignedly at Hassan. "I know you will."

I'm in.

Twenty-Eight

After the launch departed, Sarah turned to Hassan. "What did you say to him? What language was that?"

Thanks for that handy opportunity to convince you I don't understand Arabic.

"Oh, it was a blessing of sorts. An Arabic sendoff, if you will."

"Arabic, really? Will you teach me some?" Sarah asked earnestly.

Are you convinced I'm just a silly woman?

With the launch out of sight, Hassan pulled Sarah close and pressed her between his long, hard body and the wall of the deck. "Beauty such as yours needs no language." He kissed her neck, between the pearl choker and her ear.

Ah, yes. Keep the woman uneducated and in the dark. Your underestimating me will make my job worlds easier, Hassan.

Sarah glanced up to find Carlos several paces behind Hassan. Heat flushed her cheeks as she cleared her throat and gently pushed Hassan away.

Hassan gave Carlos quick instructions in Arabic. Sarah pretended not to understand when he told Carlos to bring Sarah's luggage to his suite. She watched Carlos pick up her luggage and walk past the stairway and through a door on the main deck.

"Where is he taking my luggage? My room was downstairs."

"Let me show you." He took her hand and led her in the same direction Carlos had disappeared.

Get ready to dance with the devil, Sarah.

To her own surprise, the danger of the situation only made her hotter for Hassan.

He led her into a hallway she hadn't noticed before and then through a set of heavy wooden doors.

Carlos had disappeared again, but her luggage was stacked in a neat pile just inside the doorway of a magnificent suite.

A skylight flooded the room with light. A sea breeze wafted salty air through the open windows on either side of the room. A huge, king-sized bed dominated the far wall. To her right was a long sofa underneath a row of windows. To her left stood a large sunken bathtub that looked like it could accommodate four comfortably. Considering Hassan's charms, Sarah had no doubt he could fill the tub with women just for himself. The door to the master bath appeared to be just on the other side of the tub.

Sarah loved the luxurious new world she'd found herself in.

You aren't in South Dakota anymore.

"What a beautiful suite!" Sarah moved to beneath the skylight and gazed at the azure sky above.

"It is nothing compared to your beauty," Hassan whispered as he wrapped his arms around her and bent to kiss her.

Twenty-Nine

Sarah climbed out of bed, naked except for her pearl earrings. She strutted to the huge bathtub and turned on the water. When sheets rustled behind her, she turned to see Hassan awake.

He lay on his stomach with his arms crossed under his chin. Dark hawk-like eyes were half open and watched her intently.

They had been in bed for hours and Sarah was satisfied, exhausted and hungry. By the look on his face, Sarah was pretty sure she had Hassan hooked. She let the water run as she returned his hungry stare, sashayed to the bed and sat.

He rolled over on his back exposing his tanned, well-muscled chest.

Sarah gently touched his lower lip with her forefinger and then traced a line through the short beard on his chin, down his clean, muscular chest and over the washboard of his abs until her hand arrived at the thick curls leading to his manhood.

"I'm hungry," she whispered.

"So am I." He growled as he pulled her down to him.

Until now, Sarah has considered her sex life mediocre at best. Turns out mediocre was, in all actuality, piss poor. This man was an animal and it was easier than she thought to enjoy every minute of his attentions. "No. I'm hungry...for food."

The hot water rushed out of the faucet and into the deep tub. Satisfied with the temperature, Sarah let it run while she picked up her toiletry case near the door and brought it into the bathroom. A moment later, she returned to shut off the water and slip into the tub, conscious of the fact that Hassan still watched her.

Hassan growled as he sat up and reached for the phone on the bedside table. The man wanted more of her and Sarah hoped to keep it that way. Another thirty-six hours wasn't nearly enough time to get the kind of information she needed.

Hassan spoke in Arabic as he called the galley and demanded a large lunch be sent up immediately.

Sarah leaned back into the warm water, rested her head on the edge of the tub and closed her eyes. "I hope you're having somebody bring some food. I couldn't possibly do that again without nourishment."

"Ah, so you want more?"

"Well, maybe with a few variations, but I wouldn't be averse to more. Unless, of course, you plan to send me away now that you've had me?"

Scope it out. Make him want to keep you here.

Hassan crossed the room in just a few paces. "Not just yet." He stepped into the tub and insinuated himself between her back and the wall of the tub. He wrapped his long legs around hers and let her know in no uncertain terms he wanted more.

Oh yeah, he's hooked. I think I'm in for a few more days at least.

They lay there in the tub. Hassan enveloped Sarah in his arms. Sarah had just drifted off to sleep when there was a knock on the stateroom door.

"Enter," mumbled Hassan as he kissed Sarah's neck.

Sarah opened her eyes as Jaleel walked in with a large tray piled high with fruit, cheese, bread and two bottles of water. She feigned modesty and snatched a towel from the rack to cover her body.

When Hassan glanced up to see what startled her, he seemed angry as he raised his voice in Arabic to Jaleel. "What are *you* doing in here? You know better than to interrupt me with business in here!"

"Does she understand?" Jaleel nodded toward Sarah as he spoke in Arabic.

Yeah buddy, I'm reading you loud and clear.

"Of course not, you idiot," Hassan thundered as he stepped out of the tub and wrapped a towel around his waist.

Jaleel turned his back to Sarah and spoke in very clear English. "My most humble apologies, lady. I had no idea the Sheikh had a guest."

Sarah raised an eyebrow at Hassan.

He reached into a closet and withdrew a thick, white, terrycloth robe. He held the robe open for Sarah, shielding her from Jaleel's view. She quickly slid her arms into the robe and held the front closed as she hustled into the bathroom. She'd hoped she could listen in from there without being seen.

Jaleel continued in Arabic. "Our friends are planning a surprise in Iraq and need guns and ammunition immediately. Shall I arrange a meeting with the American?"

"Yes, make it this afternoon," Hassan said dismissively. "Jaleel, never again interrupt me with this one." His voice became very stern. "I plan to keep her here for a while."

Yes! Just the way we planned.

Jaleel chuckled. "You never keep them more than three days. This one will be no different."

We'll see about that.

"I disagree. This one is different. She is strong willed. I like that in a woman. I think I'll keep her for quite a while if today is any indication of what I can expect in the future."

Noted. Performance today was good. Strong willed is a plus.

Jaleel's laughing voice came again. "We'll see." The snap of the stateroom door closing told her Jaleel had left.

Sarah ran a brush through her hair and splashed some cold water on her face. She was glad she'd had that refresher course in Arabic. Now she knew she had a chance to get more information on Hassan's network. She fluffed her hair and loosened the robe a bit before peeking out the bathroom door into the bedroom.

Hassan leaned back in a semi-reclined position against the headboard with his long legs stretched out before him. The towel had been cast aside and he lay there in his naked glory, his wolfish smile beckoned to Sarah.

First day here and you've already given us information about action in Iraq. A little more of this and you'll be giving me names and dates.

Sarah did her sexiest strut to the bed and then cat-crawled the length of him until she could reach the tray of food on the bedside table.

He smiled a broad, perfect smile as she sat astride him.

She smiled back, took an apple and then sat down beside him at the head of the bed.

Psyche!

"You tease me."

And you love it!

"Oh." Sarah pouted. "Have I angered the Sheikh?"

His lips spread in a closed smile and his eyes narrowed. "Yes, you have and now you must pay the price."

A shriek escaped Sarah's lips as Hassan pounced on her and pressed himself against the length of her. His lips pressed hard against hers. Hungry or not, she had to admit the working conditions weren't bad.

~~~

An hour later, they lay on the bed, exhausted and entwined in each other's limbs when another knock sounded on the door.

"I am occupied," Hassan yelled in English.

Kadeem called from behind the closed door. "I beg your pardon, Sheikh Hassan. The launch is approaching with your afternoon guest."

"Yes, yes. Escort him to the fly bridge."

Sarah nuzzled his neck. "But I thought you were completely mine this weekend?"

Hassan gazed into her eyes. "Mmm… I must take this meeting today. Perhaps you could swim or enjoy the sun deck for a time while I meet with this gentleman?"

"Yes, I should find a bit more sun than just the skylight over your bed," she said sarcastically, rising to open her suitcase and grab her bathing suit before she took a quick shower.

Hassan got out of bed with a sigh. He slipped on his trousers, and Sarah watched as he buttoned them and then threw his shirt on. She crossed to where he stood and began to button the buttons from the center of his chest down. When she arrived at the final button, she reached underneath and unbuttoned his trousers.

"Woman, you are insatiable." He laughed, pushing her hands away.

She gave him a blissful look. "I'm quite satisfied, but the Sheikh should tuck in his shirt." She paused for effect. "Unless, of course, the Sheikh is not satisfied."

"The Sheikh is quite satisfied." He chuckled, tucking in his shirt. "Use the phone over there." He nodded to the bedside table. "Call Tony and tell him you won't be meeting him on Monday."

"Oh, really? And when will I?" came her indignant reply.

"When the Sheikh commands." He gave a dismissive flip of his hand.

Sarah crossed her arms over her chest. "No man commands me. We'll just see where I want to be on Monday." She spun on her heel toward the bathroom.

I won't bend to another man's will again. We play this my way or not at all.

Hassan grabbed her by her shoulders, spun her around and bored into her gaze with his own. "That will change. Besides, you'll soon learn I am not like other men." He bent to kiss her gently on the lips. "Stay with me for a week, please?"

And now you're begging. Okay, I'll throw you a bone.

Sarah shook off his grip and turned toward the bathroom. "If it pleases the Sheikh, I will stay until Tuesday."

"It does," he said as he walked out the door.

Sarah found the MP3 player, plugged in the speaker and turned on the music as she prepared to shower.

"Nice moves, babe. Makes me wish I was there," Chris' voice said inside her ear.

"You couldn't handle this," she retorted, feeling quite sure of herself.

"Oh, try me. Vince is on his way for a status check. Give him a sign if everything is okay. Out."

Vince.

In all the excitement, she'd managed to push Vince out of her mind. Now he was about to show up for a status check? Sarah remembered that afternoon when he'd called her down to his cabin. A chill crept over her skin and caused gooseflesh to pop. Suddenly she felt unsure of herself.

What man wants a woman who sleeps with guys for a paycheck? Granted, I've only slept with one, but wouldn't he judge me?

The calm voice from deep within Sarah, the one that had gotten her through every tight spot she'd been in over the past several months spoke up again.

He set this up. He planted you here. He knew what you had to do and he, of all people, knows that this is a job. This is a different war with different weapons. This time, a woman is the weapon.

This was the truth of the situation. There was something between her and Vince, and they both would need to set aside their personal feelings in order to get this mission done safely. Her part in this mission shouldn't make a difference in Vince's eyes.

I have to believe that.

Sarah showered quickly and scrubbed her skin until it shone. Then she applied moisturizer and a touch of rose oil. There were several bathing suits in her case to choose from, but she decided Vince was worth a good one. The black and gold thong, topped with the black and gold push-up bikini top fit her well. After brushing her hair and applying her lipstick, she did a full turn in the mirror and decided she was ready to make an appearance.

Big Daddy, if you had a camera you would drop dead because this babe is definitely drop dead gorgeous today!

Showtime!

Thirty

Sarah grabbed the romance novel she'd brought along to assist in her cover and grabbed one of the plush towels in Hassan's bathroom before walking out to the sun deck. After she settled into a chaise and closed her eyes against the bright sun, the launch pulled up. Nicholas' voice directed someone to the fly bridge. Heavy steps trudged up the stairs to where Hassan waited. She cheered on the inside because the fly bridge was just above her and she would be able to hear the whole meeting while seemingly working on her tan.

"Good afternoon, Mr. Hennessee. Please join me for lunch."

Hennessee?

Sarah assumed he'd come by as a tourist in a boat when she should have realized he would be setting up an arms deal with Hassan.

Vince's deep voice carried well. "Sounds great. I've had a pretty long day and missed lunch."

"Cigar?" Hassan was the perfect host. "They're Cuban. The finest I've had yet."

"Don't mind if I do. Thank you."

Chris' voice interrupted Sarah's eavesdropping. "Will wants you to nick a few of those."

There was a pause in the conversation. Sarah assumed they were busy tasting their cigars.

Sarah heard Vince say pointedly, "Nice view you have here."

Thank you very much!

"Only the best." Hassan sounded happy. "Sarah, my beauty. Join us, will you?"

Here we go.

Sarah shielded her eyes from the sun as she looked up at Hassan on the deck above.

He nodded and motioned for her to join them.

Sarah slipped her sandals on and made her way up the stairs.

This should be interesting. There is a whole lot of testosterone up there. Two of the hottest men I've ever met…hmm, I wonder if they're up for a threesome?

Still hot after her athletic morning with Hassan, Sarah felt particularly empowered. She arrived on the fly bridge glowing and quite turned on by the view. Hassan wore the clothes she'd stripped off him this morning. Vince looked sexy as hell in black slacks and a gray T-shirt that stretched to show off every inch of his chiseled chest.

Boss or not, you have got one rockin' body! I'd trade this guy for you any day.

"Mr. Hennessee was just admiring you," Hassan quipped.

Yeah, I've been admiring Mr. Hennessee for quite some time now. It's about time he returned the favor.

"How generous of Mr. Hennessee. He's quite admirable himself."

Hassan smiled as he puffed thoughtfully on his cigar. "Mr. Hennessee, I'd like you to meet Sarah Stevens."

Okay, I see what you're up to.

"Very nice to meet you," Vince said between puffs on his cigar.

Sarah could see what sort of game Hassan played, as could Vince. What she wasn't ready for, was playing this game with Vince in this environment.

I assured the guys I could do this. I can do this. It's just a job and if anyone would understand that, it's Vince.

"So, is Mr. Hennessee a man of action or does he prefer to observe from a distance?" Sarah taunted Vince as she sat provocatively on Hassan's lap and crossed one long, tanned leg over the other.

Vince's eyes sparkled. He seemed to be having fun with where this was going. "Oh, I'm *definitely* a man of action."

Okay, big boy. You want to have some fun? We can play.

Sarah stood and strolled the few steps it took to stand behind Vince. She had to gauge her actions so as not to push Hassan too far, but to push him far enough to turn him on. She watched Hassan's gaze as she caressed Vince's strong, hard shoulders and arms. "Certainly there's no doubt about that…mmm," she murmured as she seductively rolled her shoulders for Hassan's benefit. "But I get enough action already, thank you very much."

She spun on her heel to walk down the stairs and back to the chaise she'd been sitting in.

That should be enough for you to play with but not enough to kick me out of your bed.

"Nice girl." Vince complimented Hassan as Sarah settled into the chaise. Sounding less distracted, he then informed Hassan. "I have the merchandise you need."

"Excellent. You didn't have any trouble procuring it, did you?"

"No more than usual. Don't worry, no one will be able to trace it, and my men and I will be able to deliver to the location you specify."

"That will be fine. Jaleel will give you the specifics."

"You'll have the balance upon delivery?"

"Yes, of course. Now, please excuse me for a moment. Stay and enjoy your cigar."

The sound of footsteps on the stairs alerted Sarah to Hassan's approach.

"Sarah, would you join me for a moment?"

Uh-oh. He sounds pretty serious.

The hair prickled on the back of Sarah's neck. She began to second-guess herself and wondered if she'd overplayed the scene. A flashback to the leggy blond who had disappeared after flirting with the bartender came to mind.

Damnit! Amateur!

Sarah opened her eyes and steeled herself for what might happen. She stole a quick glance and saw Vince looking down at her with concern.

Don't worry. I can handle this.

She didn't need him to act too concerned and blow their covers, so she smiled, stood and sauntered into the main salon where Hassan waited.

"Why did you touch him?" Hassan demanded, his mouth a grim line.

Sarah stood her ground. "Because you dared me to. I don't take challenges lightly, Hassan. Remember that and we'll get along just fine."

"Do you always fight when challenged?" His voice was husky now, instead of angry.

"Always." She stared purposefully into his eyes.

Hassan grabbed Sarah by the waist and pushed her up against the wall. He forced her head back with a long, rough kiss as he quickly unbuttoned his trousers.

Okay. I definitely nailed that scene.

Sarah knew why Vince was here. He was the man who would sell Hassan the guns his terrorist friends would use in Iraq.

Vince's brother was in Iraq so this had to be a particularly difficult scene for him to play. Her mind couldn't be on Vince now. The idea of a man like Hassan getting so hot for her he'd cut short a transaction for several tons of AK-47s made her hotter than she had ever been. She wanted Hassan as much for her own ego as he wanted her for his.

With his trousers undone and his erection longing for release, he grabbed her by the thighs and wrapped her legs around his waist. He thrust into her forcefully, pinning her to the wall and making her climax instantly. The rush of having this sort of power over him was exhilarating and she drank in every hard gulp of it. He came within minutes and released Sarah with the second most passionate kiss she'd ever had. She couldn't help but wonder why all her other lovers had been so completely inept compared to this man.

The wrong man.

"Did you enjoy that?" Hassan growled.

"You know I did."

"Good. Because there is more where that came from," he stated with a satisfied smile. "I want you to do something for me."

"Mmm…" she said as she caressed his thighs. "I'm sure I'll be happy to oblige."

"No. Not yet, but you will do that, too. I have reason to believe Mr. Hennessee may not be what he claims to be. I'd like you to conduct a little test for me."

Panic stabbed at Sarah's gut. Vince couldn't have been made so early in the game.

"What do you mean?"

"I don't trust him. I think he might enjoy seeing you in the white caftan."

"Of course he would. He's a man. Any man would enjoy seeing me in sheer nothingness. What's your point?"

Hassan lifted her chin. "I need to test his intentions and I believe you are the perfect bait. He seems quite taken with you."

Sarah pushed him away and started to walk toward his stateroom. "Look, I don't know what kind of game you're playing here, but I don't care to participate, thank you."

Hassan caught her with his long reach and grabbed her arm in his vice-like grip. "I said put on the caftan and join Mr. Hennessee on the fly bridge. Make him believe you want him. Now."

Sarah wanted to kick Hassan's sleazy ass right now, but the team was in this to win and that meant she had to play Hassan's game. She gave him a cold, hard stare.

This had been kind of fun but that brought me back to reality. Thanks. We're going to take you and your whole organization down if I have to stay here for a month.

Sarah stalked out of the salon and toward Hassan's stateroom for her wardrobe change.

The white caftan in broad daylight wasn't much more than an opaque film.

Sorry Vince, I've got a job to do and you've become my next project. Hopefully Chris has clued you in.

Sarah made her way up the stairs and through the sky lounge. Hassan sat in a corner with a drink in hand, waiting for her to bait his trap for Vince.

"Enjoy the show." Sarah glared at Hassan and strutted out to the fly bridge where Vince waited. She closed the tinted sliding glass door so Hassan might not hear what was said and then sidled up to Vince. Gently, she put her hands on Vince's shoulders and stroked downward over his chest. "Sorry, but the Sheikh has some voyeuristic qualities I wasn't briefed on. He's on to you and wants me to toy with you a little. If you don't take offense to my advances…"

"He'll know he can't trust me to do business with. If I take advantage, as much as I might enjoy it, it could get ugly."

"In a nutshell." Relief that he understood flooded Sarah.

Vince let out a heavy sigh. "Are you okay?"

"I'm fine. Now make him believe."

Sarah snaked her hand along his broad back and stood in front of him. She wasn't wearing a stitch of clothing underneath the caftan and knew the afternoon sun showed every nuance of her body through the near-sheer silk fabric."

Vince jumped to his feet. "I came here to conduct business, not disrespect my host. What are you trying to do?"

He was so convincing that Sarah startled and stumbled backwards. She caught herself on the deck rail and was steadying herself when Hassan stepped out of the sky lounge and onto the sky bridge.

"Mr. Hennessee, is there a problem?"

"No. None at all. With all due respect, if we're finished here, I have things to do. I'd like to head back now."

"Yes, of course. Jaleel will take you in the launch and discuss the delivery details."

Good job, boss.

Sarah watched Vince walk down the stairs and out of sight. The anger simmering under the surface of her skin rose to a full boil. She stalked up to Hassan, stared him in the eye and slapped him hard across the face.

Hassan raised his hand to slap her and adrenaline rushed through Sarah as her body prepared for the fight of its life.

Stay calm. Don't break eye contact. Show no fear.

Hassan lowered his hand and chuckled. "You did well, beautiful one."

Sarah turned on her high heel and walked away. It didn't matter. This time it was Vince, so there was no harm done, but if she let Hassan think he could continue these games with her as his pawn, it might get dangerous. The slap was really just for effect. He'd understand now she wouldn't play this game again.

Hell, if I'd really wanted to inflict pain, I'd have skipped the slap and gone straight to a roundhouse kick to the head!

Sarah had gone too long today without the benefit of food. She found her way to the galley where the little woman she'd seen the night before in kitchen whites appeared to be preparing meals for the staff.

"Yes, ma'am?" The woman greeted her in perfect American English.

She marveled at the woman's ability to greet her so respectfully when she was practically strolling around the ship naked. Hassan definitely kept a tight ship.

"Hi. What's your name?"

"Delia, ma'am. Is there something I can get for you?"

"Delia, I'm dying for a cheeseburger. I don't suppose you have the makings of one here?"

"Of course, ma'am. I'll have one sent up to the Sheikh's quarters immediately."

"Thank you, Delia." Sarah smiled before she turned and left the galley.

As she made her way to Hassan's cabin, she wondered what to expect after the slap. She paused a moment outside the door, took a deep breath and stepped inside.

The cabin sat empty and she let out a sigh of relief. If Hassan was to send her away, she might have enough time to enjoy a good meal before she got the boot.

The cabin was spotless. The food tray from earlier was now gone, the bed linens had been changed and Hassan was nowhere to be found. Sarah turned on some music and decided now might be a good time to do a status check with Chris.

Chris picked up on the signal. "I hear a little AC/DC going. Is that my cue?"

"Yes, it is." She didn't bother to hide her excitement at the sound of his voice. "How are we doing today?"

"Excellent, Sarah. We've got some new locations being monitored by satellite. Great idea to leave your necklace near the phone, by the way."

"Huh?" Sarah touched her neck and realized the necklace had been removed this morning. "Oh," she said. "Lucky that."

"Hey, I heard a slap that didn't sound like it went with a tickle. Are you okay?"

"Yeah, I slapped Hassan."

"Sweet." He laughed. "You got big balls for a girl. Keep up the good work." There was a pause. "Oh, make sure you bring that white thing back with you. Vince told us all about it and we're all dying for you to model it for us, too."

"He just left. Don't you guys have more important things to talk about than what I'm wearing?"

"No, not really. We're five dudes waiting for the shit to hit. You're doing all the work and from what we've heard, your wardrobe is a pretty important feature in this operation."

There was a knock on the door. Sarah turned off the music. "Come in."

A stewardess entered the room with a silver tray. In the middle of the tray sat a stunning Wedgwood china plate topped with a cheeseburger surrounded by French fries. A bottle of water and a dish of fresh strawberries rounded out the meal. Sarah's mouth watered as the aromas assailed her senses.

Well, that's not your average Happy Meal!

"Thank you. Please give Delia my compliments." Sarah took the tray and closed the stateroom door as her stomach growled in anticipation. She wolfed the whole meal down in minutes. Then she took the bottle of water and reclined on the bed to consider Hassan's next possible move.

Option one: He could be arranging for me to leave right now. Option two: He might be turned on by my nerve and want me to stay even longer. At least the day wasn't a total loss. I got good and laid, Chris said they managed to get some intel on specific locations and I ate the best cheeseburger I've had in months.

Thirty-One

Sarah opened her eyes and stretched, long and catlike. She had no idea how much time had passed since she'd fallen asleep. What she did know was the room had changed. Every tabletop was covered with a vase full of long-stemmed Sterling roses, and the air was thick with their heady, sweet scent.

She scanned the room and found Hassan reclined on the sofa by the bed with his feet up on the opposite armrest. His shirt was unbuttoned and barely hanging on to his shoulders. His chest and abs were so tanned and defined, he looked like a Greek god.

Hassan smiled at Sarah in a sleepy, seductive way that made her body respond, regardless of how bad he was and how much he'd pissed her off.

Be cool. Be cool.

"I must have fallen asleep. What time is it?"

Hassan stood. "Time for us to talk, my beauty."

Sarah sat upright and immediately took the defensive. She wasn't going without a fight. "Look, if you're upset about the slap, you had it coming, and then some, and you know it!"

He smiled his perfect, charming smile. "Perhaps I did, but never in my life has a woman, any woman, dared to correct my behavior, not even my own mother."

Well, maybe she should have.

"So, you're angry?" She arched one eyebrow in challenge and waited for his answer.

He chuckled. "Hardly." His voice softened and he brushed a strand of hair from her forehead. "I'm intrigued. Either you are very foolish or very brave. If you were foolish, I would have lost interest the moment I finished making love to you for the first time. The look in your eyes tells me you're brave. It is the look I see in a horse's eyes before he is broken. Defiant, bold and fierce. Most of all…intoxicating. It is the one thing my money and connections will not buy. Therefore I must have it."

"Excuse me?" Sarah raised an eyebrow. "Did you just compare me to a horse?"

Hassan reached under the pillow and retrieved a small black velvet box. He opened the box. "Stay with me?"

The sparkle of the yellow diamond solitaire had the effect of an atom bomb.

I love it. I want it. I'll take it.

"What did you say?" She croaked after taking a moment to collect herself. She didn't know if he'd asked her to marry him, to be kept by him or to just stick around for a few more days.

"I do not need another wife, nor do I need more bimbos looking for a free ride. What I need is a companion who understands me. You, my beauty, seem to do just that. Stay with me and this will be the first of many gifts. You will never want for anything and when we choose to part company, you will be well provided for."

Wow! Satan's retirement plan? Nobody has ever given me a diamond before.

Sarah remembered Jason, standing on the deck of their boat, holding her hands. *Keep these babies clear, Sarah.*

Oh, hell. It's a ring. I can't do rings.

She pulled her gaze away from the stunning gem and glanced up at Hassan. His features had softened. He appeared so sincere. Only a man. "I'm sorry. I can't."

His face hardened. "What?" Hassan stood and paced the length of the bed. "You are the most infuriating woman I've ever met! No woman has ever said no to such a generous offer! What kind of woman says no to yellow diamonds and Sterling Roses? Would you prefer real estate…art… horses? Name it and it shall be yours, but I will not ask again."

Ego alert! Damage control.

Sarah scrambled off the bed and stood in his way to stop his pacing.

"Hassan." She kept her voice soft while she placed her hands on his chest. The rapid beat of his heart pounded under her fingertips.

"Woman, do you have any idea who I am?"

"Be quiet." She placed a finger to his lips. Something akin to lightning flashed in his eyes. Pride and ego were definitely strong traits in this man.

He'd actually hit the roof when he thought I turned him down! I had no idea it would be so easy to manipulate you, Hassan. You are completely ruled by your ego!

Sarah spoke in a calm whisper. "I don't care who you are. The stone is gorgeous. The roses are beautiful, too. But I do not wear rings. I would like the stone set in a pendant on a chain long enough to lie¼" She took his hand and placed his fingers between the valley of her breasts. "Right here."

A smile curled the corners of his mouth and the lightning in his eyes simmered to a sparkle. "You are an infuriating woman, Sarah Stevens," he whispered as he ran his hands through her hair to the back of her head and pulled her to him for a long, seductive kiss.

Thirty-Two

Sarah could not get over the woman who stared back from the mirror. She marveled at the diamond pendant and how it sparkled around her neck. She wore a dark blue, silk gown. The plunging V-neck was perfect for showing off her assets, both old and new, while the length of the gown flowed to the floor with a long slit up her right thigh. She left her pearl necklace beside the bed, but was sure to wear the pearl earrings and bracelet.

Two weeks had passed since Hassan had given her the diamond and asked her to stay. He had been very generous, arranging for shopping trips with unlimited budgets so she could always wear the finest clothes when they entertained his business associates.

Hassan liked to conduct his daytime meetings on the fly bridge, overlooking the sun deck. He always seemed to want her on the sun deck during those meetings.

She usually gave him a hard time about it, but eventually complied in the end. Having her there provided a distraction for his associates and eventually led to him getting the better end of every deal. It was easy to listen in on his meetings if she acted the sunbathing trophy, so it worked out best for the team's mission this way. Names were always mentioned, details were passed on the movement of Hassan's associates and links were confirmed.

Chris' link analysis work on Hassan's organizational chart was coming along great because of her frequent sunbathing efforts.

Hassan generally conducted all his meetings in Arabic so he had no idea Sarah learned as much about him as she actually did, nor did he realize every word was being transmitted to an intelligence station set up on another yacht just out of sight.

Hassan seemed to adore Sarah the way a collector adores his prized possessions. She was merely another beautiful piece he'd collected. He had beautiful houses around the world, a stable of the finest Arabian horses and a collection of sports cars that would make Henry Ford weep.

A smug sense of pride washed over her. Sarah had managed to insinuate herself into the perfect position to collect a great deal of damning evidence against Hassan and his associates.

At times she had to remind herself about Hassan's dark side. On occasion, she allowed her mind to wander and wonder what her life would be like if he were a legitimate businessman and not a terrorist financier. She could have everything she'd ever wanted, a beautiful home, money, jewels, fine clothes and a man who was an attractive, attentive and passionate lover. Love wasn't a necessary part of the equation.

Why risk it?

When Sarah daydreamed about what-ifs, reality had a way of cutting in. Chris would do a status check or one of Hassan's henchmen would give her a sideways look. She had to remind herself none of this was real. This was a job and would be over soon. Then there would be another job…another target.

At times like this thoughts of all her ex boyfriends brought her back to reality. Getting dumped and letting it affect her self-esteem led to being buried in her own fat. It had killed her spirit. That old Sarah needed to die. The new Sarah would give no quarter. The new one would burn through men and take whatever gifts they were stupid enough to give.

This is a much better arrangement. He's using me and I'm using him. We both know it and accept it for what it is.

A knock resounded on the door. "Come in."

"The Sheikh demands your presence immediately." Kadeem spat. He always spoke to her disrespectfully whenever Hassan wasn't around.

Several times she'd heard him say very ungentlemanly things about her in Arabic to members of the staff. She suspected he was trying to find out if she understood Arabic. She would always smile as though oblivious and then make a mental note to kick his ass one day soon.

Sarah stood quickly, nodded to Kadeem and flashed her most charming smile. "The Sheikh is so lucky to have such a dedicated errand boy."

Before he could respond, she left the room in a rustle of silk and was on her way into the main salon where Hassan waited for her.

She smiled, quickly crossed the room to him and gave a deferential bow of her head. "I was informed the Sheikh demands my presence."

Then she whispered, "I have a few demands of my own, and the Sheikh will hear about them after his guests have gone."

Hassan stared into her eyes. "There may be times I allow you to command me but, make no mistake, it is only because I allow it that you do."

Sarah refused to back down. "You would think so, but perhaps it is I who make the allowances."

Hassan chuckled and shook his head.

She had to throw him a little sass every once in a while or he'd become bored with her. So far, she'd managed to keep his favor and the team gathered great intel because of it. Sarah spent the rest of the evening in the role of charming hostess to the international mix of movers, shakers, Democrats and mobsters. These were the people financing terrorism and ninety percent of them didn't have a clue.

"Hassan, there you are." A portly, middle-aged man Sarah thought looked familiar grabbed Hassan's hand with gusto and shook it vigorously. The young brunette with him gazed around the room as though she were looking for anyone more interesting to spend her time with.

"Senator Farlin." Hassan smiled. "How nice of you to make it. May I present my hostess, Miss Sarah Stevens."

Senator Farlin. I seem to remember a bit of a scandal with you and a Congressional intern. The woman beside you doesn't look at all like the wife you publicly reconciled with.

Sarah reached out to shake the Senator's hand and was met with a crushing handshake she hoped to never endure again. Shaking off the pain in her right hand, she assumed her most charming smile. "Welcome. It is very nice to meet you, Senator."

"Hassan, I got a little somethin' for that children's charity of yours in Iraq. I had a little get together at my place in Oklahoma last weekend and we managed to pony up a few pennies for the kids." The Senator reached into the breast pocket of his beige, Brooks Brother's jacket and handed a check to Hassan.

Hassan opened the check and, as was the Middle Eastern custom, commenced to make a fuss over it. "Oh, the Senator is very generous. On behalf of the children of Iraq, I thank you."

He showed Sarah the check and to register anything less than amazement would have been impossible and rude.

Sarah couldn't believe this American Senator had just handed a known terrorist financier a seven-figure check. She was sure to convey as much as she could verbally so Chris could get the evidence he needed to put a stop to this.

Sarah's eyes opened wide. "Two million dollars on the Senator's own account. Senator Farlin is very generous indeed."

There were people in the world who were so anxious to say they were helping humanitarian charities they would write checks to anyone. Men like Hassan who bankrolled terrorists who used jets, cars, subways, busses and babies as bombs were only too happy to relieve them of their money.

There were people who would condemn the tactics she used to get her job done, but she felt more than justified considering the fact there were so many people in the world, influential people like U.S. Senators who were gullible enough to finance mass murderers in the name of humanitarian aid.

The night grew late and the salon became heavy with cigar smoke and the noise of big egos on good Scotch. Sarah excused herself and stepped out onto the deck for some air.

As she strolled along the deck, she greeted and spoke to several of Hassan's other guests who mingled outside. She couldn't take two steps without having some celebrity or millionaire bump into her. Tonight's party was a particularly large one. There were fifty people on the guest list and all of them had shown up. Another twenty or so arrived uninvited but were made welcome all the same.

Hassan was by no means a good Muslim. A womanizer and financier of mass murderers, he still insisted on holding to the Arabic traditions of welcoming all visitors and seeing to their comfort.

Thirty-Three

"Excuse me."

Surprise and delight fluttered through Sarah's system at the sound of Vince's voice. Goose bumps rose over her bare arms. She turned to see Vince leaning against the railing, absolutely stunning in a black Armani tux.

"Oh. Hello, Mr. Hennessee. I should apologize for my behavior the last time we met. I'm sure I was simply overwhelmed by your presence."

"No need, sweetheart." Vince moved close and whispered in her ear. "You can paw me anytime you want."

"Really? I'll keep that in mind." She gave him a flirty grin and raised one eyebrow.

Sarah couldn't help the disappointment that flared through her when he pulled away to a more respectable distance. Vince pointed to her empty glass. "Can I get you a drink?"

"Thank you. White wine."

"Really?"

"Unless you know someone who can make a proper Margarita?"

"I do, but he isn't tending bar tonight. White wine it is."

"Ah...Vince."

Sarah nearly jumped at the sound of Hassan's voice. "I see you remember my hostess, Sarah."

"Who could forget her? I was about to get the lady a drink. Can I get you one, too?"

"Nonsense. You are my guest. Allow me." Hassan kissed Sarah on the cheek. "Excuse me, my beauty. I trust you'll keep Mr. Hennessee company?"

Sarah gave Hassan a deferential nod. "Of course."

Once Hassan left, Vince leaned in. "Man, that guy has a gift for sneaking up on people, doesn't he?"

"Uncanny stealth. He'll be back any minute. So, how are the boys?"

"Very well, as a matter of fact, one of the reasons I'm here tonight. My *girl* is doing exceptionally well."

Happiness bubbled inside her. "How wonderful." Sarah sat on a nearby bench and motioned for Vince to join her. "Do tell."

"She's about to break someone's heart."

"Really?" Sarah smiled a wicked grin. "She's a beautiful girl. It really is inevitable." She removed a cigarette from her cigarette case and brought it to her lips.

Vince lit her cigarette. "Yeah, tell me about it. The boys watch her every day and cry themselves to sleep every night. It's a matter of days for this guy. Could even be tomorrow."

A wave of relief washed over Sarah. "How sad for him."

"Yeah, but she needs a break. She works very hard at what she does."

"Yes, I'm sure she does."

"Your wine, my beauty, and Scotch for you, right, Vince?"

"Yes, thank you." Vince stood. "You're a very generous host, Hassan. Someday soon I'll have to return the favor. Maybe then you'll tell me where you found this lovely lady."

Hassan lifted an eyebrow to Sarah. "Perhaps I should lend her to you?"

Sarah returned his tease with a hard glare.

"A tempting offer, but I'm afraid she's far too much woman for me." Vince glanced at his watch. "It is late and I have some business to attend to with one of your other guests. If you'll excuse me?"

Sarah smiled and nodded to Vince while Hassan shook his hand and said goodbye.

I should have known you'd be stunning in a tux.

Hassan bid his other guests goodnight as he and Sarah watched them board their own launches to return to nearby islands and moored yachts.

Kadeem approached Hassan. "All of your guests have gone, sir."

Hassan nodded and dismissed Kadeem. "Thank you, Kadeem. You may finish your preparations for tomorrow. Goodnight."

Kadeem bowed slightly. "Goodnight, sir." The way Kadeem scuttled off reminded Sarah of the cockroaches she'd seen outside her barracks in Texas.

Every morning she had stepped outside before dawn for her run and had to jump out of the way of at least two Texas-sized cockroaches.

Kadeem reminded her so much of them and Sarah looked forward to the day she could crush him. A cell at Guantanamo Bay would be too good for the slime.

"Is something happening tomorrow I should know about?" Sarah turned to Hassan.

"Just business, my beauty. Nothing for you to be concerned with. I'll be leaving early and returning late. The crew will be here to care for you. You should spend the day resting. You're looking tired."

Sarah ran one finger down his chest and gave him a playful poke in the ribs. "I should be offended, but you are the reason I haven't had much sleep lately."

Thirty-Four

Sarah awoke with a start when someone shook her shoulder.

Just Hassan.

The sun was barely on the horizon. Something was different. The sunrise was on the wrong side of the boat. Panic slapped her in the face. "Where are we?"

"Just off the coast of Africa. Dress in traveling clothes, we're taking the helicopter to the mainland."

"To Africa? I thought I was staying here to rest today?" Sarah stalled.

Vince didn't say anything about this last night. I thought we had intelligence guys on the job? How can I tell Chris I'm moving? I hope we're still within transmission range for him to hear this.

"What sort of traveling clothes? Formal or casual? You really need to give a girl a day to prepare for travel, darling."

Chris, you'd better be listening to this!

"Wear riding clothes, my beauty. We'll be going to one of my homes. I want to show you my stables."

"Oh, how wonderful! I haven't been riding in ages. How long will it take to get there?" She feigned enthusiasm. Adrenaline pumped through her and her gut told her something was very wrong.

"We'll take the helicopter. It will be a short flight inland. Now, dress quickly. I have much to do today."

"But I thought…?" He had already left the room.

Riding clothes, riding clothes…too many things buzzed through her mind and if she continued to allow them, she'd appear frazzled and worse yet, nervous around Hassan.

Get a grip, Stevens.

She slipped on a pair of slim jeans and then stepped into her brown leather boots.

Good thing I took advantage of those shopping trips. This turned out to be a long weekend trip with way too many wardrobe changes.

She threw on a white cotton collared blouse and tucked it in. Then, praying nobody walked in on her, she emptied her suitcase and opened the false bottom where her knives were stashed. She slipped one small knife into the scabbard sewn into each boot, closed the false bottom of her Luis Vuitton suitcase and then heard the door open.

"What on earth are you doing?" Hassan questioned when he saw the pile of clothes and the empty suitcase.

Sarah quickly covered as she threw the pile of clothes into the suitcase. "My pearls! I can't find my pearl bracelet."

Hassan pointed to the bracelet and necklace on the bedside table. "There, on the table. Would you wake up?"

"Well, I should still be asleep, shouldn't I?"

Yes, a perturbed attitude should turn him on and make him forget what he walked in on.

"You keep me up all night entertaining your friends and then entertaining you, and now you expect me to wake up at the crack of dawn ready to go riding?"

She grabbed her pearl bracelet off the bedside table and clasped it on her wrist as she rattled on. "You might have given me some notice so I could lay my clothes out. My blouse hasn't been ironed. I don't even have time to do my hair." She pulled her hair back into a clean, tight ponytail.

Hassan's eyes became dark brown slivers under his furrowed eyebrows as the muscles in his jaw tightened and released. "I have decided I would enjoy your company on this trip. You test my patience. Do not make me regret my decision." He grabbed her by the wrist and pulled her roughly to him.

Sarah matched his tone as she pushed him away and marched out of the stateroom. "And you test my tolerance."

She proceeded to the helipad without looking behind her. She knew Hassan followed closely. Sarah was quite sure the sass he found appealing at first would soon wear thin. She only hoped she'd be able to gauge the time and place appropriately. Hassan was not a small man and she was sure he could do her serious damage if he ever got the first hit.

When she arrived at the helipad, she turned to look for Hassan. He was so close behind her she practically bumped into his chest. She recognized the depraved look in his eyes. They gleamed with desire. Sarah breathed a small sigh of relief.

Sass still works.

Kadeem waited inside the helicopter and glared at Sarah as Hassan helped her into the aircraft. "Perhaps the lady would prefer to stay here today?"

"The Sheikh is pleased with her company," Hassan answered tersely in Arabic.

Sarah snuggled up to Hassan and purred, "I adore the sound of your language. I wish I could understand what you're saying."

"I was simply telling Kadeem although you are a pain in my ass and take entirely too long to get ready, I still take pleasure in your company."

Sarah smiled and whispered in Hassan's ear. "It's too bad he's here. You'd be taking a whole lot more pleasure in my company."

Hassan gave her a sideways glance and a wicked smile.

Yeah, I've still got an edge on you. Ego and libido will be your downfall.

The helicopter flew low along the northern coast of Africa. Sarah guessed to avoid radar but left the technical issues to the pros. She hoped the team had found some way to track her. She hadn't had any contact with Chris since yesterday morning and had been unable to speak with Vince last night. The knives in her boots kept her from feeling completely vulnerable.

Thirty-Five

Vince dropped two ice cubes into his coffee and sleepily climbed the flight of stairs to the bridge. Chris had all his radio and satellite gear set up there and Vince started every day with a status check on Sarah. "Mornin', Chris. How's our girl today?"

"Just a sec, Vince." Chris rubbed his face with both his hands and keyed his microphone again. "Sarah, if you can read me, please acknowledge."

Warning sirens went off inside Vince's head. The tone of Chris' voice sounded desperate. Chris always seemed chipper when he chatted with Sarah. "Talk to me, Chris."

Chris turned his chair to face Vince. "I lost her."

Vince couldn't have heard him correctly. Chris always had contact. He must be overreacting. "Come again?"

Chris held his head in his hands. "I have no GPS signal from her watch, can't find the boat on satellite and have no audio whatsoever."

The muscles in the back of Vince's neck tensed. She wasn't just a teammate to him. She was more. It took a moment to bury his personal feelings but he did. Vince picked up his coffee, took one huge swig to finish the cup, and calmly but swiftly planned their next course of action. "Get your head out of your hands, agent. Map their last known coordinates and get them to Brian. We're moving." He pushed the intercom button. "All hands. Brian, I need you on the bridge now. Jason, prepare the war gear and weapons. Will, get your kit ready."

Vince heard the *thump-thump-thump* of someone bounding up the stairs.

Brian burst through the door to the bridge. "What's going on?"

Vince glowered at Brian. "We lost Sarah." He pointed at Chris. "Get the coordinates from Chris and get us there, balls to the wall. Chris, call Araxos and see if they can get a fix on her signature."

"Uh, Vince?" Chris interrupted.

Vince had his hand on the doorknob. "What?"

"We've got company. Small, fast mover and six personnel coming up on our aft." Chris tossed Vince the binoculars.

"Shit. We may have been made." Vince focused the binoculars on the same Zodiac they'd seen before. Only this time it was loaded with six guys and they were armed to the teeth.

If we've been made, Sarah's been made.

Jason exploded into the room. "What's up? What's happening? What's going on?"

Vince grabbed the shotgun and ammunition Jason held and tossed them to Brian. Then he took three earpieces from Chris's desk. "Plot your course, get ready to move. We need to finish these pirates. I'll tell you when to go."

Vince turned to Jason and handed him an earpiece. "Get me two shotguns and an AK for Will. You get an M-60 on that fly deck now."

"You got it." Jason tore out of the room.

Vince left the bridge and slid down the stair rails.

Will was waiting when his feet hit the floor. "What's the situation?"

"Follow me." Vince gave Will an earpiece and crossed to the aft deck. "Chris lost Sarah. No GPS, no audio. The Zodiac is back and packed with six armed men. We finish these bastards off and get to Sarah's last known location to try to track her down, if it isn't too late."

Jason arrived loaded with two Benelli shotguns and an AK-47. He handed Vince the shotguns and a large ammo pouch. "You got five rounds in each weapon and here's an extra two-hundred."

Will grabbed the AK-47. "What have I got?"

Jason pointed to the rifle. "You've got seventy-five rounds in the drum, one in the chamber." He handed Will another large round magazine for the rifle. "Here's an extra seventy-five rounds." Jason spun and ran up to the fly deck. Vince heard him through his earpiece. "Boss, I got two thousand rounds upstairs. If we can't finish them with what we've got then it's time to retire."

Vince laid his ass on the line every day and the only way he could keep on doing it was knowing he had a crew as competent as this one. He focused on the job. Now was not the time to imagine what might be happening to Sarah. "Jason, stay out of sight until we need you. Will, we're gonna ambush these bastards as they try to board." He cocked both shotguns. "If we can keep their gear and boat, all the better."

Thirty-Six

Sarah peered out the window of the helicopter in an effort to get her bearings from the terrain below. They flew inland for what seemed like hours. With a glance at her watch, she determined they'd been flying due south for the past forty-five minutes. They now flew over what appeared to be a military camp.

Camouflage netting mixed in and under the trees hid something, Sarah wasn't sure what. The untrained eye wouldn't notice, but Sarah did. She pretended not to and made silly comments about the terrain. All the while her gut twisted. What sort of situation was she flying into?

She hadn't been as concerned about her safety on the boat¾after all, she could always jump.

Vince did say they wouldn't leave her in the water for long.

But now, she flew into the heart of enemy territory, without any identification, to a continent where you couldn't spit without hitting a terrorist training camp. To say she was apprehensive would be an understatement. She prayed her charms would be enough to carry her safely through this leg of the adventure.

A large estate appeared beneath them. An immense, Mediterranean-style home stood at one end of the property. Stables graced the other and several outbuildings stood at each side of a large grassy yard clearly used for helicopter landings. The grounds were lush and full of trees. Outside the perimeter of the estate, the ground was bare. Dread sank to the bottom of her belly. She wouldn't stand a chance in such bleak terrain if she tried to make a break and run.

Two men dressed in black with white turbans stood on the ground just outside rotor range.

I hope this isn't my welcoming committee.

When the rotors stopped, Kadeem jumped out of the chopper to hold the door open for Hassan.

Hassan stepped out and then reached in to help Sarah down the stairs.

One of the men who stood a few feet away widened his eyes when he saw Sarah.

Not expecting me? Oh, good.

The man ran to Hassan and addressed him belligerently in Arabic. "What is this woman doing here? Why would you bring her with you?"

Hassan bristled and responded in Arabic. "You forget yourself, Assad. I have killed better men than you for such insolence."

"Forgive me, Sheikh, but I am concerned only for your safety." He nearly whimpered after Hassan's reprimand.

"The woman poses no threat to my safety. She is here as my guest and will receive the respect due to a guest in the house of Sheikh Hassan Abdullah Mohammed al-Rashid. I trust you understand?"

"Yes, of course. I beg the Sheikh's pardon." The man bowed low as Hassan and Sarah strode past him.

Close one. I don't think I'd care to hear that tone in Hassan's voice again. This is a dangerous game. I only hope I can play it out.

"What a scary man. You really pull out all the stops, don't you? In the United States, we keep dogs to scare away strangers." Sarah linked her arm through Hassan's and gave him one of the admiring gazes he seemed to adore as he led her away from the helicopter.

"Do you like dogs? I have two."

"Not if they're as scary as he is."

Hassan chuckled. "No, they are quite friendly."

"Then I would love to meet them," Sarah squealed in delight.

"Ah, here they are." Hassan pointed toward two beautiful specimens of the Saluki breed as they sprinted toward them.

The dossier had noted he'd kept Salukis and described all about the breed, how it was bred for its speed and skill in the desert. If she didn't understand Arabic, she certainly shouldn't know about Salukis. "Oh, they're magnificent. What breed are they?" Sarah played her socialite part as she bent to pat a very friendly black and tan dog.

"They are Saluki. Prized by the Bedouin, I keep them in honor of my ancestry."

"Really?" *Here's my chance to lay on a little ditz.* "So, are you one of those men who wear the long flowing robes, ride camels and live in those black, carpeted tents in the desert?" She smiled playfully.

"The Hollywood version but, simply put, yes. My family has a long, proud Bedouin history."

Her appearance of ignorance seemed to amuse him. Relief radiated throughout her body. Apparently she could get away with a whole lot more than the men around him as long as she put a kittenish spin on whatever she did. Of course, sleeping with their boss did give her a distinct advantage.

"Where are the horses? Do you have Arabian horses? I've never seen an Arabian horse up close before."

"Then you have never seen a true horse." Hassan stood and smiled indulgently at Sarah. "I have some business I need to attend to inside. Why don't you go to the stables and find a pretty horse you'd like to ride? I'll be down shortly to ride with you."

"That sounds dreamy," she enthused as she kissed Hassan on the cheek. She patted the flank of one of the dogs. "Come on, let's go." She jogged and laughed as the dogs ran circles around her to the stables

Well, he seems to be enjoying me so far, as long as I continue to play pussycat, I might stand a pretty good chance of making it out of here alive.

Sarah had seen stables before but Hassan's stables put the farm stables in South Dakota to shame. Every inch of wood had been polished to a high shine. The floor of the center aisle was made of fine marble and so spotless you could eat off it.

Even the horses were different. Arabians were nothing like the quarter horses and mustang ponies Sarah had seen in the United States.

Sarah counted twelve horses. Of them all, one stood out as the finest. The gold plate on his stall gate was engraved in Arabic. She looked around to be sure she was alone with the horses.

"Mu'tazz Asad. Mighty Lion? You look more like a puppy than a lion to me."

His eyes were large and a soft brown. When Sarah looked into them, she got the impression this was a very intelligent horse. Though he was a stallion, he was gentle and particularly friendly. He stood taller than the other horses, majestic with his solid black coat glistening in the sunlight coming through the high windows. His long mane draped down the side of his neck and his tail almost reached the ground.

Sarah glanced around and found a very tidy line of bins. She reached into one and grabbed a handful of oats. After her new friend relieved her of the oats, she rummaged for a brush and began to stroke his neck. He sidled up to the gate so Sarah could brush more of his back. Sarah chuckled at the animal's antics. Mighty Lion acted more like a pet dog than any horse she'd ever seen.

"Stunning creatures."

She recognized Hassan's voice behind her and continued to run the brush over the horse's neck. "Yes, they are. All of them."

"I meant you and him."

"Oh, I see. Am I another animal for your stable?"

"I would never dream of keeping you in the stable," he asserted. Hassan wrapped his arms around her from behind and growled. "But I am seriously considering taking you in the stable."

"If it pleases the Sheikh, who am I to question?" She pressed herself back against his long powerful body, feeling his arousal against her ass.

"Are you still angry with me?" He nuzzled her neck.

"Oh, I'm still angry." Sarah turned in his arms and pulled him closer to sandwich herself between him and the stable wall. "But that won't stop me from having my way with you."

She reached to unbutton his pants and free his impressive erection. She stroked him gently at first as she reached up with her other hand to unbutton his shirt.

He busied himself with unbuttoning her shirt and caressing her breasts through the delicate white lace bra.

She opened his shirt and pressed against him, raining a trail of soft kisses down his bronzed chest and rippled abs.

~~~

Sarah stood and stretched her legs. Her lips felt swollen and her shirt was still open.

A gentle finger touched her lips and then traced a line from her bottom lip to the center of her heaving breasts where the yellow diamond rested. "You wear this every day. Have you no other jewels? Am I the only man who has given you jewels?" He seemed dismayed and shocked by the possibility.

"Yes, you are." Sarah turned away from his gaze. The men she had been with before Hassan were either poor, cheap or inconsiderate.

Hassan gently gripped her shoulders and turned her to face him. He lifted her chin and forced her gaze to meet his. Sarah did all she could to mask the pain of years of wasted faith in other people. She'd given her love to men who'd tossed it away like yesterday's news. Now when she'd decided to withhold her love from the equation, fate dealt her a new hand entirely.

Funny how the worst man I've ever been involved with treats me better than all the rest combined.

"Then I shall make myself a very difficult act to follow."

Hassan's comment touched Sarah. "You already are."

Tragic you are either not long for this world or you'll spend the rest of your days locked up in Cuba.

Sarah shoved the thought to the back of her mind and focused on her act. "Now this is the horse I want to ride." She pointed at Mu'tazz. "Where are the saddles?"

"You have excellent taste." He smiled.

"Yes, I do. And so do you." She gave him a saucy wink as she buttoned her blouse.

"Can you ride an English saddle?"

"Of course, doesn't everyone?" She thanked her lucky stars she'd taken riding lessons and had chosen the English style and learned to post.

Thirty-Seven

Sarah stood by and waited as a stable hand readied the horses for her and Hassan. Once he finished, she and Hassan saddled up and headed off at a canter.

They never left the compound, yet found isolation in a lush forested area.

Sarah marveled at the hard work that must have gone into creating this fertile oasis in a desolate North African desert. Everything sat silent except for the sounds of birds and the horses' hooves.

"Are you all right?" Hassan spun in his saddle and asked from several yards ahead.

"Yes, your estate is beautiful. Go on. I'll catch up."

"Sarah, come in, damnit!" Sarah's heart leapt and hammered against her ribs when she finally heard the voice she'd been waiting for.

"Hey, stranger. What's the big idea leaving me high and dry?" she whispered.

"Technical difficulties. Our pirate friends came back for some fun. We know where you are and can be there within thirty minutes if we have to."

"Thirty minutes? It took us over forty-five to get here."

"Brian's friends have fast boats and even faster helicopters."

Brian's friends? Navy. Ah, the Sixth Fleet. Good to know who has your back.

"We've got a great picture of the top of his organization now. We're also getting some great satellite feed of the camp you're in."

"So, it is a training camp?"

"Yeah, from the satellite pictures, it looks like a staging area for something big. The boss wanted to pull you out tonight, but if you're okay, we'll leave you in a little longer."

"Yeah, I'm cool. Don't stay away so long next time."

"No problem, babe. Big Daddy will take good care of his girl. Do you know where you are?"

"Northern Africa is all I know."

"Sweetheart, you're in Libya."

"Aw, shit." Terrorism wasn't an exception in Libya. More like the rule.

"Look, Sarah. You need to know something. This isn't the first operation we've done this way. You know, with a Honey Pot. You're the second."

"Yeah, I know. So, what happened to the first? Did she play her cards right and retire on the jewelry?"

"No such happy ending. She fell in love with the target, and lost her nerve. She didn't have the guts to choose between herself and the guy. When it got ugly, she thought she could negotiate her way out. He didn't see things her way."

Oh, great. I'm already nervous and this sudden decision to tell me about a previously failed mission is not helping.

"Chris, this little pep talk of yours is not helping. Are you trying to scare me here because, in case you didn't notice, I'm in Libya with a known terrorist and it's nothing like a jaunt to the Bahamas with a boy toy, if you know what I'm saying. Why are you telling me this shit now?"

"I'll be the first to admit the lifestyle is seductive. Everything that money can buy and nobody can touch you. I've heard the guy's lines. He's smooth and, let's face it, you haven't been treated this well by a guy before. Wrap it all up in a bow and you've got the American dream. Remember we're fighting a war here. The bad guys are dressed a whole lot better, but they're still the bad guys."

What the hell! Do these guys know every wretched detail of my miserable love life?

"What happened with the girl?"

"Uh, things went tactical. She missed her window and nobody could get a shot. He took her hostage and got away in a chopper."

"So, she quit the business and retired."

"Sarah, these bad guys are real. The son of a bitch dropped her in the drink from two hundred feet once he got away. She died on impact. Jason hit the chopper with a Stinger before he went too far, but we lost her."

Sarah's anger began to reach new heights, the horse beneath her fidgeted as he sensed her agitation. "Well, clearly the experience should have taught you all a little something about your response time. I'm not impressed. As for your technical difficulties this morning¾don't you ever do that shit again. Look, I'm not going to lose my nerve and I won't ever let you guys down. You tell Brian I'm looking forward to that bottle of tequila and will be back soon to collect. I know what I'm here for and know what to do if it gets messy."

"There's a difference between knowing and doing, Sarah. We don't doubt you, but the nature of your job is to get in deep and you can't tell me you aren't. You're doing something that none of us could ever do. When you're that close to someone, sometimes they get under your skin and you begin to wonder if they could turn. They never do, Sarah. He's got great game with the ladies. You're putting on a hell of an act, but I guarantee you he's been working people over a whole lot longer than you have. Don't let your guard down."

I am so done with this conversation.

"You just better make sure you guys are on the job and not sitting around with your dicks in your hands. I'm out."

Well, Chris. You've got me pegged, haven't you? It would have been so easy with Hassan. Our relationship is perfectly superficial. You can't get your feelings hurt when you don't put your heart on the line.

Sarah's heart was on the line, though. Just not with this one. Hassan was merely a distraction to keep her mind off her feelings for someone else. Someone she could never have.

Thirty-Eight

Sarah caught up with Hassan and stayed quiet, lost in her thoughts for the rest of the ride. Chris was right. The lifestyle and Hassan were incredibly seductive. She might have toyed with the idea of what it might be like to stay with him, but never for long.

Whatever goes down in the end, it won't be pretty. I'll survive, but the old Sarah will be dead when it's all said and done.

"What troubles you, my beauty? Is Mu'tazz too much horse for you?"

Sarah snapped out of her daze. "No, no, he's a wonderful creature. Very tame for a stallion, isn't he?"

Hassan rode close beside her and took her right hand in his left. "Don't let his appearance deceive you. He can be very dangerous when he wants to be. You ride well. If you were less cooperative, he might be inclined to show you his treacherous side."

Sarah smiled and tilted her head toward Hassan.

Are we talking about the horse or you?

"He's much like his master, isn't he?"

"You're a smart woman, Sarah."

I understand both meanings of your message, Hassan. I know who you are and I know the stakes in this game. Don't worry. I'll play nice… for now.

The sun sat directly overhead as they returned to the stable. An older man waited as they rode up. With quick steps the man stood in front of Hassan's horse and held the reins.

Sarah appreciated Hassan as he dismounted the horse in a single agile move.

He really is an exceptionally attractive man.

She smiled as he helped her dismount. She didn't need the help but knew it would look better if she deferred to him in front of his help.

Hassan wrapped his large hands around Sarah's waist and lowered her down from the saddle.

Sarah placed her hands first on Hassan's rugged shoulders and slowly wrapped her arms around his neck as he lowered her along the length of his own body.

Her lips met his on the way down and she kissed him hard. His ego and body were his weaknesses. She had every intention of manipulating those weaknesses in order to allay any suspicions he may have. Maybe it was the change of location, but something didn't feel right today and she wanted Hassan to be off guard should anything get weird.

Hassan responded as she expected. A low moan rasped from his throat as her thighs and hips slid over his solid erection.

Sarah held herself close to his body and intentionally rubbed against him as he lowered her feet to the ground. She gazed into his eyes. Intense and dark brown, they burned with passion. "I want you now," she whispered.

"Come with me." He grabbed her hand and led her to the house.

Hassan opened a set of French doors off to the east of the main entrance of the house.

Sarah's eyes took a few seconds to adjust to the dim light inside the room. It came into focus as a lush bedroom suite.

Good, an opportunity to solidify my position. I'll be damned if he leaves me in Libya!

A king-sized bed stood to the right of the doors. Sarah closed the doors and pulled the curtains. When she turned back to Hassan, he was already on the bed, staring at her.

Sarah removed her boots very carefully so as not to let Hassan see the small, dark, Gerber knives tucked inside them. The woman inside her was determined to make the show worthwhile. There was something about the look in Hassan's eyes that told her she was completely bewitching.

She pushed her conversation with Chris out of her mind.

She thrust Hassan's true character out of her mind.

She forced Vince out of her mind.

Sarah gazed at Hassan and tried to see the man, the passionate lover who appreciated her company and wanted to please her. She unbuttoned her white blouse, slid it from her shoulders and let it fall to the floor. Sarah bent forward, allowing Hassan an excellent view of her breasts held close to her body by the delicate white lace bra. She slid her jeans off and then stood, allowing Hassan to drink in her full form.

He growled with wanting but continued to lie there, watching her.

She turned her back on him and with slow moves designed to tease slid off her white lace thong.

Next, she unclasped her bra and let it drop to the floor with the rest of her clothes.

Then she removed the band from her hair, allowing the long dark waves to cascade around her shoulders and over her breasts.

She slowly turned to face Hassan.

His smile was gone and his eyes had grown dark.

Sarah saw the predator in him and matched the look with one of her own. This wasn't about love or lust. She pushed her fear deep down into her gut and played the part of the consort. She was somewhere in Africa and on her own. Pleasing Hassan was about staying safe and protected until this mission was over. She needed this man to adore her and want to keep her safe. Determination pumped through her veins.

She sashayed to the bed and leaned over Hassan as she unzipped his trousers. He reached for her as he leaned back, but she pushed his hands away.

"Come here," he growled.

"Be quiet," she snarled back as she freed him from the confines of his trousers and, without pulling them off, straddled him, pinning him to the bed. He sighed and thrust his hips, trying to enter her.

"No." She glared at him.

He's dying for it and I'm going to make him wait until he can't stand it anymore.

~~~

After she had pleased him, Hassan climbed out of bed, reached for Sarah's hand and pulled her into his arms. His kiss was gentle. More gentle than he had ever been.

Nervousness stabbed at Sarah. Though his kiss was soft and warm, she knew it was either very good or really bad news. He was either falling for her or this was the final kiss off.

He led her through a door at the far end of the room and into a magnificent marble bathroom. He drew a warm bath in the huge white marble tub and motioned for her to get in.

Sarah stepped into the deep, round tub and lay back on the soft, velvet cushion Hassan placed behind her neck.

Gentle hands began to massage her feet with the hot soapy water. Waves of relaxation rippled through her body. A sigh slipped past her lips as she closed her eyes and accepted a sensual moment for what it was.

His deft fingers manipulated every muscle in her legs until Sarah barely remembered she'd been riding that day. The tightness she stored in her muscles dissolved as he worked his way up her body. The tender kneading soon relaxed her arms, shoulders and neck.

Her eyes darted open and she sat upright when she no longer felt his hands.

He smiled and reached for a shampoo bottle. "So tense."

Sarah feigned a sleepy smile as she wrestled with whether she'd ever get back to the boat or not. "Riding. It has been a while for me."

Hassan carefully poured water over her hair and began shampooing it, massaging her scalp as he did.

A sense of calm overcame Sarah while she enjoyed the soft circles Hassan made with his fingers through her sudsy hair. The tension began to melt away as she convinced herself Hassan wouldn't let any harm come to her. At least not today.

Warm water flowed over Sarah's hair as Hassan rinsed the shampoo from it. "Rest. I'll be back soon." Hassan dimmed the lights in the bathroom and closed the door on his way out.

Sarah toweled off and hoped for some time to nap as she walked out into the empty bedroom. She collapsed naked on the bed and fell asleep almost instantly.

Thirty-Nine

Sarah woke as Hassan entered the room with a large silver tray piled with several smaller covered dishes.

He crossed to the sitting area, set the tray down on the coffee table and motioned for Sarah to join him.

Sarah slipped on her thong and bra and then slid into the white shirt she'd shed earlier. She didn't bother to button it. Hassan smiled and his eyes sparkled, so she assumed getting dressed might be a wasted effort.

Hassan patted the seat next to him on the sofa.

Intrigued, Sarah sat beside him.

Hassan removed a silver cover from the first plate to reveal several large, ripe, red strawberries.

Sarah reached for one and he gently tapped her hand away.

"Hey!"

He removed the cover of the next bowl to reveal fresh whipped cream.

Sarah eyed him expectantly and waited for the third cover to be removed.

Hassan chose a strawberry, dipped it in the cream and brought it to Sarah's lips.

Wow! A girl sure could get used to this sort of treatment!

Sarah bit the tip off the strawberry and then kissed Hassan.

"What's under that one?"

"See for yourself."

Sarah removed the cover of the third dish. Her stomach did a flip flop as she stared at the most exquisite ruby and diamond choker she could ever have imagined.

Hassan smiled. "You're pleased?"

"Yes," Sarah whispered as she held the choker in her hands. "And apparently you are, too."

"You should always be adorned with beautiful things." He slipped the choker from her fingers and placed the jewels around Sarah's neck.

She was inclined to believe him.

Forty

Safely back on Blue Harem, Sarah sat in front of the vanity and stopped applying her makeup to admire the ruby and diamond choker around her neck.

One point eight million dollars. Smart move to get them insured, too. Honey Pot Rule Number One: Always make sure you get yours.

"You alone?" Chris's voice in her ear had become commonplace.

"Yes, but I'm not in the mood for any more of your failed mission stories."

"No, this is good stuff. That estate of Hassan's in Libya is apparently one of the best terrorist training camps in Africa. It is also a staging area for a pretty big operation about to happen in Iraq."

"Okay. Sounds like good intel for you to have."

"Yeah, you did great, babe. Between radio, telephone and satellite we've determined something big should happen within a few days."

"So, when do we make our move? And what do I need to do?"

Chris spoke like he read off a checklist. "Extraction tonight. Standby for Vince. He's coming in to get you."

"Wait. Is that wise? Hassan is having a dinner party. Won't that look suspect?"

"Negative. Vince has been invited to dinner. It's cool. Wearing your watch?"

"Yeah, why?"

"Brian is setting explosives under the engine room and on the launch right now. They're set for 2200 hours. Copy?"

Stunned, Sarah stared at her reflection in the mirror and absorbed what he'd just said. "Well, sounds kind of drastic, Big Daddy. What aren't you telling me?"

"The less you know the better. You'll be fine. We've got your back. You copy the time?"

"Roger. 2200," she repeated.

"Nobody leaves tonight but you and Vince. You're going to have to jump. You need to be one-hundred feet away when she blows so don't dally. Jason, Will and Brian will be standing by with a boat on the north side of the island off Blue Harem's fore deck. They'll be out to sweep and pick you up immediately after the blast. Copy?"

"Roger. Standby for Vince. Jump. Swim a hundred feet. Tick-tick-boom 2200."

Chris sighed. "Affirmative. It'll be good to see you again, babe. It's time you came home."

The word home saddened her. "I don't have a home."

"You'll always have a home with us, babe. We won't let you down."

Sarah finished dressing for dinner.

Hassan was hosting a small dinner party for several of his close associates. There would be no women tonight, but Sarah was expected to be the gracious hostess and then leave them to talk business after dessert.

The burgundy silk gown proved to be a perfect combination with the new diamond and ruby choker Hassan had bought for her. The full skirt with hidden pockets was rather handy, too. She kept her pearl earrings and bracelet on and tucked her pearl choker into the left pocket in her skirt. The yellow diamond on the long gold chain, which she never parted with, was safely attached around her waist.

The last, and most important accessory Sarah needed was in her suitcase. She slipped her Gerber Guardian Backup knife into the right pocket of her skirt. Under the folds of silk, it would be virtually undetectable even if Hassan pulled her away for a quickie.

She breezed out of Hassan's stateroom and turned to take one last look. A disappointed sigh escaped her as she stared at all she'd leave behind. *My luggage. My lingerie. My designer clothes. I've shopped in thrift stores for the better part of my life. Now I have to watch this go down with the ship. I'll especially miss the silk caftan.*

Sarah had her act down pat. She entered and owned the dining room plus everyone in it. She went directly to Hassan's side and graciously greeted his guests with him. She charmed and entertained.

Hassan, on the other hand, seemed particularly tense.

Sarah was certain she had performed to perfection and hadn't given anything away by her demeanor so she assumed he must be tense about one of his many business deals that were always riding on the coattails of these parties.

As the cocktail hour came to a close and the table prepared for dinner, Sarah noticed the one guest she expected to see was conspicuously absent. Already uneasy after her conversation with Chris, Sarah wiped her sweaty palms on her gown.

How can I possibly sit here and be the charming hostess when Vince hasn't shown up yet and Chris hasn't radioed me a change in plans?

Hassan asked his guests to be seated for dinner. As the guests took their seats, one remained empty.

Something has gone wrong. I've got to get out of here and call Chris. Vince should be here by now.

Sarah smiled across the table at Hassan. "I see we are missing a guest. If it pleases the Sheikh, I will go greet his late guest and escort him in to dinner when he arrives."

Kadeem scuttled up to Hassan at that moment and whispered something in his ear. Hassan nodded, waved him off and returned Sarah's smile with an indulgent one of his own.

"Thank you, my beauty, but there is no need. It seems Mr. Hennessee will not be joining us."

Chris' voice was in her ear. "Negative, Sarah. He called in right before boarding Blue Harem twenty minutes ago. Shit!"

The wine glass in her hand shook slightly, but Sarah continued her act. She nodded deferentially to Hassan and continued through dinner as though nothing were amiss.

Where is he? What happened? What's his status? Is he okay? I've got to find him!

Dinner continued without a hitch. Hassan and his guests spoke in Arabic unless speaking directly to Sarah.

She continued to play dumb and pretend to enjoy the sound of the language, but this conversation would prove the most crucial test of her acting skills.

Kadeem made yet another appearance, whispered something in Hassan's ear and then scuttled off.

Delia appeared to serve dessert.

Oh, Delia. You poor girl, just trying to earn a living. I'm so sorry this is your last night.

Hassan made an Arabic announcement to his guests. "My friends, it seems your timetable will need to be abbreviated. We've received information that leads us to believe our supplier may have shared information with people he shouldn't have."

Sarah's stomach turned and a surge of adrenaline ran through her veins.

Act calm. Remember to pretend I don't speak Arabic. For all I know he is making a toast. Vince was made! But how? Who? Hassan is staring. Smile.

The man to Hassan's right wasn't pleased at all. "What? We had your personal assurance the supplier could be trusted. Osama will not look favorably on this."

Hassan tried to calm the man. "My friend, I assure you the situation has been contained. My associate Kadeem is handling matters as we speak. I merely suggest you abbreviate your timetable in case something may have been leaked before we detected the issue."

I've got to find a way to get the hell out of here and find Vince.

"If it pleases the Sheikh, his guest seems unhappy. Should I speak to the chef about an ill prepared course?"

"What is your whore talking about?" demanded the man to Hassan's right.

Sarah pretended she didn't understand what the man said in Arabic and kept the concerned look on her face in wait for Hassan's answer to her question. All the while, her stomach wrenched itself into knots.

Jesus, I've got to get out of this room. Kadeem has Vince. Oh, Chris, I hope you can hear this shit.

Hassan eyed the man indignantly and lowered his voice to an angry growl. "May I remind you that you are a guest at the table of Sheikh Hassan Abdullah Mohammed al-Rashid and as such you will not disrespect him by speaking in such a manner about his hostess who does not speak Arabic and is merely concerned for your comfort?"

The man bowed his head in deference to Hassan and mumbled in English. "A thousand pardons, Sheikh Hassan."

Hassan gazed lovingly at Sarah. "There is no need, my beauty. Our guest was merely anxious to talk business before its proper time. If you will excuse us, our talk of business will only bore you. Perhaps you would care to retire for the evening?"

"Yes, of course. I am a bit tired. Please excuse me, gentlemen."

Sarah rose to leave and noticed the other men at the table seemed to look at her with almost admiration.

Yes, I know. You're all so amazed Hassan has found such a beautiful and yet subservient American mistress. Guess what, suckers? The roof is about to blow off your world tonight!

As a final rub to the rude guest, Sarah looked directly at him as she smiled graciously. "Goodnight gentlemen. It has been my great pleasure to dine with you."

All but one, the rude one, stood as Sarah left the table. They bid her a polite goodnight in English.

Sarah exited the dining room, closed the door behind her and stopped just outside it to catch her breath and figure out what to do next.

A second later, a loud thump reverberated through the deck, as though someone had fallen and then Hassan's voice boomed with indignation. "How dare you disrespect your host in such a manner?"

For the first time during this mission, Sarah was truly afraid. Her heartbeat thumped through her entire body, and every muscle was tense with adrenaline. She hurried across the hall to Hassan's stateroom.

I need more than a pocket knife for this.

When she arrived, she knew something was very wrong. Her luggage had been moved. She'd been there for weeks and the help had never moved anything of hers. Her stomach turned as she whispered urgently to Chris.

"Chris! Chris! Can you hear me? Where's Vince? Where is he? Come in, Chris. Do you read me?"

No answer. Sarah's adrenaline level rose even higher, making her blood scream through her veins. Something was definitely wrong. Her contact with Chris was like a lifeline, even when she didn't want it. Now she couldn't contact him at all?

Finally, Chris' voice crackled through. "Sarah, what's your status?"

"All secure. Vince was made. Have you got a lock on his location?"

"Last contact was when he arrived at the boat. We've got nothing, girl. He knows what he's doing. He'll be fine." Chris's voice turned urgent. "You've got to get off that boat now, Sarah."

Sarah kicked off her shoes as she rushed to her suitcase. She dumped it and opened the false bottom to get her knives. She had to act quickly, and although she moved at top speed, everything seemed to happen in slow motion.

My knives are gone!

"Knives gone. My knives are gone," she hissed, hoping Chris would hear.

No sound now but the pounding of her heartbeat in her ears. She felt for the knife in her pocket. They didn't call it the Gerber Guardian Back Up for nothing.

Sarah pressed her ear against the door and listened. No sound.

She opened the door and stepped out onto the main deck with one goal in mind.

Find Vince.

Sarah slipped through the dark along the outer deck. The moonless night helped with her cover so she could look in through the windows without being seen.

Hassan and his guests were still in the dining salon. She crawled under the windows toward the aft deck.

Time worked against her. She hurried around to the port side of the boat and ran full out in her bare feet and gown to the fore deck.

Sarah moved quietly through the shadows and thanked God the deck lights were off.

As she rounded the corner, she spotted Kadeem near the anchor with a gun in his hand.

He isn't aiming yet.

She could only assume Vince was there, too. Sarah scanned the deck to make sure Kadeem was alone with Vince.

Vince was bound and kneeling in front of Kadeem.

An execution? Not on my watch, you bastard. Not him.

She managed to sneak to within about four feet of Kadeem.

Kadeem was so focused on Vince he didn't notice Sarah approaching from his side.

She burst from the shadows and kicked the gun from his hand.

As Kadeem turned to face her, she punched him square in the jaw. He fell sprawling across the deck.

Sarah pounced on him and wrapped her fingers around his neck. The last two things they needed right now were noise and company.

This is my chance.

Sarah moved her face to within inches of Kadeem's and whispered in Arabic, "How do you feel now, you frigging cockroach? How does it feel to know you're getting your ass kicked by the cheap American whore you've been talking shit about all this time?"

Kadeem's eyes opened wide as he realized she spoke Arabic. He gasped for breath, but it couldn't come. He reached for the gun that had slid across the deck when Sarah kicked him.

He managed to grab the barrel of the gun and tried to hit Sarah but she dodged his swing just in time.

"I've got no time for your shit!" she whispered as she pulled her Gerber and slit his throat in one swift movement.

Her cut to Kadeem's jugular landed perfectly. When she saw the first rush of blood shoot from his neck, she turned his head to cap the flow.

Sarah scrambled to her feet and turned to face Vince who still knelt with his hands bound behind his back and tape covering his mouth.

Her heart leapt into her throat as she took in his condition. His face was bloody and swollen.

Kadeem had clearly planned to pistol whip him a bit more before executing him.

Sarah dropped to her knees and cut the tape around his wrists and ankles. "Thank God you're all right. We've got to get out of here, now."

Vince jumped up and into action. He ripped the tape from his mouth as he grabbed Kadeem's weapon and checked the cartridge. He moved to the corner and checked for anybody else that might come up on the scene.

The boat's engines began to rumble. The large, powerful boat suddenly lurched forward. Jumping from the fore deck would mean the equivalent to a keel haul. They'd be pushed under the body of the boat and come up just in time for the propellers to chop them into chum for the sharks.

Chris's voice came through loud and clear. "Sarah, status!"

218

"Secure plus one," Sarah whispered.

"What a relief. You guys have two minutes. Get off that boat now."

"Follow close," Vince told Sarah as he ran along the port side of the boat toward the aft deck.

Sarah followed, but Vince had a long stride and the full skirt she wore slowed her pace. She was about ten feet behind him when he rounded the corner to the aft deck.

Pain shot through her jaw as she stumbled and fell. As she slid backwards against the rail, Hassan stepped out of the shadows.

Sarah scrambled to stand but kept getting tangled in the full length of the dress she wore.

A familiar *bap-bap-bap* came from the area where Vince had disappeared. Fear sizzled down her spine. Sarah knew the sound of an AK-47.

She scanned the deck when she realized her knife had been knocked from her hand.

Shit! Focus. No weapons. High drag clothing. Hassan holding a gun. Stand and fight or get shot in the back?

Sarah stood and looked into Hassan's eyes. The dark and dangerous eyes of a predator.

Hassan pointed the business end of his Glock pistol at her nose.

She waved wide to knock the pistol from his hand, but Hassan moved faster.

He grabbed her wrist with his free hand and spun her around so her back was toward him.

Sarah stumbled and fell.

A sharp pain shot from the top of her head down to her tailbone. She fought the wave of dizziness and nausea and focused on survival. She cried out as Hassan forced her to her feet by her hair.

The bastard hit me on the head with a frigging Glock!

Hassan wrapped his free arm around Sarah's neck and held her close enough to whisper in her ear. "Going somewhere, my beauty?"

Sarah struggled to get away. She elbowed and kicked at him but he held tight. She was too close for her hits to be effective.

His grip tightened.

Cold steel pressed against her temple in addition to the pressure of Hassan's muscular forearm against her neck.

"We found some very interesting items in your suitcase, my beauty."

Vince rounded the corner slowly with an AK-47 aimed at Hassan.

"Thirty seconds!" Chris yelled in Sarah's ear.

"One more move, Mr. Hennessee, and you'll have more than blood on your hands."

Sarah's world began to spin in slow motion again.

Chris's voice broke. "Twenty-five seconds!"

She stared down the barrel of the AK-47.

"Take the shot, Vince."

I trust you.

"Let the girl go!" Vince ordered Hassan.

"Put the gun down, Mr. Hennessee."

Hassan has no idea we're all about to die.

"Twenty seconds! You have got to get out of there!"

"Get out from behind the girl, you coward," Vince bellowed.

We've got to finish this son of a bitch and I'm the only one who can. He's holding me so tight.

Hassan's hard body pressed against her. There were so many times she enjoyed being this close to the man, but now all she felt was disgust. She could feel his right thigh at her hip as he held her with his right arm and the handgun with his left. She mouthed the word "knife" to Vince and hoped he'd understand as she moved her right hand away from the arm around her throat.

"Seventeen seconds! Oh Jesus." Chris moaned.

"All right." Vince raised his hands and moved to place his gun on the deck.

"You see, my dear." Hassan sounded so confident. "In the end, I do command you and everyone else around me."

Vince bent and placed the rifle on the deck.

Sarah watched his every move.

Vince pulled a knife from his shoe and threw it to Sarah.

She managed the catch with her right hand, flipped the grip of the knife, drove the blade deep into Hassan's thigh and twisted it as she pulled it out.

Hassan screamed like he'd been struck by lightning and released his grip on Sarah.

Vince lunged for Hassan's gun.

Sarah's training took over and she spun around to her right for another cut as Hassan fell.

Vince dove a second too late. Sarah watched in slow motion as Hassan squeezed off a shot and hit Vince in the chest.

"You bastard!"

Sarah gripped the knife in her bloody hand and spun around to finish the job she'd started. She dropped to her left knee, pinning Hassan's hip, and with both hands, drove the knife straight into his heart.

In the moment his heart burst, Sarah stared into his eyes. "No man commands me."

In the same moment Hassan died, the old Sarah died, too.

"Six seconds! For fuck's sake, get out of there." Chris screamed.

Sarah lunged, grabbed the unconscious Vince by his empty shoulder holster and jumped over the short rail and off the deck with him.

She held tight as they fell into the water.

When they surfaced, Sarah held his head up with her right arm and shielded his face with her left.

She'd barely begun to tread water when the explosion went off.

The blast was deafening. Flames and black smoke filled the air. Debris flew everywhere. Sarah prayed they wouldn't get hit with any large pieces and held her breath. She breathed a sigh of relief when she realized the boat had been moving fast enough to put a safe distance between her and Vince and the shock wave.

Debris continued to rain down on them as Sarah felt inside Vince's shirt.

"Oh, Jesus, Vince. You can't check out on me. Not now. Not here. God, please be wearing a vest. Please?"

Some of the tension left her shoulders as she felt the Second Chance vest under Vince's shirt. And a cool flattened bullet molded against it.

Vince came to. "What the hell? Am I hit?"

Sarah let go of Vince. "Yeah, you were hit and you scared the shit out of me, you son of a bitch! Guess who threw your unconscious body off the boat? That's twice I saved your ass, Marine. You need to learn to take care of yourself. You really owe me now."

Vince turned around in the water to face Sarah and shed his shoes, shirt and vest.

"Damn, girl. I'm no lightweight. You can lift more than most guys I know. I'm impressed."

"Yeah, yeah... Save it." Sarah struggled against the drag her gown caused. Her arms and legs grew tired in her battle to stay afloat.

Vince reached out for her. "What's the matter? Were you hit?" He wrapped one of his strong arms protectively around her waist.

Relieved after the ordeal, Sarah wrapped her arms around his neck and gave him a hug. "Yeah, I'm fine. I've got to get this damned dress off."

Vince's eyes opened wide. "Hey, babe, I'm all for showing some serious gratitude, but now is hardly the time."

"The drag, you ass! I can't swim in this dress!"

But thanks for letting me know you're up for a romp.

"Oh, I knew that." Vince turned her around and unzipped her gown. "I was just trying to add a little levity to the moment."

"Oh, don't lie. You know you want me." Sarah shed her gown and let out a sigh of relief to be able to swim easily in her satin bra and panties. She didn't mention it to Vince, but she did check to be sure the chain around her waist and the choker at her neck were both still there.

Excellent! All gems intact.

"Hey, only a fool wouldn't take advantage of a situation like this."

Sarah stared at Vince. "Even knowing what I do for a living?"

"You sleep with them, I kill them. I think I've got you beat on being bad. Does that bother you?"

Sarah treaded closer to Vince, feeling safe and secure within arm's reach of him even though they floated in the middle of the ocean. "Correction, I killed them. And no, what you do doesn't bother me as long as you're killing the right people." She smiled.

Then she felt something that made her temper flare. "Aw, shit!"

Vince quickly wrapped his arms around Sarah protectively. "What is it?"

"I broke a nail."

They both broke out laughing. The laughter was a good release for all the tension Sarah had felt.

Sarah's earpiece crackled and she heard Chris' familiar voice. "Well, I'm glad you two are having fun! I think I just shit myself, you psycho mother fuckers! Where's Hassan?"

"Bled out at four seconds to blast," Sarah stated soberly.

I killed two men close up. No guns, no sniper rifles, just a knife. I saw the look in their eyes when they died. A look I'll never forget.

Vince pulled Sarah close and gave her a comforting squeeze around the waist. "Hey," he whispered. "We all have blood on our hands. We've all been where you are. You won't forget the look in their eyes, so don't try. Just remember it was you or him, and the best man lived."

Sarah's lower lip trembled and tears stung the backs of her eyes. She gave Vince a half smile. "So, I'm one of the guys now?"

"Babe, you've got balls. You've always been one of the guys¾just built a whole lot better."

Vince's lips were so close Sarah could kiss him and nobody would fault her, especially after all they'd been through. Their eyes met and she wondered if he thought the same thing. His breath feathered against her cheek as his arms tightened around her. Just as Vince lowered his mouth to hers, she heard the sound of a boat approaching.

Damn. I don't know if I should thank them or tell them to make another pass.

Jason stood at the front of the boat scanning the debris with a twenty-gauge shotgun.

Brian was in the back, at the controls.

Will grabbed Sarah's arm and hauled her into the boat while Vince climbed in.

Once Sarah was in the boat, four pairs of eyes seared her exposed flesh.

"Whoa, baby!" Brian cat-called. "A good look for you."

Suddenly, Sarah was acutely aware of her near nakedness. It hadn't been a big deal in the water but now it had become inconvenient.

Crap.

Brian wore a wetsuit, no help there.

Vince's shirt, vest and jacket had been dropped in the water.

"Jason, give me your shirt?"

"Sorry, hot stuff, I'd gladly give you the shirt off my back any day, but I'm a little busy looking for floaters right now." His eyes twinkled as they roamed up and down her body. "Besides, I think you look just fine."

Sarah turned pleading eyes on Will.

The corners of his blue eyes crinkled as he smiled. "I'm with Brian. I think it's a great look for you."

Aw, hell! What's the use? I'd probably do the same to any of them.

Sarah sighed, resigned to her fate. "I love you guys."

Vince's deep voice rumbled with laughter. "Yeah, and the more we see of you the more we love you, too."

She wished she could control her body's response to his voice but it was useless. He made her heart flutter and her pulse race. At least she could deny the attraction and blame it on adrenaline.

Sarah opened her hand to find the flattened bullet, the tiny lead pancake she'd pulled from inside Vince's shirt. The bullet her lover fired at the man she couldn't help but love.

When Hassan pulled that trigger, Sarah changed. There was no going back. She never wanted to go back.

Killing Kadeem had been self-defense. He'd have killed her if she hadn't killed him. Hassan would have killed her, too. There was no need to think, no thought necessary in making the decision. He tried to kill Vince and he would have killed Sarah. He simply had to die.

Sarah stroked the smooth lead with her thumb as she remembered plunging the knife into Hassan's heart and pulling it up to destroy the organ just as she'd been trained. She recalled how fast the blood seeped through the front of his perfect white shirt.

Sarah shivered from the horror of her thoughts and tucked the smooth lead coin into her bra.

"Hey, you okay?"

She stared straight into Vince's eyes, which were etched with concern. "Yeah, just a little cold."

Forty-One

Sarah glanced around from the comfort of her chaise. The sun shone brightly and Lake Mead sparkled. Sarah and the guys had all gathered on Brian's pontoon boat, known as the floating barbecue, for just that.

They'd returned from several days of detailed debrief at Ramstein Air Base in Germany and were all ready for a little rest and relaxation after their mission.

While at Ramstein, they were briefed that the British Special Air Service commandos had raided Hassan's camp at the same time American Swift destroyed his boat. The SAS nabbed six known terrorists and held fourteen more for questioning. They also collected computer records of bank accounts being used by Al Qaeda to support several other terrorist organizations. From their questioning, they'd determined the pirates that tried to board the team's boat had been associates of Hassan's and one of them told Hassan about the incident just before his last dinner party. The pirate had positively identified both Vince and Sarah.

Hassan had Sarah's luggage checked and the knives confirmed the pirate's story.

Sarah inhaled the delicious smell of steak as Brian worked the grill.

Vince's dog, Thor, quietly lounged at Vince's feet and busied himself with a T-bone steak.

Lucky dog.

Sarah took a quick look at herself, reclined on the chaise in a brand new bikini.

Gotta love that expense account.

In the midst of five well-muscled men, drinking beer and eating steaks beat even the best day on Blue Harem. She trusted these men. They were family. No games to play with these guys. When Chris leaned back and put his feet up on the end of her chaise, Sarah remembered some very important items and pulled her rucksack out from under her chair.

"This broad's so gung-ho." Jason laughed as he pointed to the camouflage rucksack. "Thousand dollar handbags and she chooses a ruck. Can I pick 'em or what?"

"Don't get too excited, Jase. I came completely unarmed today."
Sarah pulled out five small collapsible six-pack coolers and tossed one to
each of the guys.

"Now this is what I'm talking about." Will grinned. "A hot babe
bringin' me my beer! Hey." He hefted the bag. "This feels a little light."

"Yeah, baby!" Chris waggled his eyebrows at her. "What else you
got for Big Daddy? Hey! Did you manage to save the white thing?"

"Sorry, Chris. I lost everything. I know how much you were looking
forward to seeing me in the caftan." She wrinkled her nose and smiled.

"Oh, yeah. That was hot! You missed a great scene there, guys.
When the sun hit just right...hooah!" Vince stole a look at Sarah and her
body tingled.

"What the hell is this?" Vince had opened the small cooler and found
ten tight little bundles of thousand-dollar bills.

"Consider it our bonus."

The rest of the guys opened their coolers and found the same thing.

"Where the hell did you get this?" Will asked, his voice edged with
suspicion.

"Diamonds and rubies hold no value for me. I sold the pieces Hassan
gave me and felt it was only right to split the cash with you guys."

"What? Why? Those gems were amazing!" Will looked completely
confused.

Sarah leaned forward and opened her hand palm up. "What's a
diamond? I mean really? You squeeze a piece of coal long enough and
you get a diamond." She closed her hand in a tight fist. "But what's in it?
Nothing." Sarah opened her hand to emphasize the emptiness.

"I know they were equipment but I loved the pearls. A pearl, now
there's something special. It all starts with a piece of grit. A tiny grain of
sand gets into a mollusk and irritates. So, the mollusk fights back, builds
onto the grit and creates something hard and beautiful. You string a bunch
of them together and they look so perfect, but every single one of them
started with grit." Sarah leaned against the chaise lounge and took a long
pull from her beer. "I'll take pearls over diamonds any day."

Vince crossed the deck to stand by her side. "Well, if anybody knows
grit, it's you, babe. But, no. You deserve this money and we all know it.
You should keep it."

226

"Yeah, this is a nice gesture. The best. But we can't take this," Brian agreed.

"No way!" Sarah tossed her empty beer bottle into the trash can. "We're a team. We all had a part in the operation and we all came through. This is right and it's how *I* want it. Discussion over. Now somebody get me another beer…and Brian, I'm still waiting for my tequila."

"Damn, girl. All I wanted was a couple cigars." Will winked as he tossed her a cold Corona from the cooler beside him. "Hey, that reminds me. We got you a little something, too."

"What are you talking about?"

Will pulled a package wrapped in plain brown paper out from under his seat and handed it to her.

"What is this?"

Vince crossed his arms over his chest with a shrug. "Just open it."

Sarah opened the package to find a white silk caftan trimmed with gold embroidery.

She frowned at Will. "But the boat? Everything was lost."

"Vince gave me a detailed description, and I mean *de*-tailed." Will smiled as he continued. "I called a few people and found this. Is it similar?"

"Well," Vince sat and took a long swig of his beer. His face turned up in a grin. "We won't really know until she models it."

Sarah gave Will a kiss on the cheek. "This is even more beautiful than the original. Thank you so much. All those designer clothes I lost and I missed the damned caftan the most." Then she turned Vince. "How did you know?"

He shrugged. "You're a pearl girl."

Forty-Two

In the two weeks since Sarah had returned from her first mission with American Swift, she began to pull a little bit of a life together. She'd taken her cut of the cash and purchased a luxury condominium at The Residences at the MGM Grand in Las Vegas.

Sometimes at night, she'd wake up in a cold sweat after dreaming about what she'd done to Kadeem and Hassan, but those dreams were becoming fewer and farther between now.

She also cleaned out the storage unit where she'd stored the remnants of her past life. Since the old Sarah was dead, she donated everything to the Salvation Army.

Her expense account provided her with enough cash to put together a very stylish wardrobe for the new Sarah. As for the old Jeep Wrangler, she traded that in and paid cash for a new Rubicon loaded with all the bells and whistles.

If you're gonna sell your soul to the Devil, make sure you get top dollar.

Forty-Three

"Pardon me, Miss Stevens."

Sarah opened her eyes to see the familiar form of the young fitness model who made his living as a waiter at the Margarita Bar. She smiled. "Yes, Troy?"

Sarah spent every sunny afternoon by the pool and knew each waiter's voice just as they knew her and her favorite drink.

He handed her a Margarita on the rocks with no salt, just the way she liked them. "Compliments of the gentleman at the bar over there. He'd like you to join him for a drink."

Sarah accepted the drink and glanced over at the handsome, young Val Kilmer look alike who smiled as though he'd already scored. "Some fighter jockey here for a couple weeks of training at Red Flag, no doubt. Quite handsome, though, wouldn't you say, Troy?"

"Yeah, but not my type." Troy rolled his eyes.

"Troy, will you thank the gentleman for the drink but give him my apologies? Tell him I just came off a bad break-up and was looking forward to a quiet afternoon today."

"Of course, Miss Stevens."

Sarah loved how the waiters treated her like royalty. Ever since she'd moved into the Residences, she'd been a regular here and a very generous tipper. Even a glass of water would get the waiters a tip and they knew it. Sarah took another drink of the Margarita, nodded thank you to the good looking man at the bar and leaned back with her thoughts as Troy delivered the message.

"Miss Stevens?"

"Yes, Troy?" She opened her eyes and smiled again as he looked at her apologetically.

"The gentleman on the corner chaise asked me to send you a drink."

"Oh, thanks, Troy, but please explain to the gentleman I'm not drinking any more this afternoon." She gave Troy the half glass of Margarita and a ten dollar bill.

"Of course, Miss Stevens. I won't interrupt you again."

Sarah closed her eyes and relaxed in the sun, hoping to nap.

"Bring us a pitcher of Margaritas and two glasses with ice, no salt, please." The unmistakable baritone voice rumbled over her in the most delicious way.

Troy's voice sounded less apologetic and quite a bit more stern. "Sir, I'm sorry, but Miss Stevens doesn't care for any drinks or company this afternoon."

An indignant snort. "She'll drink with me."

The familiar ache at the apex of her thighs told her whose voice it was. A week had passed since she'd seen Vince and her heart leapt to know he'd sought her out.

Troy tried again. "Sir, I don't think…"

Sarah opened her eyes. "Thank you, Troy. He's okay."

Troy eyed Vince. "I can call security."

"No, that won't be necessary. Thank you very much though." Sarah gazed up at Vince, shielding her eyes from the sun. "Hey, Marine."

Is he caramel or bronze?

With the sun behind him, Vince glowed like a bronze statue. Dressed in an Armani tux, black BDU's or jeans and a white tank top, the man could only be described as stunning.

"What are you, Queen of the Margarita Bar? These boys are like bodyguards. I thought I was gonna have to rough somebody up."

She giggled as she sat up. "Yes, as a matter of fact, I am." Sarah sobered as the rest of his words sank in. "You'd do that for me?"

Vince nodded. "Absolutely. But more importantly, they'd do it for you."

They both sat in awkward silence for a moment.

God, it's good to see you.

Vince spoke first. "So, did you miss me?"

Sarah tried to play nonchalant. "A little. Where were you?"

"I had to take a little business trip."

Her insides quivered. "So soon?"

"Yeah. I had to lay some groundwork for our next little jaunt. Brush up on your Russian."

Troy returned with a pitcher of Margaritas and two glasses without salt.

"They do treat me like a queen, don't they?" She smiled at Troy. "Thank you, Troy."

Vince tipped him a twenty-dollar bill. "Sorry about that, Troy. Thanks for taking such good care of Miss Stevens."

Troy walked away happy and Vince leaned closer to Sarah. "Will that get me King for a day?"

"You'll always be a king to me." Sarah winked.

Vince sat on the empty chaise near Sarah and poured two Margaritas. "Well, that's all that matters, my queen." He handed Sarah a full glass and leaned toward her. "Congratulate me."

"What exactly am I congratulating you for? Did you find yourself a new conquest while you were gone?"

Please say no. I know I can't have you, but I don't want to know about other women.

As though he read her mind, Vince looked into his drink. "No. You know there's only one woman for me." He stared into her eyes. "It's final. I signed the papers at nine. I let her have everything. I took Thor and the truck. Thor never liked her anyway. Next time I hook up, it's pending Thor's approval."

Sarah tried to be cool while inside her chest, her heart did a happy dance. "So, you're going to try again, huh?"

"I think so."

"Well, congratulations." Sarah took a sip. "Good call letting Thor make the decision for you. Dogs are excellent judges of character." Sarah paused. "But you and Thor are homeless now. Where are you going to live?" Then she added with a coy smile, "I'd let you stay with me but I doubt you could control yourself on naked Mondays."

"Well, since I needed a place in Vegas, I bought a nice little studio just a couple floors down from you. I signed those papers at ten. He smiled wide. "Since you brought it up, you and I do have some unfinished business…and today is Monday."

Sarah's heart skipped a beat and she let out a nervous laugh. She still wanted him as much as she ever did. And loved him more than she would ever admit, but things were different now. They were a part of something big. Their last mission saved thousands of lives and very possibly the life of Vince's brother who served in Iraq. She'd screwed up so many times before by following her heart.

Don't wreck a good thing, Stevens. He's alive and he's here. Strangely, for now, that is enough.

She stared deep into Vince's eyes and realized he knew it, too. "Two floors down, huh? Good. More eye candy for around the pool."

She tapped his glass with hers, sat back to enjoy the sun, good tequila and fine company. Yeah, life was good…for now. A great way to end a very difficult year.

Enjoy A Sneak Peek Of A Taste of Liberty, Book 2 in the Task Force 125 Series

One

Sarah blinked back the sweat that rolled from her forehead and into her eyes. Her hair fell from her ponytail in long locks sticky with perspiration and clung to her cheeks. Her breath was hard and fast as she dodged hits and blocked kicks just to keep up with the man she was fighting.

My God! He's a machine.

He had about thirty pounds on her but he was wiry and fast. He was throwing everything he had into the mix. He started with Muay Thai boxing, but, when he did a Capoeira flip and spun his body in mid air from a standing position, a chill raced up her spine. She'd never seen anyone as fast as this guy. She threw punches at his face, shoulders and stomach and never made contact. He'd dodge, twist, spin and jump just barely avoiding her hits and kicks. His years of training and experience in hand-to-hand combat were obvious.

Focus, Sarah. Focus.

The midday sun in the Nevada desert beat down with a steady blast of 102 degrees. Each breath was like taking a drag off a bonfire. The heat, dehydration and near exhaustion wore her down, and Sarah slid into a reactive, defensive mode where her movements were automatic. She knew she couldn't win this way but the bright sun lulled her into not caring.

Her opponent flashed a wicked smile. His eyes sparkled like the trillions of grains of sand glinting around them. The relentless sun and heat slowed her down and he made the most of it. "Come on, sugarlips. Is that all you got?" He spun to his left.

The pain of a powerful blow to her right shoulder woke her from her daze, and her adrenaline surged.

Son of a bitch!

His teeth glistened as he grinned. "Papa's gonna take you to school."

Her jaw tensed. "Not today, Papa." Sarah saw her opening for a kick and took it. She put all of her weight behind a roundhouse kick aimed for his neck and a clothesline takedown but the soft sand beneath her feet shifted and she slipped, kicking him in the head instead.

They both fell.

Sarah scrambled to stand quickly. As she did, she turned to see the man still lying on the ground, unconscious. She dropped to her knees beside him. A chill raced up her spine despite the heat. "Jason? Jason!" She placed two fingers on his neck.

Good heartbeat. Damn. I'm gonna need some help with this sandbag.

This wasn't the first time one of them had been knocked out when they were sparring. It was becoming all too common as Sarah's fighting skills advanced. She walked over to her Jeep and pulled her phone out of the door pocket. She pressed the number *One* and then the *Send* button.

I hope he answers.

About The Author

Lisa Pietsch (pen name of Lisa Woodward) is the Publishing Director at Defiance Press and Publishing, an Air Force Veteran, former magazine publisher, multi-published author, mother of two giants, and wife to a Viking.

Lisa speaks French, Spanish, Norwegian, and Russian. She has been USAF Security Forces Leader, received specialized training as an FBI Hostage Negotiator, and worked with MI-5 on personal security details for both British and Jordanian Royals. These diverse experiences inspire her Task Force 125 series, which follows Sarah Stevens, a CIA Special Activities Division recruit, through gripping tales of espionage and paramilitary operations.

In 2020, Lisa's life took a romantic turn when she reconnected with the love of her life, the man who inspired her Task Force 125 series, launching her into her greatest adventure yet.

An avid gamer, Lisa enjoys both console and tabletop gaming, where she goes by "Geniekin" on Xbox and Roll20.

As Lisa Pietsch, she crafts thrilling paramilitary action/adventure/romance novels, while as Lisa Woodward, she weaves enchanting epic romantic fantasy tales.

www.ingramcontent.com/pod-product-compliance
Lightning Source LLC
Chambersburg PA
CBHW051105030726
47504CB00006B/1801